Two Moons: The Eternal Tide by Cameron O'Brien stands out for its imaginative world-building and the emotional weight of its themes. The title refers both to Deor's twin-moon birthmark and the recurring "eternal tide" of life, death, and rebirth—a cycle that binds Nebra's past to Earth's present and shapes the fate of these characters as they fight for survival and freedom. The reincarnation thread adds depth, tying Nebra's tragic past to Alcyone's current struggle. Moments like Deor confronting the spirits of the dead or wielding Alphym-forged weapons show how seamlessly mythology and history are woven into the narrative.

The characters feel layered—Deor's growth from hunter to leader is convincing, Sam's protective bond grounds the story, and Sage's quiet intelligence provides balance. The novel also succeeds in its pacing; quiet, reflective chapters contrast with tense escapes and looming battles, keeping the momentum fresh. The writing style is clear and heartfelt, often evoking atmosphere without drowning the reader in exposition—for instance, the description of the living forest carries both beauty and unease. The symbolic weight of the "eternal tide" and the mix of personal stakes with cosmic cycles give the book its heart. This is a strong, moving debut that leaves room for even greater complexity in future installments. This story is best for readers who enjoy epic fantasy with a spiritual edge—fans of *Eragon* or *The Inheritance Trilogy* will feel at home.

—Reviewed by Manik Chaturmutha for Readers' Favorite

Cameron O'Brien's *The Eternal Tide* is a riveting fantasy tale set in a world shaped by oppression, rebellion, family loyalty, and the cyclical nature of life and death. This captivating story will draw you in from start to finish. Deor and her siblings aren't just your typical characters fighting to survive their difficult circumstances. They are deeply linked to Merope's regime and themes of freedom and resistance. Thus, the story doesn't focus on one conflict alone. This bold narrative reveals how trauma and oppression can be repeated if not confronted. Through Deor's story, the author illustrates how individuals can face their ongoing challenges with hope, team effort, and courage. O'Brien's writing conveys the raw pain of loss, the threat of enslavement, and the sad reality of living in a world that no longer feels like home. I recommend this novel to fantasy fans who enjoy action-packed, deep, and thought-provoking reads.

—Richard Prause for Readers' Favorite

The Eternal Tide is superbly written, an epic, sprawling fantasy in which worlds are condensed in the soul of the heroine. I loved the characters and how well they are written, and the banter between Deor and her young twin siblings. While Deor is a determined and fierce fighter, the supporting cast, such as Sage with her sharp wit, intelligence, and love of life, is equally well-developed and fleshed out. Cameron O'Brien cleverly explores themes of oppression, cyclical history, family loyalty, and the search for identity. The settings of Alcyone and Merope blend post-apocalyptic earthiness with hints of lost advanced civilizations, giving the story a hauntingly plausible, lived-in atmosphere. *The Eternal Tide* is imaginative, crafted in gorgeous prose with impeccable worldbuilding. I was utterly immersed in this spellbinding narrative.

—Romuald Dzemo for Readers' Favorite

Deor, a young woman of Alcyone, chafes under the brutal occupation of the Meropans. Then, she learns that she is the reincarnation of a young woman named Lore, who lived on the planet Nebra, which was attacked and destroyed by Remus. Additionally, she discovers that the people of Merope are reincarnations of the people of Remus. She and those around her are, in fact, caught up in an eternal cycle of destruction and violence that spans worlds and generations. At the same time, in Merope, Arietis, a Meropan, has begun to question the established order in which Meropans exercise dominance over Alcyone. Lives and past lives become intertwined in Cameron O'Brien's *Two Moons: The Eternal Tide*, a genre-bending novel that blends fantasy and science fiction in a compelling, action-packed tale. This exploration of civilization and governance, as well as the indomitable resilience of the human experience, makes for a captivating narrative.

This is a well-crafted story that will grab your interest from page one, and bit by bit, word by word, pull you into an epic tale that tells the story of ancient civilizations through the eyes and experiences of characters you can not only identify with, but also empathize with.

O'Brien can create characters and scenes that, despite the fantasy aspect of the story, feel real. Action and dialogue all ring true. As the story winds its way to a most satisfying conclusion, with scores—ancient and contemporary—settled along the way, you will sit back with mixed emotions. It was—is—a tale well-told, but you will also feel a sense of sadness that there is not more. In essence, this is a story that will satisfy you, but, at the same time, whet your appetite for more.

—Charles Ray, author of the best-selling Caleb Johnson Mountain Man series

Two Moons

THE ETERNAL TIDE

Cameron O'Brien

ALKIRA
PUBLISHING

Two Moons - The Eternal Tide
Cameron O'Brien
Copyright © 2025
Published by Alkira Publishing, Australia
ABN: 32736122056
http://www.alkirapublishing.com

ISBN: 978-1-922329-97-4

To my children: Daisy, Sam, Eliza, Olivia and Rose.
To the memory of my mother, who always pushed me to explore
my potential fully.

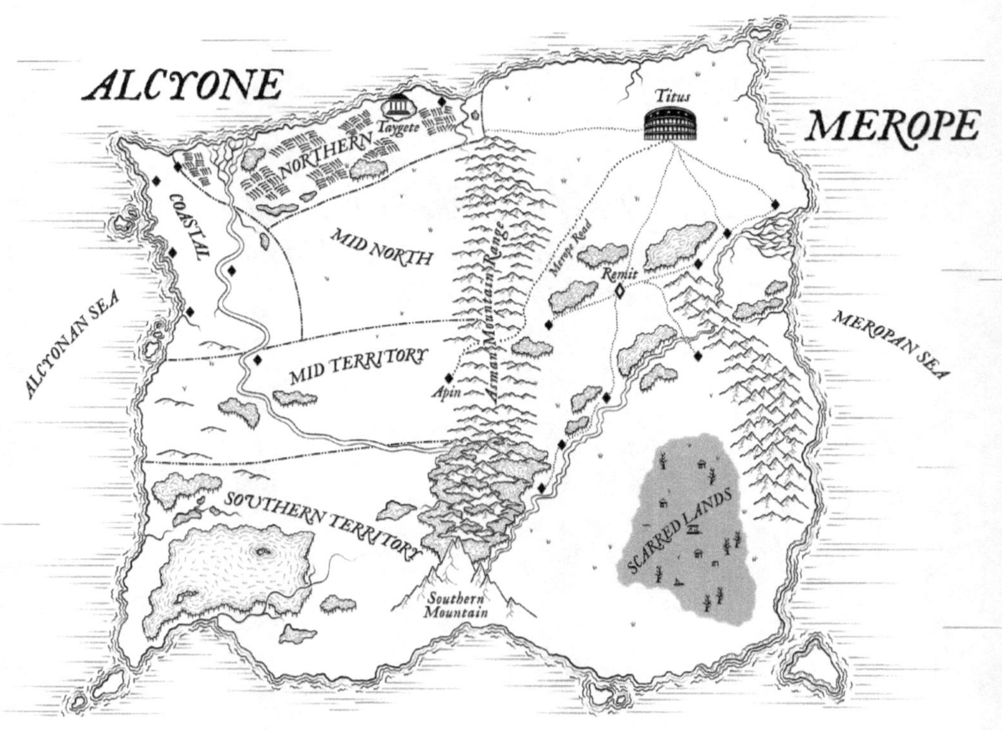

ALCYONE
MEROPE
NORTHERN
Taygete
Titus
COASTAL
MID NORTH
Merope Road
Remit
ALCYONAN SEA
Arman Mountain Range
MEROPAN SEA
MID TERRITORY
Apin
SOUTHERN TERRITORY
SCARRED LANDS
Southern Mountain

Deor scanned the trees ahead, hunting for prey, as always. The vast Asman Range stretched away in front and behind her, mountains she knew well. Her brother Sam stopped beside her and pointed. He'd seen something. Deor followed his gaze. Perhaps thirty metres in front of them, two hares, nearly a foot tall, nibbled on low grass. Youths, inexperienced, unused to listening out for humans, they hadn't heard them coming. These should make easy targets. Sam drew his bow while Deor pulled a light spear from her sling.

Thankfully, she'd tied her dark, light curls back into a braid—much better not to have them in her eyes when hunting. Sam had a similar colour and curls, but he wore his hair much shorter.

Deor aimed at the hare on the right, as her brother aimed at the one on the left in an unspoken instruction: fire at the one on your side, and do not fire across one another's line. Trusting her instinct, Deor launched her spear as Sam fired his arrow. Both hares collapsed immediately. Dinner.

'Slim pickings,' Sam said, as they picked up their prey. 'Would give a leg to see a bison one of these days.'

Deor nodded. 'I haven't seen a bison in months.' Its thick frame and meaty legs would be a welcome sight and target. 'Maybe a year.'

'I'm pretty sure the patrollers shoot them for fun when they see them. Even they couldn't miss a bison,' Sam said.

'Such a waste,' Deor said. Since the invasion, fresh meat was hard enough to come by without the patrollers taking more away. They already took everything else in the town; why couldn't they leave the game alone? Deor tied her hare to her kit and walked on through the forest with her brother. Ideally, they'd find another couple of hares. Or at least a decent-sized bird or two. There were five mouths to feed in her family, and her younger siblings were too young to help out much yet, except in the garden. For now, anyway. They could make four of these small hares stretch for a week. Or they could use two of the hares to trade.

'Let's head for the clearing,' Deor said. 'There's sometimes game there. Maybe we'll see a sabre.'

'Dangerous hunting sabres.' Sam shook his head. 'Miss, and you're mauled.'

They rounded a hill, and Deor froze. Instinctively, she put her hand on Sam's arm, stopping him. Ahead, in the clearing, six patrollers sat in a rough circle in the middle. The furthest one away, facing her, looked up and saw her. Silence for a moment as their eyes locked. That is until he stood and raised his rifle.

'Run!' Urgency taking over, Deor turned and sprinted away with Sam at her side, while shots rang out from the patroller. She didn't look back, just raced hard up the mountain with several shots fizzing past her. Fear washed over her as she ran.

'Higher!' Sam yelled.

The higher they went, the greater their position in relation to the patrollers, and the less the patrollers could look down to spot them and pick them off. Deor breathed hard but trusted her fitness and that of her brother. The patrollers carried cumbersome packs, whereas Deor only had her light sling. Perhaps the patrollers would give up after a little if they could put some space between them.

Shots continued to burst through the air, though, and they weren't getting further away. A tree in front of Deor spat bark as a bullet smashed into it. She winced—it must have missed her head by centimetres only. Vaguely, she heard birds fleeing from trees higher up as more bullets continued to fly by.

She and Sam ran a criss-cross pattern up the hill, hoping to throw off the patrollers' aim. Why were they shooting, though? What had she and Sam done wrong? They hadn't crossed the border into Merope; they hadn't broken any rules; they weren't out after curfew. Why was this happening? Answers to those questions would have to wait; right now, all she could do was run. Her legs burned, though; her muscles strained. Desperate for relief, she suddenly saw a small ravine cut into the mountain; it led away laterally and offered some cover. It could hide them.

Deor spotted a way in. 'Here!' she called to Sam, her voice hoarse and short.

She dropped into the ravine and took off, leading the way. She ran along its spine, hunting along the ravine wall as she ran, searching for cover. Soon enough, she found a small gap between two large stones, obelisks even. Why were there stones like this high up the mountain, and in a ravine? They differed from the surrounding rocks, so were probably erratics, rocks brought in from somewhere else, but how? She didn't have time to ponder that now, though. She darted in through the opening and crouched in the dark interior a few metres inside, her back pressed against the cave wall. Sam followed her and crouched opposite. The cave seemed to go back several metres further, perhaps more, but she couldn't see much. Barely breathing, just enough to try to recover a little from the run, Deor sat and listened for the patrollers. They were getting closer.

Sam began to fidget. He preferred to confront the danger and fight if necessary. She reached across and touched his arm. Now that her eyes had adjusted to the dim light, Deor could just make out his face, a face she'd known all of her life, kind and calm. She pressed her finger to her lips and whispered, 'Shhh …' as she held his arm.

Sam nodded slightly; his face calmed.

The patrollers' footsteps grew louder. They were at the edge of the ravine. This was the moment; would they recognise where she and Sam had gone? Had they left any tracks in their haste? Deor sat as still as possible, listening and waiting. Her heart pounded hard in her chest; adrenaline coursed through her body. She slowed her breathing, deeply in, slowly out, deeply in, slowly out.

'Where are they?' one patroller yelled, his voice bouncing down the ravine, echoing past the cave entrance.

Deor held her breath. The ground shook a little.

'I don't know!' another called. This one sounded more authoritative. Perhaps he was the one in charge. 'If you weren't so slow to react, we'd have had them! I'm certain they're part of the group, that's what we're bloody well here to do, isn't it? And you had them in your sights!'

A shot rang out. The bang echoed and throbbed throughout the mountain and the ravine, like a bolt from Pleid.

'Throw his worthless body down this ditch!' the leader called out.

Muffled sounds of people moving about came down the ravine. After a few moments, something heavy landed on the ground outside, and the dead patroller came to rest at the cave entrance, lying on his back. He had a bullet wound in his forehead. His now-lifeless eyes locked with Deor's again, as they first had in the clearing. Deor stifled a gasp and quickly looked away. Ironically, the dead patroller had found his prey, though he was in no position to do anything about it.

'Let's bloody well go. Those mountain rats will be hidden away by now in some miserable hole,' the head patroller said above them. The patrollers' steps began to subside as they headed back down the mountain.

After a long pause, Deor allowed herself a breath. That was close.

'We have to go,' Sam said, running his hands through his hair. 'We have to get off this mountain.'

'I know, Sam,' Deor said, but the cave was intriguing with those stones at its entrance. Turning away, she stepped further into the cave. Her eyes had adjusted to the dark completely now, but still she couldn't make much out, except for the vague outline of the walls.

'What are you doing?' Sam asked.

'Just a minute.' Deor ventured further into the cave. She sensed something and wanted to see what was back there. Still, the darkness obscured all. 'What is this place? I haven't seen this cave before. Didn't you see the stones out front? There's something strange about all of this.' Without consciously recognising it, she touched the birthmark on her left shoulder.

'We can't investigate now!' Sam whispered urgently. 'And for all we know, there could be animals back there! We can come back another day!'

'Yes, just a minute.' Deor took another step. A low growl

assaulted her from the darkness: a cave lion, about a metre in front of her. Deor's heart stopped; adrenaline again washed through her body. She turned and sprinted for the cave entrance, yelling, 'Run, Sam!'

Dodging the body of the dead patroller, Deor and Sam raced out of the ravine. Once out, she glanced back, but the cave lion hadn't followed them out. Thank Pleid.

'That was too close, Dee,' Sam said, when they were a safe distance from the ravine.

Yeah, it was too close. She didn't want to take on a cave lion, that was for sure. But there was something about that cave that she needed to investigate, though not now. 'The bigger issue for now is the patrollers. We need to get down the mountain, and be on high alert.'

'What do you think they were doing here?' Sam asked. 'Why were they up here in the mountains?'

It was unlike them to be in such a large group and to be up in the mountains. 'It's troubling,' she said. 'They must've been looking for someone. Perhaps they're pursuing people who've been hiding out up here. They said something about a group. I don't know. But I don't like it. Six of them up here like that. I don't like it.'

Sam nodded. 'Generally, there's just two. And generally, they're just patrolling, making sure no one is crossing the mountain range. And sure, they're rough, but they didn't even call out to us; they just fired on us. What the hell is going on?'

'This group they're after, they must have broken the rules,' Deor said. 'Maybe they're on the run from another territory. Whatever they did, it must've been pretty serious. The patrollers can get pretty vicious when they need to, beastly even.'

'Beastly, definitely. We know they're that. And we've all heard the rumours.'

'The Age of Defilement.' Deor shuddered. The Age of Defilement was the term the patrollers apparently used to refer to the Day of Procurement. It made her skin crawl.

'Yeah, that,' Sam said. 'I hope it's just a rumour that they call it that.'

'It's coming up, you know, the Day of Procurement. Sage will be very nervous. She's thirteen now, and they take one in ten of the girls away. I remember how I felt five years ago. I was lucky, I wasn't one of the ten per cent, but Arunet wasn't so lucky.'

'Taken away as the property of Merope.' Sam mimicked the language of the officials who come in on that day.

Deor wondered now, as she had many times, what had happened to her friend Arunet. All the girls were taken to the capital of Merope, Titus, but beyond that she knew nothing. She expected they were then used as servants—as slaves, in reality, but no one had ever seen any of the procured girls again.

She and Sam made their way steadily down the mountain, and, thankfully, they didn't encounter the patrollers again. At the bottom, Deor scanned the thinly wooded stretch that led to her town, but it seemed all clear. They made their way through the thin woods and slipped back into the town. Evening was falling; the curfew would soon come into effect, so they quickly made their way to the town square and towards the old courthouse, where in a couple of weeks, the Day of Procurement list would be nailed.

As they approached the courthouse, Deor kissed the ring on her right hand. It'd been her mother's. Her mother had been wearing it on that day, nearly ten years ago, when she was shot and killed for protesting in front of the courthouse. Six innocent lives were taken, just for protesting against the occupation. Deor had worn the ring in her memory ever since, both in memory of her mother and to mark the day her childhood ended.

The courthouse hadn't served in its titular fashion since the invasion. Now, it was used as headquarters for the incumbent patrollers of the area. Every town in her territory—the Mid Territory—was the same: a garrison of patrollers stationed there to maintain a *pax Meropa* and to ensure that the valuable resources of each town and territory were diverted successfully back to Titus and to Merope more widely. A garrison in every town, in every territory, throughout every territory of Alcyone. This was what life was like; her people being used as cattle to farm resources for Merope. She kicked the dirt angrily. It tore at her deep inside her soul.

They passed the courthouse, and a patroller appeared from around the corner, carrying a rifle. Deor's heart skipped a beat, but she didn't think he was one of the remaining five from the mountain, though she hadn't seen them all clearly.

'What the hell are you two doing out still?' He poked his rifle into Sam's chest.

'We're heading home, right now.' Sam tried to move away from the rifle's nose.

The patroller had his trigger finger dangerously close to the trigger, and Deor could smell alcohol on his breath. She looked around for escape routes.

'You'd better be doing that. It's nearly curfew, and you wouldn't want to be found to be still out after curfew, skinny man.' The patroller turned to Deor. A leering smile broke out across his pasty features. He rubbed his three-day growth and looked her up and down.

A wave of revulsion surged through her body. Thankfully, at least, it meant he lowered the rifle.

'Though you, my sweet little rat, you could stay out after

curfew with me anytime you want. You're well past the Age of Procurement, I can see that, but I'm betting no one has ruined you yet. A pure little mountain rat, that's what we have here.'

The patroller reached forward to grab at Deor, but she quickly moved out of his way, and just as quickly, Sam got between them. The patroller took the butt of his rifle and slammed it into Sam's stomach, making him double over in pain.

'Sam!' Deor put her arm around him and tried to get him to walk away. Though in great pain, he tried to walk with her as she held him up.

'Get back to your little holes, you disgusting mountain rats!' the patroller yelled and then spat on the ground in front of himself. 'Or next time I see you, I won't be so polite!'

'We're going!' Deor said, the anger welling up inside her. Everything about the patrollers and the Meropan occupation of Alcyone angered her. More than that, it enraged her. She'd felt the anger all her life, the rage at the situation her people were in. Occupied, oppressed, dominated by Merope. 'Asshole,' she added quietly.

'Yeah.' Sam groaned and attempted to stand up straight as they walked. 'And drunk too.'

The sun began to set as Deor helped Sam down the street. Step by step, he regained his breath, though she suspected he'd have a nasty bruise forming on his stomach. Something he would no doubt show off to the girls who followed him around town. Deor smiled at the thought and of what her younger sister, Sage, would say if she saw it happen. Sage had her brother's measure, that was for sure.

Deor led Sam through the door of their house, and he straightened himself up as best he could to avoid any questions from their father, Cyrus, who was busy preparing vegetables for a stew at the small bench. Alexi and Sage, her twin younger siblings, were helping him.

'How did you go?' Cyrus asked, turning to greet them. His grey hair hung down close to his eyes, hiding some of the lines that life had added to his brow in the last few years. He saw the two hares as he turned. 'Well, it's something.'

Deor and Sam took the hares out back of the house. Quickly and expertly, they skinned them and cleaned the skins. The hares were lean, with not a great deal of meat on the bones. They took the skins back inside and hung them on hooks in the corner of the room. They would dry them out and treat them so they'd last, then they could trade them in the town.

Back inside, Deor and Sam quickly broke the two hares down into pieces. They stored most of the meat away and added the rest to the pot of vegetables their father was preparing. It was modest, but it would be enough. At least they had some meat. Deor had grown tired of plain vegetable stew.

'When are you going to take me hunting?' Sage asked, coming up to Deor and staring up at her. Sage took Deor's arm in her own, and smiled up at her with her best *do this for me, won't you, please?* smile.

Deor laughed and kissed her sister's forehead. Sage brought Deor nothing but joy with her sharp wit, her intelligence and her love of life. 'Soon enough, my beautiful Sage,' she said.

'She's still too young,' Cyrus said matter-of-factly.

'She's thirteen; I was hunting at that age.' In fact, she'd been hunting when she was nine. She always had a gift for it and always loved it. Even when she was small, she saw the mountains and longed to explore them. She felt as though she had been born to hunt.

'You were different, Deor,' her father said. 'I want Sage to learn, to go through the school until the end. I wish we'd done that with you and Sam.'

'We couldn't do that with me,' Deor said. 'The mine doesn't pay you enough. We were all starving to death; we couldn't rely just on Sam hunting. Things got hard after Mum died.' There was a long pause in the room. They didn't talk about her death often.

'I know …' Cyrus eventually said wearily, with great sadness in his voice.

Deor had lost her mother; Cyrus had lost his wife. To his credit, Cyrus had never let himself fall apart. He kept going, no doubt hurting inside, but still moving forward for their family.

'What about Alexi?' Sam asked, breaking the silence.

'Yeah, what about me?' said Alexi. His teenage voice cracked and squeaked slightly.

'I want them both to go through the school to the end, if we can manage it,' Cyrus said. 'In the fight against Merope, we need thinkers as much as warriors.'

Deor laughed. 'There is no fight against Merope, Dad, there's only the Meropans occupying our territory, taking our resources, taking our children. We're an oppressed people. If there were a fight, at least we'd have a fighting chance. But we have sticks, while they have guns.'

'Yes, but perhaps one day there will be a fight,' Cyrus said. 'You two were too young—and Alexi and Sage, you weren't even born yet—but I remember freedom before this occupation. I remember what Alcyone was like. I hunted in those hills at your age too, Deor, and without the fear of being shot by a patroller. One day, maybe those days can return. In the other territories too. I visited the Northern as a young man and saw our capital. We aren't even allowed to leave our own territory anymore, let alone see the capital.'

Deor thought about what that must have been like while Cyrus served up the stew. They all sat at the table to eat together. Freedom in Alcyone; it must have been so liberating. She'd never felt it, to be free. When she and Sam went into the mountains, they always had one eye over their shoulder looking out for a patroller. That's how she lived her life, looking out for a patroller. She always had, and yet even though it was the only way of life she knew, she also knew it wasn't right. Part of Deor knew that life wasn't supposed to be this way, that she had rights, and they'd been taken away by Merope. It burned inside her, somewhere deep, beyond the reach of her thoughts.

'We saw some today,' she said as they ate.

'Saw what?' Cyrus asked.

'Some patrollers in the mountains. Six of them in a group. They chased us … and shot at us.'

'Deor!' Cyrus said. 'What had you done?'

'Nothing!' Sam said quickly. 'We'd done nothing. We came into a clearing, and they were sitting in a circle. One of them saw us and immediately stood and fired. We ran, and we got away.'

Cyrus' eyes widened in shock. 'My God … Why would they shoot at you?'

Sam shrugged. 'I don't know. But we think they were looking for someone or a group of people. Perhaps they thought that was us.'

'The mountains are getting too dangerous, then.' Cyrus shook his head. 'You may have to stay away from them for a while.'

Deor rolled her eyes. There was no way that was going to happen. 'We can't stay away from the mountains, Dad.

We have to hunt. If we don't hunt, we don't have meat, and we have nothing to trade. We have to go there, but we'll be careful, I promise.'

Silence descended on the room as fog descended on the Asman Range nearby. It began to rain. Deor thought of the dead patroller and wondered if he was still lying at the entrance to the cave. Most likely, the cave lion had taken him.

'Well, at least give it a few days, Deor,' Cyrus said. 'You turn eighteen tomorrow, and Sam turns nineteen, do something for your birthdays tomorrow instead. Go out to the tavern.'

'One of the few places the patrollers let us have,' Sam said.

'Yes, but not beyond curfew,' Deor said. 'Never beyond curfew.'

'We could go there tomorrow afternoon, Dee, see if any of our friends are there. It's the end of the week. Usually there's a crowd then.'

'You mean, see if any of your girlfriends are there …' Sage piped up.

Deor laughed. Sage had a way of making Deor laugh like no one else could.

'I see them,' Sage continued, 'how they look at you. How you look at them. They giggle like they have a mental condition.'

Deor nearly spat out a piece of rabbit. Sage was just thirteen, but she sure had a hold of her older brother.

'I have *friends* …' Sam said, glaring at Sage. 'And some of them will likely be at the tavern for a little while tomorrow. Leon may be there. Deor, it's our birthday, we're going. That's final.'

'Sure, it'll be fun, I'm certain. I'm going to bring Mini, though.' Mini was her smallest spear, more like a dagger, strongly built and with a strong and sharp blade. Deor could conceal it well in her clothes but have it out in a flash.

Sam laughed. 'How fitting that Mini isn't the name of a friend of yours, but of a weapon. We'll have fun; you'll see.'

Deor feigned hurt. 'Harsh!' Though he was kind of right. She didn't really go out to make friends. Though she always kept an arunet flower in her room.

'Good,' her father said, 'and in the morning, instead of heading up to the mountain, we can all spend some time in the garden. The vegetables are coming along well.'

Sam shook his head. 'The garden is more Sage's thing, not mine. I'm going to sleep in.'

'Don't let him in the garden, Dad,' Sage said. 'He's a brown thumb; everything he touches out there dies! Maybe he should try that with his girlfriends …'

Deor stifled a laugh.

'Very funny, Sage,' Sam said, 'but they're not my girlfriends.'

'I'm going to go out early, just for a little while,' Deor said. 'There's something I want to check out.' The obelisks and the cave plagued her thoughts. Those rocks had been placed there, she was sure of it, but why? And also, somewhere inside, they reminded her of something. She didn't know what; she just knew she had to go back there.

'Don't go far,' her father said. 'If there's an increased presence of patrollers on the mountain, then it isn't worth the risk.'

'Okay, I won't,' Deor lied.

CHAPTER 2

Deor stood in front of the cave again as the sun began to rise in the east. She'd snuck out before dawn and made it up the mountain unseen. The patroller's body was gone. Probably taken by the cave lion, though there were no marks indicating it had been dragged inside. Lots of other animals in these woods could have dragged it away, though.

She and Sam had been rushed yesterday. There had been no time to examine these stones properly, but now, in the dawn light, she had more time to look at them. They'd definitely been placed here; no other stones like this existed anywhere she'd been in the Mid Territory. And they weren't random; they were shaped. Obelisks. Worked stone. But where had they come from? Why had they been placed here?

She ran her hand over the surface of the one on the right side of the entrance. Smooth and cold. Something on the stone drew her eye, and her heart skipped a beat. Embossed on the stone, two crescent moons faced one another. This couldn't be … She pulled down her shirt a little, revealing her birthmark. She looked from the stone to her birthmark and back again. Identical. Someone had embossed her birthmark on these stones … How could this be possible?

'What the hell is going on here?' she said to herself, then quickly realised how small her voice sounded in the vast isolation of the mountains. She checked the stone on the left. Same thing. Her birthmark, embossed on it at approximately head height. Deor inwardly referred to her birthmark as her *two moons* because of how clearly it resembled two crescent moons facing one another. Nearly perfectly shaped, slender crescent moons facing one another on her shoulder. Of course she'd had them all her life, so to see them now replicated on these stones was startling. Why were they here?

She had to find out what was happening. She just had to. She scanned the woods surrounding her; no sign of anyone around. Safe, for now, from patrollers. Nervously, slowly, she entered the cave, waited for her eyes to adjust to the dark, then looked around. Like yesterday, she could see the cave walls stretching into the darkness. She had Mini in her hand and other spears in her pack. If the cave lion was here and it charged her, at least she'd be ready.

Deor walked slowly forward into the cave. After a few steps, she again heard a low growl in front of her, unmistakably a cave lion. She moved back quickly to the cave entrance, but not out into the light. She couldn't see the lion, nor any sign of movement. Something wasn't right here …

Moving slowly, Deor crept back into the darkness of the cave and returned to the spot she'd been in before. Again, a low growl rumbled at her from around a metre away. Instinctively, she held out Mini in front of herself, ready to fight if necessary. She peered into the darkness of the cave, but she still couldn't make out anything specific.

Something didn't feel right. *Why can't I smell it? This cave should reek of lion.* Deor crept slowly to her right, away from the sound, then with the greatest of caution, she crept forward, small step by small step. After a few steps, she heard a deeper growl, in front of her again now. Instinctively, she lunged forward with Mini, ready to wound the lion but hoping to scare it away. Suddenly, the sound disappeared, and she stepped into a lit cavern with torches on the walls. She turned quickly and looked behind her but saw only darkness, yet here was light. The light hadn't been there a moment before, but it was there now. And there was no sign of the cave lion.

What the hell is going on here? She turned and looked at her surroundings. Tunnels led off each side, and another one before her led into the mountain, but a door stood at the far end of it. A green door. Completely confused as to what was going on, and moving carefully in case the cave lion—or anything else—might jump out at her, Deor made her way to the door. She tried it. Locked.

Deor gathered her thoughts and tried to make sense of things. The cave was dark, she heard a cave lion, then all of a sudden, she was in a lit cavern with a locked door leading into the mountain. And her birthmark was embossed on the stones out the front!

She tried the door again, but it was still locked, of course. Summoning up courage, she knocked on the door. 'Hello …?' she called. 'Is anyone there?'

Nothing but silence from the other side of the door. She waited a few seconds, then knocked again. 'Hello?' this time a little louder. She waited, but no response came. She tried to force the door handle to open, but it was locked firm.

Frustrated, Deor turned to walk back towards the cave entrance. She didn't know what to make of any of this, or what to do next. The tunnels coming off the side of the cavern just led away into darkness, and she had no desire to explore them. She walked out of the lit cavern, back into the darkness of the cave, and turned to look back at the cavern, but it had disappeared once more. What magic had created this strange place? The cave lion growled again.

'Oh, you're not really there!' she said loudly, waving Mini in its general direction. 'You're just put there somehow to try to frighten me. I'm onto your game, lion!'

She turned and made her way out of the cave. Though frustrated by the lack of answers, she couldn't stay here. She couldn't risk being on the mountain for long, given the recent patroller activity. She had to get home. After touching the two moons on the obelisks one more time, she turned her back to the ravine and the cave and made her way back down the mountain.

As she walked, Deor kept pondering the cave and what it could mean, especially the two moons on the obelisks. Why were they there? Where did that door lead? Who was behind all of this? Lost in her thoughts, she was jolted back to reality by the loud bang of a gunshot.

Adrenaline swept through her body; her senses heightened. It came from the right. Close by. She turned to look and saw a commotion coming through the trees. Five men emerged, running wildly. One of them saw her; fear and panic flooded his face.

'Run!' yelled the man. Behind the five young men, five patrollers chased them, guns pointed. She had to go. Right now. Deor sprinted straight down the mountain, dodging trees as she went. She leaped over a fallen log, then barely avoided a rut in the forest floor that nearly sent her sprawling. Recovering her balance and maintaining her stride, she glanced over her shoulder and saw the patrollers still in pursuit of the young men. She kept running hard, then heard another explosion as one of the patrollers fired. She spun around and saw one of the men collapse on the ground. The others ran on.

Deor turned right to run down the hill and across it to get further away from the patrollers. She headed in the direction of the thin wood just outside her town, running fast. She turned a couple of times to look back, but it seemed they hadn't seen her. She'd gotten lucky. Eventually, she reached the bottom and the beginning of the thin wood. Her breath came in sharp, hitched bursts. Adrenaline still washed through her. She'd just seen a man shot. Shot and killed by the same five patrollers she'd seen yesterday. Why were they shooting people?

She walked back through the thin woods, her hands on her hips, sweat on her neck, recovering her breath. 'I'm already fit,' she mumbled to herself. 'I don't need all this extra running, especially when it's from bullets.'

More questions filled Deor's head now than when she'd left home earlier in the morning, and worse, she hadn't gotten any answers. She still felt baffled as to what the cave and cavern were for, and now she'd seen a person killed. Her father was right; it was too dangerous in the mountains. Those patrollers were clearly under orders to shoot the group they pursued on sight. She realised how lucky she and Sam had gotten yesterday.

Back home, Deor slipped in through the front door, hoping to go unnoticed. No luck; her family were up and eating breakfast—leftover stew from the night before.

'Where have you been?' Cyrus asked.

'Nowhere. I just went for a stroll on my birthday, that's all.'

Sam stifled a laugh. Cyrus looked at her suspiciously.

She lied to her father more and more, but she had to find out what was behind that door.

The afternoon grew longer; Deor played with her hair a little as she prepared to go to the tavern with Sam. Nerves agitated her when something social was coming up. She found socialising awkward at best. People talked about such meaningless and menial things; she found it hard to pay attention and harder to care. Usually, she'd just stand there, nodding, until she eventually realised they'd stopped talking and were waiting for her to respond.

'That's great,' was her go-to line in these situations. This had led to an awkward situation about a year ago, when a girl she used to go to school with told her that her father had died.

'It's great?' the girl, whose name Deor couldn't remember, had replied.

Deor had quickly realised that she hadn't been listening, and panic rushed her senses like a mugger.

'I mean, awful, awful, not great,' had been her clumsy save.

Now, as she got ready, anxiety twisted inside her. She would be sure to bring Mini. She didn't plan on stabbing anyone, but it made her feel better to have it with her.

Sam had returned from the town, where he and Alexi had gone to trade. Money was scarce. Officials in Titus controlled the finances of Alcyone, and they paid her father a pittance for working in the mine, so the majority of their goods they acquired were through trade.

'They deliberately keep us in poverty,' Deor had said to her father earlier that day. 'When we're kept that way, we're easier to control, to keep in line. They deny us our rights, our freedoms, so we can be used as servants of their empire. The sweat from our brow oils the machinery of it.'

Cyrus agreed. He and Deor shared the same political views,

the same take on the Meropan occupation of their homeland.

Deor had spent a chunk of the morning in the garden with Sage and Cyrus. The garden wasn't really Deor's thing, but Sage had a talent for it, and she delighted in being able to not only tell Deor what to do but also to chide her when she did it wrong.

'Don't worry,' Sage had said, 'when I harvest this emmer wheat, I'll teach you how to make bread. You may assist me.'

Sage had been growing many vegetables, including peas, broccoli, beans, potatoes and parsnips, as well as some goosefoot and nettles. For the first time, they were growing emmer wheat. In the last few centuries, as the ice had properly melted away, the people of Alcyone had gotten good at turning emmer wheat into bread, and Sage was keen to try it. Deor was extremely proud of her bright, sassy little sister, and though she knew Sage wanted to learn to hunt, Deor secretly wished a different life for her. She couldn't bear to think that the wheels of the Meropan machine would inevitably grind her sister down, like emmer wheat ground down for bread. The light that shone from Sage deserved to remain undimmed.

'Dee,' Sam said, putting his goods from the town on the table. Sage immediately began rummaging through them. 'Are we going to the tavern or what? I want to have some fun!'

'What's this?' Sage was never one to pay attention to what Sam was saying. She'd picked something up.

Deor didn't see what it was before Sam snatched it back. 'Sage!' he whispered abruptly.

'Tavern?' Deor said. 'Sure, why not? I'm ready.' She'd done exactly zero to get ready, still wearing what she'd run from the patrollers in.

'Well, you're not going to wear that, are you?' Sam asked. 'We're not going hunting, after all.'

'I'll find something to wear,' she retorted, though she'd much prefer to stay in her hiking clothes. Deor avoided dressing up—it was almost always coupled with socialising.

'Good,' Sam said, 'but first, come over here.'

Though suspicious of Sam's request, she walked over to the table.

Sage smiled at her. However, it was her father who spoke up. 'Deor, you're eighteen years old today, and I know you don't want to make a big deal about it, but we all wanted you to have something nice on this day. Sam?'

Deor looked at Sam. He came over and hugged her, then placed something in her hands. 'Happy birthday, Dee. We love you.'

'Is that …' Deor looked in her hands. Sam had put a pendant in it, and the sunlight sparkled on the gem inside. Deor stumbled over words, not sure what to say—she knew what was in her hands.

Cyrus nodded. 'It's a Minerva gem. We traded for it. And it's for you.'

'No, you—you must have traded … how much did this cost?' She held the gem up to the light. Its refractions sprayed drops of sunlight on the walls.

'It doesn't matter,' Sam said. 'It's something we worked on for a while with a merchant in town. He was good to us; we struck up a deal. It exists from before the invasion, so this is something the Meropans have never gotten their hands on. This pendant was made when Alcyone was free; it was owned by free Alcyonans. It's from all of us, your family, always. Now you have a part of our land as a part of you. A part of our heritage.'

Deor looked at the gem again. This was so generous. A lot of the people of the Mid Territory worked in the mines, extracting the valuable Minerva gems, but Merope took them all away for very little pay. This was the life her father led. Stealing one of the Minerva gems would get you shot. Or worse.

'I don't know what to say …' She again held it up to the light. 'It's too much.'

'No,' Cyrus said, 'it's not. We know who you are; we see you. Your light deserves to shine, like this gem.'

Deor hugged Sam, and then her father. 'Thank you.'

Alexi gave her a hug too, and Sage took her hand. 'And now I'll help you find something to wear that matches it.'

Soon afterward, Deor and Sam walked into the town. Deor wore the pendant but kept it underneath her clothing. She wasn't about to take a chance, not with patrollers around who might think she stole it. She couldn't help bringing it out to look at it in the afternoon sunlight, though. It glimmered dazzlingly. Minerva gems were especially beautiful when allowed to see the sunlight, and this one hadn't seen much sunlight for a long while.

They arrived at the tavern and found it fairly full—common on a non-workday. Of all the buildings that had been available to the townsfolk before the invasion, Merope had only allowed them to keep the tavern, a recreational hall, the school and the temple. The courthouse, the police building, the library, the town forum and other buildings had all been either taken over by the patrollers or forbidden to be used. The school maintained a small library that the children used, but the records of the last few hundred years of life in their territory— going back to when the ice had begun to melt away and the territories were formed—and the collection of manuscripts on matters of philosophy, medicine and mathematics, were now unavailable. They sat unused in the town library. Locked away.

The police headquarters had become the patrollers' barracks and the courthouse their headquarters. No legal acts happened there anymore.

'The Meropans are cunning,' Deor said, as they approached the tavern. 'They occupy our territory, take all our resources, but still let us have a few small things, such as the tavern, just to placate us and stop people rising against them. It's not through generosity; it's through strategy that we can use this place.'

Sam nodded in agreement. 'Even the fact that they have two patrollers stationed at the tavern entrance is strategic; it's them saying, *You can have this, but only while we allow it.*'

'They want us to feel grateful to them,' Deor said, 'for these small mercies. As though they're magnanimous. It makes me despise them even more.'

In the tavern, several of Sam's friends and one or two people that Deor remembered from her few years in school stood about socialising. They greeted her with small smiles, familiar but not close. Deor returned the same smile.

Deor and Sam headed to the bar, got a drink each and found a table to sit at. Deor had barely taken a sip of her drink when she noticed Sam's friend Leon making his way towards them. He had a large drink in his hand and had someone with him, a stranger, though to Deor his face looked familiar.

'Sammu, my friend!' Leon said, embracing Sam. 'Always good to see you! And if it isn't baby sister, Deor! Hello, my lovely!' Leon was a little bit drunk.

'Hello, Leon,' Deor said, awkwardly returning the hug he offered.

Leon was Sam's best friend, and Deor had known him most of her life. He was a good man, normally a sensible and quiet man. Today he was letting himself loose, clearly.

'We will sit with you!' Leon declared, sitting himself down next to Sam.

His friend sat next to Deor. He had a confident smile, tanned skin and wavy blond hair. He was very attractive. She guessed he was a couple of years older than her, and he looked like he came from the Coastal Territory. He gave her a smile that showed he knew he was attractive and was perfectly okay with flaunting it and flirting with it.

Deor smiled in return, but she couldn't pinpoint where the familiarity she sensed came from. She knew him, but from where?

'Well, are you going to introduce us to your friend?' Sam asked.

'Pleid forgive me!' Leon bellowed. 'Where are my manners! Sammu, Deor, this is my friend Dolus! He has only recently come to our territory.' On saying that, Leon checked himself. 'Though I shouldn't say that too loudly, should I?' he added in a whisper.

'Charmed to meet you,' Dolus said, taking Deor's hand and kissing it. 'Leon did not tell me your territory had such beautiful women. Your eyes, they are striking, one green and one blue. I don't think I've ever seen that before. And both of them so deep, like endless wells.'

'Oh God, we have a smooth talker, do we?' Sam took Dolus' hand out of Deor's to shake it and introduce himself. 'I am Sam. This is *my sister* Deor.'

Deor chuckled inwardly. Sam was very protective of her.

Dolus shook his hand and nodded to Sam. 'Nice to meet you too, Sam, and my, what a firm grip you have with your handshake. Almost too firm! I like that, though; it shows a man of character, a man who knows what he wants! I respect that.'

Sam finally relinquished his grip. Deor smiled; Dolus was

trying not to show that his hand hurt.

'How are you finding the Mid Territory?' Deor asked. It was maddening that she couldn't place where she knew him from.

'Very different to mine, but beautiful. I come from the Coastal. In summer back home the ocean breeze makes the afternoons a joy, and the water is a nice temperature to bathe in, especially in these days when Alcyone seems to get a little warmer each year.'

'Sounds ideal.' Deor sipped her drink. 'What made you leave it to come here, then? We're just mountain rats round here.'

'Enough about that!' Leon bellowed, surprising Deor. 'Because I want to make a toast! My good friend Sammu, it's your birthday today, if I'm not mistaken? Hmm? You didn't think your oldest friend Leon would forget your birthday, did you? Nineteen years old today, he is! So … a toast!' With that, Leon abruptly stood on the table, wobbled and called out, 'A toast!'

Some people in the tavern laughed. One of the patrollers at the door outside turned to look at what was going on.

'To my best friend, Sammu, on his nineteenth birthday! He is the strongest, wisest, most noble man I know! Pleid himself would be proud to have him as a brother! To Sammu!'

'To Sammu!' some of the others called out in response.

Sam mouthed the words, 'I'm sorry' to Deor. She smiled and shrugged. It was funny to see Leon like this. Much more enjoyable than making small talk with school friends whose names she couldn't remember.

The patroller who'd taken an interest strode into the tavern and up to Leon. 'Off the table!' he yelled.

Leon did what he was told. 'Sorry, sir, sorry,' Leon said with feigned deference. 'I will never do it again, your excellentness.'

The patroller, on whom sarcasm was clearly lost, seemed satisfied by this. He grunted and returned to guarding the front door.

'Thank you, Leon,' Sam said, 'but it's also Deor's birthday, remember? She is exactly one year younger than me.'

Leon looked horrified. 'Oh, my queen!' he spluttered. 'I am so sorry! How could I forget; of course, it's also your birthday. How could I have been so … what can I do to fix this? I know! A TOAST!' He rose from his seat to get on the table once again, but Sam and Dolus both reacted quickly as Deor laughed.

'No!' they called out simultaneously, both restraining Leon from getting on the table. They successfully sat him back down again.

'Let's not have another toast, Leon!' Dolus said. 'I don't want your oafish patroller friend joining our little party again. Something tells me it might be the end of it, and I've only just met your friends. I'd hate to see it end so soon.' He smiled at Deor as he spoke.

By Pleid, he was a flirt. She inwardly rolled her eyes. Then a lightning bolt of memory hit her. He was one of the young men she'd seen on the mountain, the one who yelled at her to run. The shock of realisation must have shown on her face.

'Unless that is not agreeable, Deor …' Dolus said.

'No, sorry, that's fine,' she said, regaining her composure. 'I just thought of something, doesn't matter. Sorry. Yes.'

'Fantastic!' Dolus said, sitting back down. 'So, Leon, how do you know Sam and Deor?'

'Oh, well, that's a funny story. Very funny indeed! We went to school together.'

Silence from Dolus, Deor and Sam.

'That's it?' Dolus eventually asked. 'That's not a very funny story, Leon.'

'Oh, but the funny things we did!' Leon said. 'Like when the patrollers were at school that day and you threw a fig at one, and they thought it was me, and they nearly shot me! Fun times!'

'Always had a bit of trouble with the patrollers, have you, Sam?' Dolus asked.

'Dee and I both,' Sam replied. 'And seemingly more of late. I don't know why, but they seem to have stepped up their aggression in the area.'

Dolus frowned. 'Have they now …'

Deor turned to Dolus and studied his expression as she spoke. 'Yes; in fact, I think they may be looking for people. Specific people, or a group of people, I'm not sure. Do you know anything about that?'

A strange smile came across his face. 'Deor, what is that?' he asked, indicating her birthmark.

The top Sage had picked out for her didn't hide the mark. She chided herself. Normally, she hid it when she went out in public. It didn't embarrass her, but when she was younger, she was a little self-conscious about it, and the habit of hiding it away had stuck.

'It's nothing,' she said, touching her two moons, 'just a birthmark.'

Dolus nodded. 'A birthmark, yes, I can see that, but it's very distinctive. May I see it again?'

Reluctantly, Deor pulled her fingers away from her shoulder, showing her birthmark.

'Remarkable!' Dolus said. 'It's like two perfect crescent moons facing one another! Don't you think, Deor?'

'Yes. I've always thought of them as the two moons.' Where

was he going with this? She wanted to get the conversation back to the patrollers and try to find out more about what was happening in the mountains.

'The two moons,' Dolus echoed. 'Exactly. That's exactly what it looks like. Leon? Have you noticed this before?'

'Ah, I don't, I don't think I …' Leon stammered.

'That's okay; it's just quite remarkable.' Dolus paused in thought for a moment before continuing. 'Tell me, Deor, what do you know about this place?'

'What, this tavern?'

'No, not this tavern, this place, this land mass we live on, us and the Meropans. What do you know about it? How much do you know?'

Deor shrugged. 'Not a great deal; for all my life as far as I can remember we've been occupied by Merope. That doesn't exactly leave a lot of time for sightseeing.'

Dolus chuckled. 'Have you ever been to any of the other territories?'

Deor shot Sam a quick look. They'd done a little border exploring before, but it was perilous; you were at risk of running into patrollers tasked with stopping you from doing exactly that. They'd explored the top of the Asman mountains occasionally, which marked the boundary between Merope and Alcyone, though they'd gone no further. They had seen into Meropan territory, though not far. On occasion, they'd journeyed into the territory to their north when hunting—the Mid North. Never far, though. They hadn't journeyed south. Everyone said that territory was unoccupied.

She replied with a partial lie. 'Not really. I only know what I hear from people who've been there or come from there. Like you.'

'What about the rest of the world?' Dolus asked. 'What

do you know about that?'

'Rest of the world?' Sam asked. 'What do you mean, the rest of the world? The lands beyond Alcyone and Merope?'

'Yes, beyond this land,' Dolus said. 'This island, or land mass, that we're on, we share with the Meropans. We are the only two peoples on this place, as far as we know. Beyond the seas that surround us, though, there are other lands. From some parts of the coast, for example where I'm from, on a clear day you can see them.'

'How far away are they?' Sam asked.

'Hard to know,' Dolus replied. 'But I do know they used to be a lot closer. Centuries ago, when there was still a lot of ice covering parts of Alcyone and Merope, the ocean was lower, revealing more land, so those other lands were closer to us.'

Sam frowned. 'Wait. How do you mean they were closer to us? They can't have moved.'

'No, they haven't moved; the seas have risen,' Dolus said. 'And as a result, the coastlines of Alcyone and Merope have receded with the rising seas, as have the coastlines of the other lands. Centuries ago, therefore, they were closer.'

'Well, what do you know about those other lands?' Deor asked. In school, the history teachers had made vague mentions about people on other lands and the time in the past when ice covered some of the country, but they'd received little information. What she could mainly remember was that her distant ancestors had once lived in caves, before they built Alcyone and Merope.

'What I've been told by others,' Dolus said, 'is that the people in my territory have always lived on the water; we are fishermen and women. We catch a lot of seafood for our diets. At least, we used to. Since the invasion, the patrollers have us catching it mainly for them. We get to keep precious little.

Like you and the Minerva gems that are abundant under the ground here. Your ground.'

Anger at Merope washed through Deor again. 'Yes. Our ground, but they take from it.' She unconsciously felt for the Minerva gem around her neck. Her Minerva gem. Her piece of their history.

'They do it everywhere, Deor,' Dolus said, 'in every territory across Alcyone. The patrollers, on behalf of Merope, use us like slaves to extract food, resources, minerals, elements from the ground, trees or sea that they want and need. They use it to sustain their garrisons across Alcyone and send it back to Merope as well. They enrich themselves at our expense. So the fish and other seafood that we used to catch to sustain us now largely goes to sustaining and strengthening the garrisons in my territory, and it gets sent off to other territories as well. If you ever see a patroller eating fish, it was caught by one of my people and sent here. It is our fish.'

'What does this have to do with other lands, though?' Sam asked.

'That's what I am getting to,' Dolus replied. 'You see, we have this civilisation here, in Alcyone and in Merope. Do any of you know what the Meropan civilisation is like?'

Deor shook her head. 'No, none of us have ever been there.' Curiosity got the better of her from time to time with Sam, but there was no way she was going to go on an adventure into Meropan land.

'Neither have I,' Dolus said, 'and I bet going there would be a one-way journey, like on the Day of Procurement. However, I'm told they're more advanced than us. Large buildings in a capital, Titus, where they have central command of their country. Of course, these things flow on from having the resources of both countries to draw on. Merope is the most advanced civilisation the world has ever seen. We have nothing like that in Alcyone, though we do have territories, and we have a capital that they've locked down. The rest of the world? The lands beyond here? Nothing like this. The people live in caves and don't have language. They form tribes and hunt animals and war with neighbouring tribes. There are no buildings. There is no civilisation.'

'How do you know this?' Sam asked.

'Because my people, before the invasion, had sailed there and seen it, several times. They explored the possibility of new lands for what they might offer, but only encountered savages who live in caves and who attacked them if they came too close. Our people decided to stop going back. The last trip was a few years before the invasion took place.'

'So we've built up a civilisation, and so have Merope. Maybe the others will in time,' Deor said, hoping to end the conversation and redirect it back to more present matters: the events on the mountain.

'Maybe,' Dolus said. 'But my point is, why has it happened this way? Why do we have civilisation, but the rest of the world are savages? Why is it different here? Why are Alcyone and Merope so much more advanced than the rest of the world? And how did we do it all so quickly? Only a few hundred years ago, ice covered a lot of these lands, and we lived in caves. We know this. Our civilisation, all our buildings, our capital, it's all only a few hundred years old, and we've built all this in that short time. Not to mention what they've built in Titus. How did we do it so fast, from being cave dwellers like the rest of the world?'

'Dolus,' Sam said, 'this is a very deep conversation for birthday drinks. It's very interesting, I'm sure, but I have no idea in the world why we have a civilisation and the rest of the world do not. Until you mentioned that there were people on those other lands, I'd never even thought about that possibility. It's pretty interesting, but why are they savages and don't have civilisation like we do? I have no idea …'

'Deor?' Dolus turned to her. 'Care to offer a theory?'

'I don't know,' she replied, trying again to end the conversation. But maybe if she had a go at an answer, the conversation would finish. She thought for a moment. School. They'd talked about the requirements of humankind. She liked school. She thought back to history lessons. 'More animals, more land, better access to more water? All these things we need to live. It's hard to build a civilisation if you need to spend all your time searching for food and water.'

'Yes, very true, and this is part of it,' Dolus said. 'Resources. You must have resources. And there's more of that here than over there.' He waved off in a generally westerly direction. 'But that's not all of it.'

Deor and Sam had finished their drinks. Sam got up to get them another. 'Can I get you two a drink?' he asked.

Dolus replied before Leon had the chance. 'No, we'd better not; I really should get Leon home without having another, unless he agitates those patrollers again.'

'Boooooo!' Leon called.

'But will you do one thing for me, Sam, Deor?' Dolus asked.

'That depends on what it is,' Sam replied.

'Tomorrow, will you come and meet some people with us? I think you'd be very interested to meet them. They may be able to give you the answer to that question I've asked.'

'Okay …' Sam said, 'but who are they?'

'You'll see tomorrow. Deor? Will you come?'

Deor thought for a moment. She looked again at Dolus, sure he was the young man from the mountain that morning.

She liked him well enough, but she didn't know enough about him yet to trust him. But she wanted to hear more and find out what was going on with the patrollers, so she'd cautiously trust him for now. She nodded. 'Count me in.'

A broad smile came across Dolus' face. 'Fantastic! Leon and I will come by your place in the morning, bright and early!'

'Not too bloody early and bright!' Leon said, stumbling as he got up.

'Goodbye, Sam; goodbye, Deor,' Dolus said. 'It was my pleasure, and surprise, to meet you. I look forward to finding out more about you.'

'And I, you,' Deor said. She had to know more about what he'd been doing on the mountain, what led to them being chased. She would find out tomorrow.

Leon and Dolus left the tavern, the patrollers giving them a stare as they did.

'What do you think that was all about?' Sam asked, having gone and returned with drinks.

Deor shook her head. 'I really don't know. But I guess we'll find out tomorrow.'

Deor sipped her drink. Two girls across the bar looked giddily over at Sam. He gave them a wave. Deor rolled her eyes.

'What?' Sam said sheepishly. 'They're friends of mine!'

Deor smiled. 'What would Sage make of this?'

'You don't tell Sage anything! She doesn't need any more information!'

The two girls came over and sat down to talk to Sam. They didn't even look at Deor, which was fine with her.

She sat pondering the questions Dolus had raised. The answers to those questions resonated with something inside her, but she just couldn't get to it. All her life, she'd felt as though there were things she couldn't remember but needed to. Like there was some past, some memory she couldn't reach. The feeling constantly gnawed at her, and now it did so more than ever.

CHAPTER 3

Deor stepped out into the pre-dawn darkness, Sam by her side. They had both risen early and snuck out without waking anyone. Dolus and Leon waited out front, as promised. Keeping quiet, they headed to the Asman Range.

Deor had again tied her hair in a braid, despite no prospect of hunting, but habits are what habits are. Dolus led the way south along the edge of the mountains. Sam walked alongside Leon, and Deor followed behind. Leon was less effusive than the previous evening.

'Feeling okay this morning, my friend?' Sam asked.

'Yes, yes, I'm fine now,' Leon said. 'I may have had a little too much merriment last night, but Dolus got me back home, and I slept it off. It's good to be out in this beautiful morning air.'

Leon was right. The morning was stunning today in Alcyone. Each year, the mornings were brighter and more beautiful. In school, they'd talked about how the country used to have a lot of ice covering it centuries ago, when their ancestors lived in caves, but that the world had warmed since then. It continued to do so, creating stunning mornings like this one. The sun was creeping above the top of the Asman Range in the east, spilling sunlight across the land like water flooding a basin. Deor smiled as she looked up at the vast mountain range marking the eastern border of her country. She hated the occupation with all of her soul, but she loved the beauty of her country.

'Glad to hear it,' Sam said. 'I feared you were going to get us into a fight with some patrollers there last night! Speaking of being out in the morning air, though, where exactly are we going? And who are we going to meet?'

'It's better if you see when we get there. Better to show and explain rather than explain on its own.'

'Well,' Sam said, 'I've known you a long time, my friend, and you've been—how should I say it—somewhat secretive from time to time. There've been many instances where you're gone for a few days, and when you come back, you pretend you haven't been away at all.'

Leon stifled a laugh.

'And I know,' Sam continued, 'that you've been involved in some sort of secretive venture. You've occasionally slipped up and alluded to it, usually when you've been merry like last night. Is it perhaps something to do with that?'

Leon paused before responding. 'Yes, it is to do with that. I think you might be interested in it. And that's all I'll say. For now. All will be revealed, Sam, don't worry.'

They headed south for a couple of hours, mostly in silence, staying close to the tree line at the bottom of the mountain. They didn't want to be out in the open in case they might be spotted. Eventually, they turned up the mountain, then came down a small trench in the hillside to an opening in the side of the mountain—a cave, closed off now. It was the site of an old mine, disused. Deor had never been to this part of the mountains before.

'The very first mine in our territory,' Leon said. 'It was nicknamed Minerva, because this is the first place our people found Minerva gems, around one hundred and fifty years ago now. The locals dug it out and fortified it, and little by little they extracted all the gems. It hasn't been used in fifty years. The patrollers are never down this way and don't know it exists. They have no reason to; it has no gems left. It's been mined out.'

Deor looked at Sam, a little confused. Why had they walked all this way to look at a disused mine?

'Let's go in,' Dolus said. 'Follow me.'

Timber bound together by rope barricaded the entrance to stop people or animals wandering in and coming to harm. Deor couldn't see any way in, but Dolus walked up to the barricaded entrance and vanished.

'What in the name of Pleid!' Deor exclaimed, alarmed. He'd disappeared in an instant. He hadn't walked through a door. He hadn't turned a corner. He hadn't fallen. He had vanished. Gone.

Leon smiled. 'It's okay; let me show you.' He walked up to the entrance and also vanished. Gone. However, a moment later, he reappeared, walking back to them.

'Leon …' Sam said, 'what's going on here? Did you somehow spike our drinks last night?'

Leon chuckled. 'Just follow me in.'

Reluctantly, Deor and Sam walked behind him towards the barricade. Deor thought of the cave from yesterday and the disappearing room. She took a few steps, and before she knew it, they stood right in front of the barricade with Leon and Dolus. Deor reached out and touched the timber. It was real, but there was another opening into the mine to their left.

She hadn't seen that until she'd come close.

'You can't see that from the outside,' Leon explained. 'There's a veil over the entrance that keeps that door hidden from view. The veil is extremely fine, made from gossamer harvested from jakelopes. They're ancient creatures that live in the southern parts of this mountain range. They spin webs, like spiders, but not to catch prey. They spin them to protect their young. The webs are as light as air and clear, see through, but they can project, reflect and refract light. The people who live in the South have learned to work with the gossamer and turn it into materials they can use. They turned this one into a material so fine that it weighs no more than the air, and made it into a veil that hangs invisibly over the front. It enables the light from the barricade to come through, but reflects the light of everything around it, so when you're standing outside, you see nothing more than the barricade. Even when Dolus stood here in front of the door, you couldn't see him, as his light was refracted and reflected away, while the barricade remained projected out.'

'Amazing …' Deor still touched the timber barricades, making sure they were real. She turned around to touch the veil, but her hands felt nothing, just the air. She couldn't feel or see anything except the forest they'd just walked through. 'Where is it?' she asked. 'I can't feel it.'

'You won't be able to feel it,' Dolus said. 'It's an amazing substance, incredibly fine and made finer by the people who live in the South. They call it jakel hair. Here, come and I'll show you.'

Deor followed Dolus out the front. She put her hands up as she walked through where she supposed the veil was, expecting to feel something, but felt nothing. They turned and looked at the entrance again. Deor couldn't see the veil, even though she looked for it. All she could see was the barricade, and she could no longer see the side entrance to the cave.

'Come around here.' Dolus walked towards the right of the entrance. Deor and Sam followed. When Dolus was nearly lateral to the door, he stopped. 'Look from this angle. Can you see anything?'

Deor looked at where she knew the second entrance to the cave was, but she couldn't see it, just darkness the shade of the mountain itself. 'What am I looking for?' she asked.

'Here,' Dolus said, 'hanging in the air, the faintest outline, like the finest mist in the morning, but thinner than a strand of hair. Can you see?'

Then Deor saw it. The faintest shimmering line through the air, like a ghostly, impossibly thin wave. It was more like a shift of perspective than something physical. The shift seemed to wrap around the front of the entrance, then turn to join the hillside and arch over the top of the entrance in the same way. When Deor moved her head to the left, it vanished, and when she moved to the right, it also vanished. Only when she positioned herself at just the right angle could she see it at all, and even then, only briefly and faintly. If she didn't know what to look for, or where to look, she would never see it.

Again, Deor tried to touch it with her hands, without success. 'Incredible.'

'The creatures that live in the south of this mountain range are exotic,' Leon said. 'They exist nowhere else on the continent. Jakelopes are large insects with eight legs. They crawl around and grow to around a metre long. The Southerners have become expert at using the jakel hair as a cloak, as a veil. It helps keep their existence largely a secret from Merope. They helped us to make this, to keep this place a secret.'

'What is this place?' Sam asked. 'It must be more than just an old mine, then?'

Leon nodded. 'It is, and it's time to show you.' He led them back through the gossamer and along the passageway into the mountain.

Deor tried to wrap her head around all this. A veil made from the web of a metre-long, eight-legged insect that lived in the southern mountains. Bizarre.

A door stood just inside the passageway. Leon had a key, which he used to unlock the bolt across the door. He opened it and led them inside. 'This way.' The passageway cut into the rock was fortified by timber beams along the walls and across the roof, sturdy beams secured by grooves cut into the timber. The floor was also timber, but it didn't bend as they walked on it.

'What's in the flooring?' Sam asked. 'It feels solid.'

Leon nodded. 'The tunnel is secured into the bedrock of the cave itself, the beams supported by the bedrock, cut into it. It took years to build all this and what you're about to see.'

'This isn't part of the original mine?' Sam asked.

'No. It's all been built since the invasion. The mine is a front only, a distraction for anyone passing by. Secrecy is vital.'

The passageway came to a turn. They'd been travelling east, but now it turned to the north. At each vertical beam, a small lantern provided light.

'Remember what we were talking about at the tavern yesterday?' Dolus asked as they walked. 'About our civilisation and how quickly we've come along?'

Deor nodded. 'Yes, I have. It makes sense, because it has happened, and yet it's surprising too.'

'Yes, and there's more yet,' Dolus said. 'But this passageway we're in, the mine itself we've left behind, the ability to build that … Cave dwellers can't build these things, Deor. The towns we have, the buildings, your tavern, the courthouse, the school, reading and writing, maths! All of this in a few hundred years, from cave dwellers? Doesn't that seem strange?'

'More and more things are seeming strange to me of late,' Deor replied. The patrollers on the mountain shooting at Dolus and his friends, this underground thing, whatever it was. They had to be related.

'How did we manage to work it all out so quickly?' Dolus said. 'Tens of thousands of years, presumably, of being cave dwellers in an ice age, then a few hundred years later we have done all of this? How?'

They'd arrived at the end of the passageway, where a double door waited for them, closed and locked. Leon again produced a key.

'It's almost as though we already knew how to do it, don't you think?' Dolus asked.

Leon opened the large doors.

Deor's heart skipped a beat at what she saw inside: a huge hall stretched out ahead of her, its ceiling towering far above. What appeared to be shafts in the roof brought in light from outside, making it well lit. The end of the hall was in the distance, far from where she stood.

Leon followed Deor's gaze and pointed at the walls. 'Magma, all of it. This mountain was once a volcano, a very long time ago. The rock is hardened lava.'

Deor looked in wonder at the sheer size of the room and the height of the dark rock walls. The beauty of it contrasted with the brooding dark colour and the nature of the rock, formed from the power of a volcano itself, the blood of the earth solidified. It was power and rage mixed with sheer beauty and majesty. Deor looked up at the roof far above her and at the shafts, which shot up further, shining light into the room.

Leon looked up at the shafts. 'Light and ventilation. They go up to the surface, to hidden parts of the mountain range. There's a rocky valley up there that's very hard to get into and out of. There's no reason for anyone to go in there, least of all the patrollers.'

'I know that valley; I know where we are,' Deor said with a touch of excitement. 'I've chased game into that valley many times. They know to run there if they're in danger from humans.'

'And have you ever gone in there to pursue the game?' Leon asked.

Deor shook her head. 'No, never. It's not worth it. Much too dangerous in there for people. It's a perfect sanctuary for a hunted animal, though.'

Leon nodded. 'Exactly. That's why this room was built right here under it. No one will ever discover the shafts in there. Welcome to the Great Hall.'

Deor walked into the hall. Many tables stretched away from her, down the length of it. Off each side were several smaller rooms. Further down, Deor could see what looked to be a large kitchen area. Other rooms seemed to be for recreation or relaxation. Others still were windowless; they could've been sleeping quarters. It was a mini-city down here, an underground city.

'What's it all for?' Sam asked.

'This is the headquarters of our movement,' Leon replied. 'This is the thing you've sensed I've been involved in, but I haven't told you about. This is how we win back freedom for Alcyone. Freedom from the occupation by Merope, freedom from the patrollers, freedom to enjoy our land once again and live in peace.'

'Sounds dangerous,' Sam said.

Deor's heart leapt with excitement. 'Count me in.' Whatever it was Leon was involved in, if it meant rebellion against Merope, then she wanted to be a part of it. Her brain was trying to take it all in. Already she was wondering how many people were involved and what the plans were.

Leon laughed. 'It will be dangerous, definitely—when the time comes. But we have to risk danger to regain our freedom.'

Leon's calmness and sureness of words was in stark contrast to the very convivial Leon from the tavern the day before. How had he kept this to himself this long, kept it from Sam and others?

'Are you the leader of all this?' Deor asked.

Leon chuckled. 'No, not at all. But you'll get to meet our leader soon enough.'

Dolus interrupted. 'Deor, there's someone I'd like you to meet. Will you come with me?'

'Yeah, I guess …' Deor replied, still unsure if she could trust him or not. He always seemed to be hiding something, but she couldn't put her finger on it.

Dolus led her away while Leon and Sam continued to talk. Dolus led her to a small room with a table and some chairs. Seated in one of the chairs was a woman about forty years old. Deor stopped when she saw her, stunned. She knew this woman. She knew her. Somehow. She'd never seen this woman before, but she felt an immediate connection, something she couldn't describe or discern, but that she could feel within herself. She was sure of it, though; she knew her.

Deor stared at the woman. How could this be? She had a birthmark on her forehead: the two moons. *What the Pleid …*

Dolus smiled. 'Deor, I would like you to meet Eve.'

'Hello, Deor,' Eve said, coming around the table to greet

her. 'It's great to finally meet you. I have waited a long time to do so.'

Deor didn't know what to say. Her mouth opened, then closed again. No words came out. She kept looking at Eve's birthmark on her forehead, trying to work out what it meant, at the same time sensing that she knew this woman somehow. How could she know her? And how could she have the same birthmark? She felt deep within that she knew this woman, but couldn't work out why or how.

'I see you've noticed my birthmark,' Eve said, 'and I see you have the same one on your shoulder. Two moons.'

'Yes, two moons,' Deor said, finally able to talk and absentmindedly touching her shoulder. She felt as though she'd stepped outside herself, as though she heard her own voice from afar. 'But how can you have the same exact birthmark?'

'Do you mind if I touch it?' Eve asked.

A strange question, but Deor felt she could trust Eve. 'I guess that would be okay.'

Eve reached slowly towards Deor's shoulder and gently pressed her index and middle fingers onto Deor's birthmark.

A wave of energy surged throughout Deor's body and shook her for a moment. A vision flashed into her mind, another place not anywhere near Alcyone, a distant place, and she was there, standing on a landscape filled with destruction and chaos, fire and smoke and crippling heat. Destruction lay ahead of her. Among the destruction, she saw two large obelisks, like the ones at the cave, but far bigger. Everything around them was scorched, but the obelisks remained intact. She couldn't see much else around her, and her ears were ringing. She turned to her left and saw a young woman yelling at her to run with her, to get away. Deor couldn't hear her through the noise and the ringing in her ears, but she turned to run, and the vision ended.

Eve had taken her fingers off Deor's shoulder. Deor's head hurt, but she was back in the room again, the vision over. Sweat stung her eyes. She could still hear the ringing in her ears, could still smell the smoke and feel the heat, but the sensations were all fading. What was that place? What had she just seen? It felt familiar, but at the same time it was alien and remote.

'What did you see?' Dolus asked.

Again, words would not come out. What had happened? Thoughts raced through her mind. Where had that been? Was that her? It felt like her memory. It was her, but it was also not her at the same time. 'I don't know,' she eventually said, 'I don't know what I saw. Destruction, chaos, fire and smoke. A war zone. And someone was there with me. And there was great sadness. I felt great, incomprehensible sadness.'

Dolus and Eve exchanged a look.

'What's going on?' Deor asked. 'What did I see? Where was that?'

'Deor,' Dolus said, 'Eve is a seer. She has gifts of vision, both into the past, and sometimes into the future. She can help you.'

Deor's mind began to function again. 'And why do you have the same birthmark as me?' This all had to be linked, somehow.

'All of this can be explained,' Eve said, 'but it will take some time. Will you sit with me?'

Deor nodded.

'I'll leave you two alone.' Dolus left the room and closed the door, leaving the two of them in complete privacy from the rest of the hall.

Two armchairs stood in the corner of the room. Eve

invited Deor to join her there, and they both sat down.

'What is going on here?' Deor asked. Her birthmark felt warm, as though it were still feeling the heat from the vision.

'Do you ever feel as though you know someone, even though you've just met them?' Eve asked.

'Yes, sometimes, with some people. I felt that way with my sister, Sage, when she came into our family. I always have.' The moment she'd seen Sage, she'd felt like she'd always known her. Like Sage had come home to her.

'Have you felt that way about anyone else?'

Deor stopped. Her answer was going to sound strange. *Stuff it*, she thought, *everything seems strange right now*. 'Well, this is a little awkward, but I felt that way when I met you just now. That I knew you.'

Eve nodded. 'And do you ever feel as though there's something that you can't remember, something you need to remember? Something in your past?'

'Every day of my life.' Deor realised that Eve was able to see her, to understand what she'd been struggling with. 'I'm constantly trying to work out what it is. I feel it's very important, but I can't work it out. Some past, some memory. I feel like it relates to something I need to do, but I don't know what. That how things are right now isn't the extent of it, not all I'm meant to do and be.'

Eve nodded. 'What you saw, Deor, wasn't a vision, it was a memory. But it's not a memory of anything you've seen on Alcyone. It's a memory from a past life.'

'A past life? You mean, a life I had before this one?'

'Yes, that is exactly what I mean. Most of us have had many past lives; usually, we don't remember anything about them, but sometimes in our dreams, or in visions, or in guided sessions, we can bring them back up as memories. Did it feel like it was you? Did it feel like a memory?'

'Yes.' Deor leaned forward in her chair. 'It definitely felt like it was a memory. That's what was strangest. I felt like it was me, but it wasn't me at the same time.'

'That's a fairly accurate way to describe it,' Eve said. 'That woman was you, the part of her that is you lives on in this life and did so in earlier lives. That part of you does not die. That is the essence of you; we call it your *bakh*, or your soul, the thing that carries on beyond life and into the next one.'

'Well, where was I? Where was that? What was happening at that place? There was a woman there with me also. Who was she?'

Eve paused before answering. 'Perhaps the best way to answer those questions is to take you back there. I can guide you back so you can see more and learn more about who you were, about where that place was. Would you like to do that?'

'I think I would, but at the same time that was a frightening place, a war zone seemingly.'

'Your vision thrust you back into that moment because it was a moment of great trauma, and I believe it may have been soon before the woman that you were died. That is a traumatic memory, and it's natural that it would be the first one to come to the surface. You have a lot of questions about who that woman was, and we can answer those by going back again but taking you back further, before the destruction and war you saw. Would you like to do that?'

Deor nodded. 'Yes, I would. I want to know who that was. I want to know what that place was. If that's my past, I want to know about it.' This could be where the answers she'd been seeking lay.

'Okay, then,' Eve said, 'if you like, we can begin now.' She brought her chair closer to Deor's, so they were nearly touching.

'Listen to the sound of my voice,' she said. 'I am going to count down from ten to zero. With each number, you will feel more and more relaxed, and slip more and more into a meditative state. When I get to zero, I'm going to put my hand on your shoulder again, on your birthmark. You won't rush into a vision as violently as you did earlier; you'll be more relaxed, and you should slip into a memory state much more gently, but more fully. Does that sound okay?'

'Yes.' Deor felt more relaxed now. Eve's voice calmed her, like listening to rain at night.

'Okay. Try to relax, I'm going to count down now, starting with the number ten. You can close your eyes now if you wish. Nine. You are going to go back into a previous life, back before this life … The life of the woman you saw in your vision earlier—did you get her name?'

'No …' Deor's words came out slowly, with more difficulty. 'I don't think, don't think I did …'

'Eight. That's okay, you'll get her name soon enough. The important thing is that you are going back to an earlier time than where you were before, okay? Seven. You are going to go back years earlier, when there wasn't the destruction and violence present. Six.'

Eve's slow and measured words carried weight, and they seemed to fall down onto Deor like heavy raindrops, pushing her further down inside herself.

'Find a time in her past when it was peaceful, and you can find out more about her, before the destruction began. Five. Perhaps it's just a few years earlier; perhaps she's at home. Four. She may have friends or family with her. You may recognise some of them; you may even remember their names.'

'Friends …' Deor's voice seemed to rise up through her as though out of a deep well. 'Family, from then? Or … or from now?'

'They can be both,' Eve said. 'You may see some people that you recognise as family or friends then, and you may know who they are in this life as well. Three. We often travel through these lives together, with the same people, our family and our friends. Our *bakhs* remain linked. Two. You are down deep now and nearly ready to come out into the memories of the previous life. Just relax and let yourself become her again; see her memories; see her life; rediscover who she was. One. We are nearly there. You are almost her again …'

'Wait …' Deor interrupted slowly, feeling her words as she said it from deep within, like she spoke from inside the centre of the Earth, and Eve's voice came from far away at the top. 'You keep saying her … how do you know I was a woman? I didn't say that.'

'No, you didn't say that.' Eve chuckled while reaching forward towards Deor's shoulder. 'I know you were a woman, Deor, because I was there too. Zero …'

CHAPTER 4

Eve touched Deor on her birthmark, and Deor reacted instantly, her body jolting. Eve was careful to be gentle with her, to ease her down into her vision. Deor's eyes were closed, and she seemed all right. She wasn't in distress, so Eve felt it was okay to continue with the session. She'd regressed many people in her time on Earth, but she'd been waiting all this time to meet Deor. Finally, the day had come.

'Lore,' Deor said. 'My name is Lore.' Deor's voice had deepened and gained an accent. She sounded very different from a minute ago.

Eve recognised the change of voice. She knew it well. She heard it often in her dreams. 'You can see yourself?' she asked.

'Yes, I'm standing outside. It's evening, I think. I know this place. This is where I'm from. This is home. I'm Lore. This is … this place is Nebra. It's my home.'

'You're sure of that?' Eve asked. She had to guide Deor in this regression, but at the same time, it was important to get the details right. Deor would have full memory of her vision when she came out of it, but Eve may still have to fill in some gaps for her.

'Yes,' Deor replied. 'I'm sure. This is Nebra. I am Lore. I can see the sky. The sun is just beginning to set. I can see … we have two moons. There are two moons in the sky. Two crescents facing each other. I know what this is; it's Two Moons' Day! We celebrate this day when our two moons align like this, both crescents, facing one another. It only happens once in every five years or so.'

'You're sure it's Two Moons' Day?' Eve's brow furrowed in thought. Why did Deor not go back further than Two Moons' Day, which was around five years before her last vision? 'That's a strange day for you to choose to go back to, if I'm thinking correctly.'

'Yes, it's definitely Two Moons' Day. There'll be celebrations tonight to mark it, and festivities throughout the day. I'll be out with my family tonight: my parents and my brother and sister. My parents are officials in our country … that's not the right word. They govern.'

Again, Eve reminded herself to get the details. 'How old are you in this time?' Details would help Deor not only when she came out of her vision but also so she could be rooted in facts if she had further visions, which was likely. Generally, when the human mind opens itself up to past-life regression, the link remains open, at least to some degree, unless Eve explicitly closes it for them.

'I am … I'm about the age I am now, about eighteen years old. The years are slightly different on Nebra, though, longer. Eighteen is … eighteen is older than eighteen on Earth. I don't know; I can't work it out … a year is four hundred and forty-four days. But the days are shorter, only twenty-two hours. I don't know. I'm a little older.'

'So Nebra is not on Earth?' Eve needed to make sure Deor was fully immersed in her regression and understood where she was.

Deor laughed at this. 'No, it's not on Earth. This is Nebra; I told you. Our sun is called Alcyone. Our star. We've lived here for more than a million years. Woah. More than a million years. But we have. This is our home. This is my home. I am Lore, and I am Nebran. I have always been Nebran.'

'Do you know where Alcyone and Nebra are?' Eve asked.

'Yes, Pleid. This system is called the Pleid. Us and other stars nearby, like … oh … like Merope. Part of the Pleid system. It's close to Earth; we see it in the sky at night from Earth, but it's far from Earth as well.'

'Yes.' Eve smiled. The regression was going well. Deor was seeing her past life as Lore and was—importantly—also gaining the understanding that Lore had. 'We do see it. Our ancestors here on Earth believed those stars represented our God and named it Pleid. Do you know why?'

'Yes, our memory. It's in our memory. The Pleid, Alcyone, Merope, everything. It's there, just beyond reach. It has always been there. We've built civilisation on Nebra and have lived there for more than a million years, from ancient times. I'm from Nebra, but why am I on Earth now? Why am I not on Nebra? I belong on Nebra.'

'What else can you see, Lore?' Eve asked. Much better if Deor found those answers herself through the regression. 'Is anyone else there?'

'Yes. I can see my family. We'll be going out soon for the Two Moons celebrations. We're at home. The Great Park is nearby. I can see the two giant obelisks that mark its southern entrance. My brother is …' Deor spoke more quickly now. 'My brother is here, and it is my brother, it's Sam! He's not Sam, but it is him. His name is Zephir. He's my brother then, as he is now. He tries to protect me, ha! Even then as now.

My parents are here too, my mother and father. They govern our region, but they're not the politicians; it's a duocracy. We don't have such a thing on Earth. Separated heads of state between the polit—the elected leaders—and the pharit, which is my family. Separate roles, separated powers. This is what my family do.'

'Do you recognise them, Deor? Are they also in this life with you?'

Deor paused before responding, trying to see more clearly. 'I don't think I do,' she finally said. 'Their names are Octus and Ada. They are my parents, but I don't know them in this life.'

'And you said you have a sister? Can you see her?'

'Yes, I can. She's Sofi. She's younger.'

'Do you know her in this life?' Eve asked.

Again, Deor paused before responding. 'This is, this is, I think. Oh, I see now, yes. She is Sage. She's again my sister. I don't understand because Sage is a twin. I don't understand if Alexi is also Sofi. No, he's not. Alexi is Sage's twin in this life, but he's not her twin on Nebra. I don't know if Alexi is on Nebra.'

'Is there anything else you can tell me of significance from this day?' Eve asked.

'I can see … I can see later in the day. I'm at the park; the celebrations are beginning soon. I'm with Pythus and Phela. They are two of my oldest friends.'

'Do you recognise them in this life, on Earth?' Eve asked, leaning forward in her chair.

Deor concentrated, seeming to look hard, though her eyes remained closed. Then a smile came across her face. 'Ha!' she said. 'Pythus is you, Eve! You were my friend on Nebra. And you were a seer, an oracle, then too.'

Eve smiled broadly. All her life she'd remembered Nebra

and her friendship with Lore. Deor had finally reconnected with it. 'Yes, my friend, I was Pythus. And I was on Nebra with you. For all our lives, we were friends. Tell me, do you know Phela? Have you found her on Earth?'

Deor again concentrated, then her shoulders and head slumped slightly. 'Yes, I recognise her now. I knew her when I was younger. She was my friend. Her name was Arunet. Phela was Arunet.'

'Was?' Eve asked.

'Yes, was. She was taken on the Day of Procurement, five years ago.'

Eve fell silent when Deor mentioned the Day of Procurement. Phela had been their friend, and Eve had hoped to meet her again in this life. She bowed her head at the news, then sought to move the vision forward. 'What else do you see, Deor?'

'Now it's later, just Pythus and I. We're at the celebrations in the evening, but something is happening. People are worried. We're outside at a large gathering for Two Moons, but something isn't right, there's … oh no …'

'Do you want to stop?' Eve knew that what Deor was about to see would be distressing.

'No, I need to see … there's a ship, and we're under attack. They come from Remus, a planet in the Meropan system. Oh no … We're running, fleeing the gathering, but they've fired on it; they've fired on the people, and many people are dead. My parents … I think my parents …'

Eve needed to bring her back. 'Deor, I am going to count up from one to ten, and with each number, you will release yourself from the memories and come back to Deor, back to Earth, back to this room.'

Deor interrupted her. 'No. I need to see it. I need to see

all of it.'

'Okay.' Eve hesitated. 'We'll continue. What else can you see?'

'They fired on us without provocation and destroyed a lot of our city. It was the capital of the region. Thousands have died, including my parents. It's going to become war; it has to. I can see that in the coming days we attempted to communicate with Remus, but they didn't reply. Nebra had to respond. We attacked their ships in orbit and sent warships off to Remus. The war began.'

'Why do you think Remus attacked Nebra?' Eve asked. The regression had gone in a stressful direction, but Eve knew the fierceness of Lore's resolve, which no doubt would now be in Deor.

'We've been fighting them all my life, and longer, on and off. We seem to always be fighting with Remus. It goes back well before my life. This has escalated it, though. This was an invasion from the Meropan system, from Remus. They've invaded us, and we've fought back.'

'What else do you see?'

'I see the war. Remus fought back. They tried to attack Nebra again, but we were more ready this time. It turned into an ongoing battle for the next … the next two or three years, I think. My brother Zephir and myself are involved. With my parents killed, the roles of pharit have fallen to him and me. We've led the battle and deployed our military against them. They have troops fighting us on Nebran soil, and we have troops on Remus fighting them. There are many fronts fighting on both planets, and the damage is catastrophic. It goes on, four years of fighting, and millions have died. This is awful …'

Deor paused, becoming more emotional as her vision

continued. Eve feared the damage this regression could cause and mustered a calm voice, as much as she could. 'Deor, we can stop at any time. I can bring you back at any time. You don't have to see all this now.'

'I do,' Deor said with a fierceness to her voice. 'I am Lore. This is my home. They are destroying Nebra, and we are destroying Remus. Cities have collapsed in ruin across both planets. The ground is scorched. The water is poisoned. Constant attacks have devastated the land and the oceans. Life … life is dying …'

'Deor …' Eve attempted to speak, but her words trailed off.

'Neither planet will stop. I will not stop. We cannot. It has gone so far, and we can't turn it around. We're destroying one another, and there's no way back. We have lost so many people.' Deor paused.

'You're right,' Eve said eventually. 'By that time, there was no way back. What are you seeing now?'

When she responded, Deor's voice was lower again, raspy now and hoarse. She sounded as if she'd aged many years. Tears ran down her face. Eve wanted to bring her back, to shield Deor from all of these memories. This wasn't fair to her, to have to bear the burden of Nebra. But Lore, reborn as Deor, would want to know everything that had happened.

'It's the final days,' Deor said wearily. 'There's almost no one left to fight on Nebra or Remus. The devastation is complete. Nearly everyone is dead. Zeph and Sofi are dead. Remus is cooling. The damage was so severe that the planet has been blown off its orbit. The same has happened on Nebra, with parts blown off like chunks chipped off a rock. Parts of the planet are floating away into space, or have been drawn back in and rain down on us as meteors. Nebra is on a destabilised orbit and is drawing closer to Alcyone. No one will survive here much longer. The heat has risen drastically. Remus has been knocked further away from Merope, and it freezes while Nebra burns. No one can survive. We have sent each other to hell.'

Deor paused again for a few minutes. Tears ran down her cheeks; Eve gently stroked her hand. Lore had been her closest friend all their lives on Nebra. A wave of sorrow flooded Eve as she watched this beautiful young woman try to deal with the grief of Nebra and Lore.

Eventually, Deor continued, her voice gravelly and grief-stricken. 'It's my last day. I'm here with you, Pythus, and Phela. We're with four others, Gideon, Xander, Nikita and Milo. We seven are together at the end. Fire is everywhere; the planet is too hot. We die here now; I know this. Xander has made something, a brand, oh—I see now. Xander has made a brand of the two moons. We've burned it in the fire and are burning ourselves with it, so we do not forget Nebra. Pythus, you burned the two moons into me, on my shoulder. I burned it onto you, on your forehead. We burned it there for you to retain your vision in the next life, in this life. You were a powerful seer, Pythus, and we wanted you to retain that sight. Nikita and Phela have branded one another, and Xander, Gideon and Milo have branded one another also. It's so we'll not forget Nebra, not forget what happened here, and so we'll come together in the next life to rebuild. I see it now … That's why we are here on Earth, to rebuild our civilisation. To rebuild Nebra, on Earth.'

Eve's head dropped to her chest. 'Yes. That is why we are here. To start again … What are you seeing now?'

'The end. I am seeing the end of Nebra. We've died; everyone has died. Remus is adrift in space, a frozen rock drifting further away from its sun, and we're a ball of fire circling ever closer to ours. Our planet and our people have been burned to death.' Deor grew more upset. The regression was becoming too much for her.

Eve worried about Deor's mental state if she stayed in the vision. 'Deor,' she said, 'I'm bringing you back to the present now. Back to Earth, back to your life today, as Deor.'

Deor didn't respond. Perhaps Deor couldn't hear her anymore? Eve spoke more quickly and loudly. 'I'm going to count up to ten, and you will be back. One, you are moving away from Nebra now, away to come back to Earth. Two, you are removing yourself from those memories. Three, coming back to Deor's body. Four, back to Earth. Five, you will remember what you saw, but you will know that was the past life, not now. Six, you are feeling yourself inside your body as Deor again. Seven, coming back into this room, Deor. Eight, breathing the air, Earth's air. Nine, you are back here again. Deor, when I say it, you will wake completely and look at me. Ten.'

No movement. For a moment. Then Deor opened her eyes, fierce and blazing with the fires she'd seen on Nebra, one blue and one green. Lore the warrior shone through her eyes, staring through the distance of space and time. She remained silent for a moment, her eyes flashing with rage as she stared into Eve's *bakh*, the *bakh* of Pythus, but then she screamed, roared a guttural cry from her soul, one of anguish and despair and helplessness, of torment and anger, but most of all of loss. She felt the loss of her entire people, of her world, of her family, of herself. She felt the ache inside that only true loss can bring, knowing and loving what there was, and is now gone. Deor screamed and screamed, and when her breath began to run out, she sobbed.

Eve sat with her and held her, trying to calm her. The

memories of what had happened on Nebra would still be coming back to her. Eve held her as Deor sobbed and tried to console her. Deor wept in Eve's arms, and Eve remembered how they'd held each other on Nebra as they died together. As they held one another then, so Eve held Deor now. The tears spilled down Deor's face, weeping for all that had been lost.

CHAPTER 5

Deor sat with Eve, recovering her strength little by little as she listened to Sam, Dolus and Leon talk. Eve had brought her in to join them. The memories still appeared in her mind, like flashes, fragments of scenes from when she was Lore. She saw other parts of her life in these flashes, random things like she and Pythus at school together when they were young, or she with Zeph and Sofi and their parents on a holiday. Eve had told her that this would happen. Her mind had been opened to this past-life memory, and Eve hadn't closed the link down, so they would slip into her mind randomly and also into her dreams. Eve had asked if Deor wanted the link shut down to stop the memories coming through. She'd said no.

Deor had regained some energy, though, and wanted to join the conversation with the others. They'd been filling Sam in on the movement and also on the war on Nebra.

'It's a story all of us here know by now,' Leon was saying. He'd been doing a lot of the talking, apparently quite influential in the movement. Deor had never seen this side of him before: authoritative, a leader. 'Most of us have seen Eve ourselves for a regression and have seen parts of what happened. I suspect you, Deor, may have seen more. This battle isn't just between us and Merope in the present, this battle has been going on in the past, over and over.'

'Over and over?' Sam frowned. 'You mean we've fought them many different times?'

'Many different times,' Eve said. 'And not just on Nebra. On other planets before that. It's an ancient battle, fought between our two peoples throughout time.'

Leon kept glancing into the hall. Deor had wondered why, and it looked like the reason would soon become clear when he said, 'There's someone else we want you to meet before we go any further. He's the head of our movement, the man who started all this.' He stood and opened the door. 'Deor, Sam, meet the head of our movement.'

Cyrus walked in, a wry smile on his face.

'Dad?' Deor said. 'No way …' How could he have kept this from them all this time?

Cyrus walked over and hugged her. 'I'm sorry, my love,' he said quietly. 'I know what you just went through with Eve must have been hard.'

'You're the head of all this?' Deor's mind raced. 'You started it? What's going on?'

Cyrus nodded. 'I know, I know. I have a few things to explain. I'm sorry I've kept you in the dark about it for all this time, but it was necessary, so I didn't put you at risk. I couldn't expose you to this when you were younger. I had to keep you safe. I decided to wait until you were eighteen.

'Eve and I started this movement soon after the invasion happened, around fifteen years ago. I was looking to gather people who were resistant to Merope and would be willing to build a movement against the occupation. That's how I found

Eve. Until then, I didn't know anything about the past, about Nebra, about any of it. Eve had retained her memories from Nebra in this life. When the invasion happened, she could see it was beginning to happen again, our war with Remus, only now they are known as Merope, the name of their sun in the Pleid system. She told me about the past on Nebra. At first, I didn't believe her, but when I had my own regression, I also saw the past. I, too, died in the war against Remus.'

'Deor,' Eve said, 'that war, that destruction that you saw, that happened around five hundred years ago. From what I can gather, our people began coming to Earth soon after that. A decision was made to start anew, and Earth was chosen. Earth was seen as a new world, a young world, with humans ready to take the next step in their evolution, so the decision was made for our people to be reborn here. It started with our ancestors on Nebra, those who had passed before the war began. After the war destroyed Nebra, they began to reincarnate here on Earth and take the steps to build civilisation.'

'So our ancestors, here in Alcyone, they were also Nebran?' Deor asked. If all Nebrans were now on Earth rebuilding their society, then the process had begun centuries before.

Eve nodded. 'Yes. At least from a few hundred years ago and onwards, they were. This is how intelligent life spreads throughout the cosmos, how civilisation spreads. Not by long-distance space travel—the universe is far too big—but by civilisations reincarnating on new worlds. The seeds of civilisation and all the beauty of intelligent life lie in wait in their *bakh*. The eternal tide of life flows throughout the universe in this way. Our Nebran ancestors took the first steps towards building civilisation here. Forearmed with knowledge, they developed language, homes, agriculture, and with each generation after that as more Nebrans came here to be reborn, civilisation developed more and more quickly.'

Dolus nodded in agreement. 'This is how we've built up so quickly, both here and in Merope, because we have the innate knowledge within us, brought here from our past, from our long history of civilisation on Nebra, and they from their history on Remus. What we know, though, is that Merope—thanks to access to our resources since the invasion, as well as their own—are now developing much more quickly than us. We have spies in Merope who report back that their development is far outstripping our own. While we live hand to mouth in whatever meagre existence we can eke out and are allowed by the patrollers, they take all the spoils of our land and grow stronger. We're in danger of being made into a slave race, unless we can fight back. If things progress as they have since the invasion, we will grow weaker as they continue to grow stronger, until they are so much more advanced in every way than us that they can dispose of us at their will. And if history tells us anything—and it always does—then what they did to us on Nebra shows that they only have one ending in mind: our destruction. Once they're done using us for our resources, we will be destroyed. That is their plan.'

'If history tells us anything,' Deor said, 'then maybe we are doomed to destroy one another yet again. Like what I saw on Nebra. The destruction … the annihilation … it was hell. We brought hell to our planets, and we unleashed it on one another.' The final moments on Nebra as the planet burned up, destroyed by the war, lingered in her memory. She and Pythus had held one another in those final moments.

'We must not repeat the mistakes of the past,' Dolus said. 'Eve says that one of the purposes of being reborn is to set right things that were wrong. To make up for past mistakes. To learn from the past.'

'That being said,' Cyrus said, 'Dolus is right, the destruction of Alcyone is their plan. The reports we get from our spies are that the Meropans consider us an inferior race, or an inferior species even, compared to them.'

'Mountain rats,' Deor said. How many thousands of times throughout her life had she been called that? It always grated on her. The patrollers wanted to dehumanise her. Perhaps it made it easier to justify the invasion.

Cyrus nodded. 'Yes, mountain rats. That's what they think of us.'

'The Day of Procurement is ten days away,' Leon said, 'and we have plans to disrupt that. This is our starting point in fighting back. Our spies have managed to get us the list of the ten percent of thirteen-year-olds they plan on taking that day from this territory. We are quietly moving those kids to safety.'

Deor's heart skipped a beat. 'Was Sage on that list?'

'No, she was not,' Cyrus said.

A wave of relief washed over Deor.

'Thankfully, she was missed,' Cyrus continued. 'This gives me hope that they still don't know about the movement. If they knew about it and knew about me, they certainly would've taken her. This is why I kept this from you for so long. I had to protect you.'

'Do you think they have spies in Alcyone?' Sam asked.

Cyrus shook his head. 'I don't know, but I think possibly not. They have the patrollers here. A garrison occupies every town in every territory; what need would they have of spies as well?'

Sam nodded cautiously. 'But what will they do on the Day of Procurement when the thirteen-year-olds aren't around?'

'I'm sure there'll be trouble, but we've been gathering weapons, and if a fight begins, we'll be prepared.'

'We can't win a fight against Merope, Dad,' Deor said, looking down. The notion of a battle with them was absurd.

'No, we can't right now,' Cyrus said with a diplomatic pause. 'But what we can do is begin to push back. The goal is to free one town, our town Apin, then another, from the stationed patrollers. If we can drive them out of one town, we can drive them out of others, then when a territory is freed, we can start on another.'

'We've been steadily and quietly growing,' Leon said, 'across our territory, the Coastal and the Northern. We're trying to centralise planning to this territory, to this group, since it has the most secure base. The plan is to start the resistance here, first, free this town of patrollers. We'll get help from other territories, which is why Dolus has come down here. He represents his people, and more will come. If all the territories work together covertly, we can begin to push them back.'

Dolus nodded. 'My people are ready to send reinforcements when the time comes. Our movement is growing in number. We use coastal caverns that the patrollers don't know about to meet and to build up and store resources. We've built a network among these caverns under the ground along our shoreline.'

'Don't they flood?' Deor asked. She'd never been to the Coastal Territory, though it sounded quite beautiful from what she'd heard. The most stunning coastline in all of Alcyone, apparently, beaches with pristine sand and towns built directly on hills that rose up from the shore. However, since the invasion, it may as well be on the other side of the world.

Dolus smiled, amused. 'We know our coastline inside out, Deor. The only ones that flood are the ones we lead the patrollers to.'

'Others are doing similar things in the Northern Territory,' Leon continued, 'all covertly. Steadily building our base across the country for when the pushback begins.'

Deor sat up with more energy. 'Well, I want to be involved. I've lived my life as a member of an occupied race, and it galls me. It crushes me to the core of my being to live this way. It crushes me in my *bakh*.'

'And you know why it galls you so much, Deor?' Eve asked, smiling at Deor's choice of words. 'Because you've fought this battle before, fought this enemy before. You experienced the worst war possible, one that destroyed both worlds who fought in it. You died fighting that battle until the very end. And now you're reborn here, oppressed by the very people who destroyed your world.'

'As did you, Pythus,' Deor said. The memory replayed repeatedly in her head.

Eve nodded. 'As did I. Yes, as Pythus. And I've had the memories of that war, and especially that final day when you and I died together, with me since I was very young in this life. We wanted to ensure my gifts of seeing were brought to this life, and they were. It's a blessing and a curse. I live each night when I sleep with memories of Nebra and how it turned to fire. And I've waited all of my life to finally meet you again.'

'Wait a minute,' Sam said, 'are you saying that not only did Deor, and you, Eve, and I guess some others, all get reborn here in Alcyone after, what, countless lives on Nebra, but that Meropans did too?'

'I am saying, Sam,' Eve said, 'that every person on this continent is reborn here from either Nebra or Remus. Everyone. Most of the Alcyonans don't know they're reborn from Nebra. They may just sense something in their past that they can't quite grasp.'

'So I lived my past life on Nebra too, then?' he asked.

'Yes, Sam, you did,' Deor said. Zephir had been a good

man. 'I saw you in my vision. You were my brother then too. Your name was Zephir.'

'How did I die?' Sam asked. 'Wait … do I want to know that?'

'I don't know how you died, Sam,' Deor said. 'I didn't see that in my vision.'

'Also,' Eve continued, 'we have to assume that if we know we're Nebrans reborn, then at least some of the Meropans will know they're reborn from Remus. We're sure those in power are aware of this.'

'And if that's true,' Cyrus said, 'then we know they'll stop at nothing to destroy us. They will resume the Remusan mission, this time from Merope.'

Dolus spoke up, nodding. 'Which is why we have to act now, or very soon, before Merope gets too strong for us to resist. What we know from our spies in Merope is that they have a strong military, but more than half of that military are posted in the garrisons throughout the territories of Alcyone as patrollers. This weakens their capital, Titus, because as a result, they don't have as strong a military presence there as they would like. They conscript their children at age fifteen to train for service, so that they have people coming through to fill the ranks. However, those youths are not grown men; the majority of the men in their military are patrollers in Alcyone. Their military, therefore, has some weaknesses at home.'

'That doesn't do us much good, though,' Deor said, 'because we're in no position to attack their capital or any of their towns.'

'No, we aren't,' Dolus said, 'but it may give us other options.'

'Regardless, we have to start here, at home,' Cyrus said, 'and we have to start with freeing one town. And that's going to be here, in Apin.'

The group discussed plans for a while longer. They discussed what other towns might be ready to try to push back on patrollers, what resources the Coastal Territory had stored, what connections they might be able to make in the Northern Territory. No one had any information about the Mid North, though. Deor tried to process her vision while talking with the group, but she needed time. What she saw in her vision was real. She was Lore; she was Nebran, and now she was on Earth to rebuild as Deor.

Eventually, the discussions finished, and Dolus led Deor and Sam away. 'I'll take you back home,' he said, 'though not the way we came in. I want to show you both something, one last thing, before I leave you be.'

He led them out the far end of the Great Hall. Deor looked at some of the other people. She recognised a couple of the faces of the young men—from the mountain the morning before? That morning seemed like a month ago. In another of the small rooms off the hall sat a strange-looking man. He had long blond hair, but an earthy blond, not like Dolus' beach-streaked blond. He looked at Deor as she passed. His eyes were a deep green, and she felt a familiarity, but she couldn't place it. Absentmindedly, she touched her two-moons birthmark.

Dolus took them down a passageway similar to the one they'd used to enter but at the other end of the hall. It seemed to go on for several hundred metres.

'You know, I saw you the other day,' Deor said, 'in the morning, on the mountain.'

Dolus stopped walking. 'Which day?'

'Yesterday at first light. You and four others. You were being chased by patrollers. One of them was shot.'

Sam's eyes widened. 'Deor! You saw the patrollers shoot someone? Why were you up there? Of course you were up there!'

'I did,' she said, 'and I think I know why there's been so many patrollers around. They were looking for Dolus and his friends. They found them, and they killed one of them.'

Dolus' head hung down. He rubbed his eyes. 'Yes, they did find us, and yes, they shot Archer, my friend. He was from my territory, as were the others you saw. Yes, we were fleeing the patrollers. Yes, they found us. That's why there's an increased presence of patrollers in your territory. Some of the patrollers saw us when we crossed over into your territory. They've been looking for us since then. Unfortunately, it cost Archer his life.'

'So it was you who brought this extra attention on us?' Deor said. 'We don't need any more attention from the patrollers.'

'No, you don't,' Dolus said, 'and for that I am sorry. But the bigger picture here is the mission and our freedom. We have to remember that. We have to remember what the goal is in everything we do. Come, I have something to show you.'

They came to the end of the long passageway. At the end of it stood a small square platform surrounded by a wooden rail on all sides except for a gap in one corner, making an entryway to the platform. Ropes went up from each side of the platform, up into the darkness above.

'Come on, then,' Dolus said. 'Get in.'

He walked onto the platform and ushered Deor and Sam to do the same. The timber rail enclosed them on all four sides. A wooden beam came up from the floor in the middle of the platform with another beam mounted across it at waist height.

Dolus took hold of the horizontal beam. 'When we push this beam around in this direction, we go up ...'

He showed them what to do, and the three of them pushed the beam around in a circle. It turned the beam to which it was attached, which turned something under the platform, and their platform rose, being pulled up the ropes. Deor felt unsteady on her feet as the platform rose from the ground underneath her. This day just kept getting more and more bizarre.

'Fantastic!' Sam said as they continued pushing and the platform continued rising. 'How did you build this?'

'It's like I keep saying, Sam,' Dolus replied. 'Isn't it funny what cave dwellers can do?'

The platform rose and rose as they pushed the lever around, up into the darkness. Wheels and cogs underneath the platform pulled ropes through efficiently with every push. Soon, they reached the top. Deor looked down over the edge. The bottom was just a faint circle of light. She stepped out into a small room. Next to the platform sat another platform, just the same as this one. Dolus used his foot to push a lever in the corner. This triggered the winding lever to wind back in the other direction, sending it back down into the depths of the chamber.

'We always keep one up the top,' he said, indicating the other platform, 'and one down the bottom. One is always available at each end.'

Dolus led them to a large door at the end of the room; like all the others, it was bolted shut. He produced a key and unlocked the bolt, then led them through, locking the door behind them on the other side.

Deor looked around. They'd come out into a large cavern with dark tunnels heading off into the mountain on both sides. Ahead, light came in from outside through an opening about the size of a door, about twenty metres away—the cavern she'd found yesterday! She turned to look at the door through which they'd come, unsurprised to recognise the green locked door she'd found the day before.

'So this is where that door led!' Deor said. 'I found this cavern yesterday! This is what it was hiding! The Great Hall! The cave lion … although there is no cave lion, is there? It's all to keep people away.'

Dolus looked surprised and impressed. 'Yes, exactly. Come, walk here.' He took a few steps towards the entrance, then turned. Deor and Sam turned with him, looking back. The cavern had disappeared, and the cave lion's low growl emerged from the darkness that had replaced it. 'And now, walk back through,' Dolus said.

With just one step, they returned to the cavern.

'Another jakelope veil?' Deor asked. Who were these mysterious people in the South?

'Exactly,' Dolus replied. 'It hides the door and the rest of the cavern, shrouds it in darkness. Jakel hair is remarkable. Not only can it reflect, refract and bend light, but it can also hold sound. This veil was made to project a dark cave outward, and it holds the sound of a cave lion. When the people in the South made this, they made it for us to protect this cave. It's the perfect way to keep people from entering too far into this cave and discovering the entrance to our base.'

'So there was no mountain lion all along?' Sam asked.

Dolus nodded. 'That's right. It's supposed to keep people out of here. Though clearly it didn't work with Deor.'

She shrugged. 'I had to know what was here. I had to. I can be pretty determined when I need to be.'

Dolus smiled. 'Yes. I'm beginning to see that. Remind me not to get on your bad side …'

CHAPTER 6

Lore and Pythus walked into the park in the middle of the city. A large park—called the Great Park—dominated the city, taking up more than three square kilometres, with their home city, Damas, built around it on every side, stretching out as far as they could see. Nebra being a big planet, the cities used the space available, but still the places people most wanted to live surrounded the park. Lore's family had a villa at the southern end, and she and Pythus walked from there. They passed between the two enormous obelisks that marked the gateway at the southern end of the park. Similar obelisks marked the eastern, northern and western gateways. The obelisks had been quarried from great quartz mines in the north of Nebra and were nearly indestructible. Each of the obelisks displayed the embossed insignia of Nebra: the two moons. On entering the park, Lore touched the two-moons symbol on the obelisk to her right—something she often did.

The centre of the park featured a large lawn area, an open quadrangle, often used for public events or large gatherings. Today, being Two Moons' Day, many thousands of people had congregated. A large platform stood at the northern end.

Lore's parents, as co-pharit, would speak there later. They attended in a celebratory fashion but also in an official one. The public roles of the public faces of the duocracy were rarely simply celebratory.

'You seeing that boy tonight? Julius, isn't it? When am I going to get to meet him?' Pythus asked as they walked past a lake, heading towards the central quadrangle.

On the lake several species of bird life congregated. Lore admired them. The beauty of Damas filled her *bakh* with joy. She felt at home here, like she'd always been here. 'Maybe,' she said, 'if he's lucky. He's been a bit absent lately, though.'

Pythus shrugged. 'Maybe he's trying to play hard to get.'

'Hard to get!' Lore laughed. 'Julius couldn't play hard to get if he hid at the bottom of the ocean. The boy flirts with everything that moves …'

Pythus laughed. 'Well, if you're seeing him tonight, I'm coming too. I need to check him out. I'll find out all his secrets, don't worry.'

'Haha, of course you will! I don't know if I'll see him tonight. I'm not committing myself to some boy anyway,' Lore said. 'Much more important things to do with my time than pampering to the facile needs of an asinine boy.'

'Ouch!' Pythus grinned. 'Lore, you are one fierce woman!'

'Don't doubt it.' Lore stopped. In the sky above the clearing, a large ship had materialised. It hadn't been there a moment before, but it now hovered only metres above the ground. Shouts and commotion came from the public below.

'What is that?' Pythus asked nervously.

Dread rose in Lore's stomach. She knew. The ship bore the insignia of Remus on its side. 'How …?'

'Lore, we have to go.' Pythus turned to leave. 'Right now!'

'But my parents are there!' Without thinking, Lore ran

towards the quadrangle.

Pythus followed.

When Lore reached the quadrangle, the shooting began. The platform exploded in the first volley of gunfire and flash bombs dropped from the ship. Large cannons mounted on the front of the ship tore holes in the structure as they strafed it, while the flash bombs destroyed its foundations and set it on fire. Panic set in, with people attempting to flee as quickly as they could, but the crowd was too big. The civilians in the quadrangle fell *en masse* to the flash bombs, a weapon of close-up destruction the Remusans used often. Hundreds of people were killed while attempting to escape.

'No!' Lore yelled. She tried to get past the people fleeing the area. She had to get in there; she had to find her parents.

'Lore, we must go!' Pythus cried, grabbing her friend. 'If we go in there, we die!'

Pythus pulled Lore away, wrenching her out of her panicked focus on the quadrangle, and Lore ran with Pythus to the nearby woods beyond the lake. Somewhere in her brain, Lore noticed that the birds had fled.

'Keep running!' Pythus yelled, leading the way.

'How did they get through?' Lore yelled back, anger rising.

'I don't know, just run!'

A screeching, whistling sound came from the east of the city as missiles fired from the air force base east of Damas tore towards the Remusan vessel. It rose up quickly and—obviously ready for such an attack—fired missiles back at them. An explosion like a bomb going off rocked the park as the missiles collided at the eastern end. The noise and shockwave rippled through the park, knocking Lore and Pythus off their feet.

'What the hell is going on?' Lore yelled, getting up quickly and continuing to run.

The Remusan vessel rose higher and flew west, away from the park, dropping flash bombs on buildings as it rose. From the east, on the heels of the missiles, two Nebran fighter ships, smaller and more agile than the larger Remusan vessel, tore into the area in pursuit. The jets screamed by overhead, the wash knocking Lore down again. As they roared over the lake, a wall of water blasted up and sprayed out over the nearby trees and grass.

The fighters rose quickly in pursuit of the Remusan vessel, firing at it from guns mounted above the wings. Lore quickly rose again to look, not noticing the blood dripping from her forehead. The Nebran fighters had missiles loaded under each wing. In unison, they launched each of them at the Remusan ship as it continued to rise. As they launched, though, the Remusan ship vanished. Cloaked again. The missiles continued on their path to where the ship had just been, but hit no target.

Lore's shoulders dropped. They had gotten away. The fighters broke off their pursuit and wheeled back around to the south.

In the park, several thousand lay dead. At the northern end of the quadrangle, the platform, burning fiercely, lay collapsed—destroyed. Lore's parents, the co-pharit of Nebra, were among the dead under the wreckage.

The vision shifted; Lore was back at her family's villa with Pythus and her remaining family. Zeph was nearby. Sofi cried on Lore's lap. Security advisers tried to talk to Lore about what they needed to do, what she needed to do, what Zeph needed to do, but she didn't hear them. Her mind was a blur. Remus had attacked Nebra; they had attacked her city. Damas was badly damaged, and her parents were dead. Lore stared blankly into nothing, numb.

Deor awoke, and the memory became blurry, distorted. A moment ago, she'd been Lore, feeling a whirlwind of emotions, seeing the attack, then sitting in her villa. Now, on waking, she slowly regained her sense of being Deor. She sat up in her bed, wiping tears from her cheeks.

For three mornings now, in the five days since the Great Hall, she'd woken with dreams of Nebra. All three times, the dreams centred around Two Moons' Day, when the attack from Remus came. The thing that stood out for her, aside from the obvious destruction and the loss Lore had suffered, was how it happened. Lore was clearly stunned that this had been able to happen, that the Remusan ship had been able to get through the surveillance and defence systems of Nebra. Not only that, but the dreams had revealed this hadn't just happened in Damas. It had happened in more than twenty cities across Nebra. The attack had been systematic, planned, widespread and devastating. How had they managed to get through? The dreams tried to tell her something, give her a message, something she needed to know as Deor.

Noises came through from the other room. Someone was up in the kitchen. The familiar rustling sounds of food being prepared. Her stomach grumbled in response. Alluring smells of something delicious being cooked wafted into Deor's room, along with the peaceful sounds of a family member preparing food in the next room. *Hurry up.*

'Good morning,' Deor said as she entered the kitchen. Sage turned and smiled brightly. She'd been busy. A freshly baked loaf of bread, made from the emmer wheat she'd grown in their garden, sat cooling on the bench. The smell of freshly cooked hot bread teased the air. Deor salivated, and her stomach rumbled again. She headed straight to it, but Sage slapped her hand away.

'Wait!' she said. 'Until the rest is ready!'

Deor smiled. Feisty Sage. 'Sorry, boss …'

Sage stirred the pot on the stovetop, reheating some of the stew they had for dinner the previous evening. She poured some into each of five bowls and set them on the table, with a spoon each. Next, she went back to the bread and cut off five slices. She placed one next to each of the bowls. The others had arrived at the table. 'Breakfast is served!' Sage said proudly.

Deor sat and picked up the bread. The outside crackled and crunched between her fingers, while the warm middle brushed against her thumb softly. She took a bite of the crust, her senses overloaded. 'Oh, Sage, this is delicious,' she said. 'This is from our garden? The emmer wheat?'

'Yes, it is. I ground the wheat myself, then used it to bake the bread. I also ground some goosefoot in there for extra flavour.'

'Oh, it's amazing!' Deor said. Sage was so smart, so clever in learning these new skills, and so talented in executing them so well. Deor's heart swelled as Sage smiled at them all from where she stood in the kitchen.

'That's just the crust,' Sage said. 'It's supposed to be crunchy like that, but you have your stew, dip a little of the bread in the sauce and eat it.'

The stew didn't contain much meat, but the broth was made from animal bones, so it had a deep meaty flavour. Cyrus had thickened it using a little of the ground emmer wheat, and the sauce oozed invitingly.

Deor dipped her bread into it and scooped some up. 'Oh, stop it!' she said. 'This is ridiculous! Sam! Have you tried this? Sage, you're a genius!'

Sage beamed broadly. She loved the garden, and she loved to cook. The satisfaction she got from them all enjoying her food showed on her face. Deor's heart swelled even more.

'You're welcome,' Sage said, her smile not diminishing.

The other three tucked into their breakfast as well. Alexi made little chortling, snorting noises of happiness as he ate.

Cyrus smiled at his daughter, his face glowing with happiness. 'Sage, this bread is fantastic. You really do have a talent, my love.'

'Hear, hear!' Sam gurgled his words through chunks of bread and stew.

'Sage,' Deor said, 'come and sit next to me. Enjoy your meal too.'

'I will.' She took a step towards the table.

Outside, three large bangs sounded on the door.

Deor and Sam jumped up.

'Open!' someone yelled.

Before anyone had a chance to react, the door exploded inwards, its top half smashed off the wall. It hung crookedly like a tree struck by lightning. Cyrus and Alexi sprang to their feet, but two patrollers stormed through the broken opening.

'Welcome to the Day of Procurement, you mountain rats!' one announced. 'We're here for you, little miss rat, Sage!'

The patroller started towards Sage, who stood in shock in the kitchen, unable to move. Instinctively, Deor moved in front of her sister to protect her.

'No!' Cyrus said. 'That's still five days away! That is not today! You cannot take Sage!'

The patroller shoved Cyrus out of the way. 'Word came down from Titus. We've been told to bring it forward. Today is the day! And she is on the list!' He held up a scroll with a list of names written on it.

Cyrus took the list and scanned it. His face dropped. 'No … She can't be …'

'Stay behind me!' Deor whispered, holding Sage close to her back.

Sam grappled with the other patroller, trying to stop him from gaining further entrance to the house.

The first patroller continued into the room. Alexi stepped in front of him, trying to bar his way. 'You're not taking my sister!' he cried.

The patroller tried to push Alexi aside, but Alexi nimbly stepped around behind him and swept the patroller's legs from under him, crashing him to the ground. Alexi seized the moment and leaped on top of the patroller, getting a quick punch in on his face. The patroller blocked his second punch, though, and rose quickly. He was much bigger than Alexi, and with one hand, he picked Alexi up by the throat and shoved him against the wall.

'Try that again, you mangy little rat, and I'll break your spine!' He threw Alexi across the room, where he thudded into the far wall. The patroller turned to Deor.

'You will not take her!' Deor reached with her left hand to hold Sage closer and fumbled for something—anything—she could find on the bench to use as a weapon.

'My, my,' the patroller said, 'such ferocity in your voice. Such spirit. It's a shame you weren't taken on the Day of Procurement, little rat; we would have enjoyed you!'

Deor found the knife that Sage had used to cut the bread and slashed out at the patroller. More ready for a surprise attack this time, though, he raised an arm and fended it off. Still, the knife sliced into his left arm, opening a gash that soaked his uniform with blood. The patroller tried to punch Deor, but she avoided it and sliced at the patroller again. He dodged her, then grabbed her by the shoulders and slung her to the ground. Deor got up, but the patroller picked up Sage and hoisted her over his shoulder.

'Deor, help!' Sage screamed.

Deor sprung towards the patroller. He held her away with his blood-soaked left arm. She wrestled at his arm, but he was strong and held her in place with Sage over his shoulder. Sage pounded her fists on his back, but it didn't move him. Deor wrestled with his blood-soaked arm. She had to find a way to get Sage off his back.

Three other patrollers had entered the house, having heard the chaos inside. One had his arm against Cyrus' throat. 'Dare me to do it!' the patroller yelled, brandishing his knife.

Sam still wrestled with a patroller, but now that patroller had help, and they pinned Sam down. Another patroller pushed between Sage and Deor. Deor attacked him with the knife, but he grabbed her arms and held her back. She tried to release her arms from his grip, but he punched her hard in the face. Her ears rang, and bruising pain flooded her left eye. Deor fell to the ground against the back wall of the kitchen.

'Stay down, if you know what's good for you!' the patroller barked at her.

She sprang up and ran at the patroller, but he grabbed her and threw her back against the wall. She slammed into the wall hard. He left her gasping, unable to regain her breath.

The patroller with Sage carried her out the front door, still slung over his shoulder. Cyrus tried unsuccessfully to free himself, and Alexi—groggy from being thrown into the wall—staggered to his feet, but he couldn't stop the patroller who carried Sage outside.

'No!' Sage screamed. 'Let me go! Deor! Sam! Help! Let me go!'

Deor scrambled to her feet, still gasping, unable to get air. She tried to follow the patroller outside, but the one who had punched her held her back. Still gasping, she could only watch as the first patroller took Sage to a large wooden cage secured on wheels. Many other young girls were already in it. The patroller pushed her inside.

'No!' Sage continued to yell. 'Help me! Deor! Sam! Dad! Help!'

At the order of the patroller, the cage moved off, pulled by oxen, driven by another patroller, who pushed them on towards the town square. The remaining patrollers left the house, rejoined the group, and they all headed into the town. Deor, Sam, Cyrus and Alexi followed them outside. Finally, Deor could get a breath again. She gulped air back into her lungs.

'Stay back from us!' one of the patrollers ordered, pulling a gun from his uniform. 'Any more of that and one of you dies!'

Deor tried to go after them. She had to do something.

Sam held her back. 'Dee,' he said, restraining her, 'we can't fight them. They'll shoot you.'

'We can't just let them take her!' she said, her voice raspy from the fight. 'We have to get Sage back!' Fear, panic and rage swept through her body: fear that she was losing Sage, panic about what she could do about it, and most of all—bubbling under the surface of her ocean like lava inside the Earth—rage that it happened at all, that it even *could* happen.

Deor followed the patrollers to the town square, looking for a way to get to Sage. Inside the square sat several more mounted cages drawn by oxen. They'd come in from all sides of the town, all at once. Deor was taken aback. What was going on here? The cages held far more thirteen-year-olds than ten percent of the population. Those captured from throughout the territory must have been brought here as well. All the families ambushed all at once. Many of those families had made their way into the town square, desperate to try to get their children back, but there was an increased presence of patrollers, and they made a ring around the square. No one could get through.

'Welcome to the Day of Procurement!' a man announced. He stood on a platform in the middle of the square and looked more official than the patrollers. 'Every year, you donate ten percent of your juvenile girls to Merope. By donating these girls, they are spared a life of impoverishment in Alcyone, scrapping and scraping all their lives like hungry dogs just to get by, and are given a better life in the service of the glorious Meropan nation. This is your price for the privilege of the *pax Meropa* you enjoy. This is the tax you pay. The list of girls you have donated is nailed to the courthouse door. Inspect it at your leisure.'

The official pointed to the courthouse, where two patrollers stood guarding the list. The ox-drawn troops began moving out of the town square, headed towards the road that eventually led through a valley between two of the mountains in the Asman Range. The Merope Road. From there, the road led to Titus.

Deor was straining to try to see Sage. There were too many people in her way. The oxen were leaving the square. She had to act. Quickly, she ran through the crowd, around the perimeter of patrollers, trying to get to the other side, from where they would leave.

'Move!' she called out, as stupefied townsfolk blocked her way. 'Move out of my way!' She pushed through the crowd, jostling and shoving her way around the square. She had to get to Sage. She had to.

'Some of you may get lofty ideas, foolish notions in your heads,' the official continued, 'about following us and attempting to take back your donation. I advise against it. These girls are now the property of Merope, and any attempts to take away the property of Merope will be met with force.'

One man broke through the ring of patrollers. He sprinted towards the departing line of cages. 'Erin!' he yelled. 'I'm coming!'

The official turned and pulled a gun. With one swift, lethal motion, he turned and fired. The man hit the ground, dead instantly.

'The property of Merope shall not be trifled with!' the official continued. 'What is given can easily be taken away. What is given is given as a gift, born out of the generosity of Merope, but punishment is swift for those who would take our generosity as something else. Learn your lesson from this man. Your taxes have been paid for this next year.'

Deor finally made it to the other side of the square. She pushed past more townsfolk to get to the line of carts leaving it. The cages were just metres away, but the patrollers still formed a line preventing anyone from getting closer. Deor frantically scanned them leaving the square. In the second to last one, she saw Sage. 'Sage!' she yelled out. 'Sage, I'm here!'

Sage saw her and grabbed at the bars of the cage. Tears and dirt smudged together on her cheeks. 'Deor!' she cried. 'Help me! What's going to happen to me?'

'I'll find you!' Deor called. 'Sage! Stay alive! I'll find you! I will find you!'

The patroller in front of her laughed and pushed her back. 'You'll find her? Not if we find you first, mountain rat!'

'Stay alive, Sage!' Deor again called. 'I will find you! I will find you!'

The carts rolled away. Sage cried, looking back at Deor as Deor called out to her, telling her to stay safe. The patrollers held everyone back. Slowly, Sage got smaller and smaller, the carts getting further and further away, until Deor could no longer see her; her sister taken by Merope in little more than an instant.

Deor collapsed, the energy drained from her. She sat on the ground, her head buried in her hands. She'd never felt more helpless, more unable to act. She'd been powerless to stop them breaking into her house and kidnapping her sister under the guise of Meropan law. Waves of grief washed up on her shore, but even as they did, behind them and beneath them bubbled the rage, boiling up from beneath the surface.

Feeling more anger and resentment at Merope than she ever had, Deor got up and made her way back around the square. Her father stood on the steps of the courthouse in strained discussions with Leon, Sam and Dolus. Alexi stood to the side, injured and lost. Deor took slow, long breaths. She needed to calm herself. Rage would not help right now. The time for rage would come. Later.

She took Alexi's hand. 'Come with me,' she said, leading him away. 'I'll take you home.' They walked off together towards home. Deor turned to her younger brother. 'You were very brave, standing up to those patrollers.'

'She's my twin sister,' Alexi said. 'It's not fair that this happens. It's not fair that they can just come in and take people. They stole her, kidnapped her. How can that be right?'

'It's not,' Deor said, 'not at all. This is how we live right now, an abused, dominated, occupied people. We deserve better than that. We have rights, and they have taken them away.'

At home, the front door half hung from the wall. Inside, the kitchen, eating area and small front room looked like a cyclone had hit. Things had been knocked over throughout all three rooms in the struggle. The careless destruction of their small possessions signalled more clearly than ever to Deor the realities of her life as an Alcyonan. Merope did not care about them.

She and Alexi began the process of tidying up the three rooms. Chairs had been overturned in the struggle and holes knocked through walls. Where Alexi had landed when thrown, a small side table lay shattered. In the kitchen, everything normally on the benches now lay on the ground. Plates were smashed. The only thing left undisturbed was Sage's stew, sitting on the table uneaten, her freshly cut piece of bread still next to it.

CHAPTER 7

Arieitis woke with a start from a dream she had regularly, one that never resolved. She called it a frustration dream. It took different forms but always had the same format: she tried to do something but kept being frustrated from achieving it by something external to her. In this one she'd been trying to walk down the street to get to a place she desperately needed to be, but people walked in the opposite direction, pushing back against her. She tried to push through the crowd, but couldn't make any ground, getting pushed further back. She turned and walked with the traffic so she could get out of it by going to the side, then crossed the street and walked down that side, but a barricade blocked her way. People were doing work on the road, and she couldn't go through.

She walked down a different street to see if there was a way around, but found a dead end. She turned down another street, but it went further away from where she needed to be. Every way she turned, she ended up further and further away from her destination. She turned back towards the first street on which she'd walked but couldn't find it anymore. The streets had changed. The thing she had to get to was further away than ever, and no matter what Arieitis did, she couldn't get around these obstacles to get where she needed to be. It infuriated her.

'Pleid above!' she muttered as she rose in her bed. 'I hate those dreams! Oh well, at least they're better than the other ones, I guess.'

She sprang out of bed. The day had dawned bright and clear. In early summer, like this, Titus shone like a gem. The sun streamed in from outside, making her strawberry-blonde hair glow like a gentle, warming fire. She turned her green eyes to it and basked in the warmth.

From her second-storey window on the western side of her room, she looked down and across the strata to the forum. Already, many people congregated there. Some would be going about their business for the day, others meeting with one another, discussing everything from business to philosophy, to the weather and the crops. Quetzl, her brother, would likely already be down there. At the western end of the forum, basking in the sun, rose the top of the new temple dedicated to Pleid. Only a few weeks to go until her father, the Emperor Barritus, would open it. On the summer solstice. The radiant dawn light illuminated the face of Pleid on his throne, sitting in his temple at the western end of the city.

'All the light of the sun illuminating all of Merope, from the rising sun in the east to the face of Pleid in the west; the world beginning and ending with Merope.' Her father had been practicing his speech constantly of late.

Arieitis dressed and went downstairs to their large dining area. In the scullery adjacent, their servants prepared breakfast. Her sister, Veronica, sat in the dining area eating, next to their father, Barritus.

'Good morning, Daughter,' Barritus said.

Arietis sat. 'Good morning, Father,' she said, and nodded at Veronica, who simply glanced sideways at her. 'Where is Quetzl this morning?'

'You can probably guess,' Barritus said, attacking a pile of pork sausages on his plate. 'Already at the forum, discussing politics with the senex.'

'They may as well just give him a position already.' Arieitis looked away from her father's mutilation of the pork. 'Or he'll hound them until they do.'

'I think they're afraid of both options,' Barritus said.

Arieitis' personal servant, Missy, came to her side with breakfast offerings. Arieitis took some fruit and fresh bread. The table was stocked with several preserves, some made by the Meropans in the farmlands outside the city walls, others imported from Alcyone.

'Thank you, Missy.' Arieitis took a preserve that she liked most, one from the farming territory of Alcyone in the North. They made beautiful sweet and savoury preserves. They also harvested tea both in Alcyone and Merope, but Arieitis preferred the tea they harvested in Alcyone. It came from further north and a cooler climate than the tea fields of Merope, which were in Merope's mid-west. Different weather, distinctly different flavours. The tea from Alcyone had enhanced flavours with more depth and complexity. The Meropan tea was okay, but more uniform in flavour, and somewhat harsh.

The preserve spread easily on the freshly baked bread, melting into the warm middle. Arietis took a bite and poured herself some tea. Most mornings, her breakfast was this or something similar.

Veronica watched. 'Missy,' Veronica said, turning to her, 'Arieitis' breakfast is made up nearly entirely of things from your childhood home, Alcyone. They make fine foods to bring to our capital. Fine foods. Tell me, did you ever eat these foods when you were a child?'

Missy looked at Arieitis, her hands clasped together nervously, but answered Veronica. 'No, Domina,' she said. 'I have never been to the Northern Territory, where they farm these. I never saw these foods.'

Arieitis glared at Veronica, but Veronica ignored her. She pursued this line of questioning often.

'But you see them now, correct?' Veronica continued. 'When we've finished eating? You get to have some bread and some Alcyone preserve, some tea, if you choose? You are given the finest foods now?'

'Yes, Domina,' Missy said. 'When you are done, we take a little bread and tea.'

'Thank you, Missy,' Arieitis interrupted. 'That will—'

'That's good,' Veronica interrupted back. 'My sister sometimes expresses regret that we *take* these foods from Alcyone. She has a soft heart and too giving a nature. She labours under the delusion that Alcyone would be better off if they ran their own affairs. But you were never able to have these foods as a child, you lived a life stricken by poverty, unable to be properly nourished, whereas now, nurtured here in and by the generosity of Titus, you can have them and flourish. Is this correct?'

'Yes, Domina,' Missy said, her head bowed.

'That's what I thought. You're dismissed, Missy,' Veronica said.

'Pro-Alcyonan sentiment is only a distraction,' Barritus said. He finished his sausage and wiped grease from his mouth. 'In an empire there will always be those who say we should not expand, but expansion is a positive both for the empire and for those whose lands we expand into. Alcyone were an unorganised rabble before our intervention, incapable of self-governance, incapable of large-scale organisation, incapable of civilisation. They are an inferior people whose lives are made better by the introduction of Meropan civilisation. Our *pax Meropa* instils peace in their regions and organisation in their lives, giving them food and health while also feeding the empire itself. Alcyone is infinitely the better for it.'

'Yes, I know all of this, Father,' Arieitis said, and—with a little smile—added, 'I have heard your speeches many times. It doesn't mean I don't wonder if they are as thrilled about the situation as we are in Titus.'

Veronica snorted. 'That is irrelevant. As Father said, they are an inferior race. You spend far too much time pondering them.'

'Well, I love their foods. It would be nice to visit the Northern Territory where they come from one day.' They shared a border, after all.

'Visit?' Barritus said in shock. 'Why on earth would you want to visit? The only ones I pity in those territories are the poor patrollers whom we have to station there to mind them and guard against uprising. To visit … We don't visit the dog where he sleeps in his kennel. This is the same.'

Arieitis failed to bite her tongue. 'Perhaps the fact that we have to station patrollers there to guard against uprising is argument enough about the validity of our occupation.'

'Nonsense!' Barritus barked. 'To extend the analogy, even a dog will bite its master if it thinks it can get a better one. It doesn't mean the dog is correct or the master is mean. All it means is that the dog is merely a dumb beast, hoping for a better meal.'

Arieitis lowered her eyes. This conversation came up

regularly enough. She never won it. Her father's position was that Merope was expanding as an empire and that by taking over the territories of Alcyone, they served a dual purpose of expansion and civilisation. But at what cost were these things achieved? Almost no one except patrollers and occasionally those tasked with the administration of the territories ever went to Alcyone. She longed to go to see it. They shared a border with the Northern Territory, but it was a world away.

Arieitis took the remainder of her fruit and left the table. She walked into the large lounge and entertaining room that abutted the dining room. 'Missy,' she called out, 'would you attend me in here, please?'

Missy entered from the kitchen and, with tentative steps and head bowed, made her way across the dining room and into the entertaining room.

'Walk with me for a little,' Arieitis said, strolling across the room towards the glass doors that led out to their large courtyard. She opened them and walked towards the central fountain.

The lawns stretched beyond it to the back of the property, where the servants maintained a small orchard. At the eastern boundary, private baths bubbled softly with running water flowing in from a nearby spring. Barritus had several baths of varying temperatures built here. On the western boundary, a small creek flowed through, entering the property at the north through an arch built in their wall and exiting through a similar arch further down. Her father had diverted that creek specifically to add to the charm of their courtyard.

'Yes, Domina?' Missy asked after a reasonable pause.

'I've told you, Missy,' Arieitis whispered, pulling Missy in close, 'when it's just you and me, you don't have to call me Domina. You can call me Ari. I insist.'

Missy blushed. 'I know you've said that, but I find it very hard to get used to. I feel if I'm caught calling you anything but Domina, your father—or worse, your sister—will flog me.'

'You leave them to me,' Ari said. 'Though you're right to be careful.'

'What did you want to ask me, Ari?' Missy asked nervously.

Ari smiled. 'I know I've asked you before, but you generally evade the questions, and I want to bring it up again.'

Missy paused before answering. 'You want to ask me about Alcyone.'

'Yes.' Ari did bring it up with Missy fairly regularly, but she was Ari's only source of information about Alcyone. That is, except for what Ari was told by the state—*Pax Meropa* and all that rhetoric. Hang that; she wanted to hear about the real thing. 'I do want to ask you,' she continued. 'We purchased you five years ago. Do you regret being made to come here?'

Missy again paused. 'Ari, I don't know how to answer that. I feel as though both answers are right, and both are wrong. In your father's house, I am protected and well looked after. Veronica is right in that I am nourished and fed well enough. I have a bed to sleep in, a room I share with another. I know that servants in other houses have it much harder than me. Your father rarely beats me, and he does not ... well, he does not take advantage of me. And I feel that you do care for me, Ari. I appreciate those things. At the same time, I wear a permanent mark on my back that shows that I belong to this house. I am property. I wasn't property in Alcyone.'

'Do you miss it?' Ari wanted to ask what it was like where she came from. What were the mountains like? Had she ever travelled to the South? These questions were difficult for Missy, so Ari held back.

'I cannot answer that question, Ari,' Missy said. 'I cannot

bring myself to do it.'

Ari thought for a moment. One thought came to her a lot and sometimes kept her awake at night. She had to ask it. 'Missy, if you had that day again, would you change it so you didn't come here?'

Missy dropped her head and looked at the ground. 'I do not know, Ari. I do not know.'

❨❨❨

Across the strata, in the forum, Quetzl strode down a long corridor, the Great Arcade. Columns of marble towered above him on either side, bearing the weight of the gable roof above, but Quetzl paid them no heed. A large man, he strode quickly. Others got out of his way, leaving the middle of the corridor to him. His long dark hair swayed with his shoulders in time with his stride.

Quetzl had his father's height and breadth and certainly his bluster. While his father used such physical presence to great effect as a commander on the battlefield, having been the man who led the invasion of Alcyone sixteen years earlier, Quetzl preferred to use it to great effect politically. His jaw clenched and unclenched, and he ground his teeth as he walked, frustrated.

Quetzl had applied for consideration as a candidate in the next senex election, but Vespus, the head of the senex, denied his application. Why? At twenty-five, he had reached the required age to be a senator and had more than enough qualifications to be considered. Did his status as the emperor's son go against him?

'Quetzl!' a man called out as Quetzl blustered past him.

Quetzl turned and stopped. 'Oh, Senator Traspus. I didn't

see you.'

'No, indeed, you nearly knocked me over!' the senator said. 'Where are you off to in such a rush?'

'I'm looking for Vespus! He has denied my application to be a candidate at the next senex elections. I demand to know why!'

'I think he's in the southern pavilion, young Master Quetzl.' Traspus indicated back the way Quetzl had come. 'Tell me, though, while I have you, have you had a chance to tour the new amphitheatre? It opens for Merope Week. The word is that your father will have many days of games to celebrate both.'

'The new amphitheatre!' Quetzl bristled at the thought of it. 'Games! Titus does nothing more than play these days, and now we have more games! I have no time for games!'

Quetzl turned back the way he'd come and marched on. He headed through the Great Arcade and around the southern side of the forum, walking on until he came to the southern pavilion. Within it, he found Vespus reclining on a lounge, picking at some fruit. Two young women reclined with him. *Questionably young*, Quetzl thought.

'Vespus!' Quetzl stormed into the pavilion. 'What is the meaning of denying my application to be a candidate in the next senex elections?'

'Do come in,' Vespus said, rolling his eyes. 'Good morning, Quetzl. I understand you've heard, then.'

He had heard the previous evening. Vespus released the information in the evening in an attempt to calm him down, knowing he wouldn't be able to get a hearing with Vespus until the next day.

Quetzl ground his teeth some more. 'Yes. I have heard. Why have you denied my application?'

'Girls.' Vespus waved a hand, and they got up and left the pavilion. 'Quetzl, why do you want to become a senator?'

'I want to become a senator, Vespus, to serve Titus. I have studied our law, our art, our philosophy and our literature. I'm more learned than any other my age or older. I'm a master of mathematics and science. Seven years I have studied beyond my schooling to learn everything there is to learn in our great civilisation. And I have learned it. I am the most qualified person to next be considered for the senex. And you deny my application?'

'And what would you do if you became a senator?' Vespus asked.

'Serve Titus for the good, of course! Shape laws that make a better society! That improve our civilisation! Lift up higher the might of Merope!'

'You think our civilisation needs improving, Master Quetzl?' Vespus asked.

'Civilisation is the very act of improving! Civilisation is not an end; it is a means! The end is greater lives!'

'And how would you go about improving our civilisation?'

'In many ways!' Quetzl replied. 'Greater standard of living for all Meropans, greater study of food production to improve agriculture, ensuring all Meropans receive better educations to better understand the world around them, developing all Meropans to their greatest potential!'

Vespus nodded. 'Noble ideals. But you know what happens if you do that? If you educate everyone? If you teach them how to develop to their greatest potential? They start to wonder why they have senators, Master Quetzl. They start to wonder why the senators and those in power have more money than them, greater property than them, more women than them. They start to believe they are our equal. The great civilisation of Merope is honourable and worthy, and it is benevolent, and nowhere is civilisation greater than here in Titus. But Master Quetzl, the harmony of civilisation rests not on greater knowledge or greater education. The delicate balance that produces the harmony that Titus enjoys relies on one thing: everyone knowing their place and everyone staying in that place. You won't find that in your books, Master Quetzl. When you learn that, then you will truly be learned, and I will then consider your application to be a candidate in the senex elections.'

'You deny me because my father is emperor!' Quetzl ground his teeth again. 'Even though I am the most qualified candidate. I know that the senex and the emperor do not see eye to eye on most things.'

'We may not see eye to eye on *some* things,' Vespus said, 'but we certainly see eye to eye on one thing: the survival of our duocracy, with the emperor as our leader and commander, and the senex as our lawmakers. Both depend on the subjugation of the people to the might of both heads of state. As I like to say, he makes the wars, while we make the laws. Anyone who threatens that position is not a friend of the senex or the emperor. You have some learning to do yet, Master Quetzl. Rest assured, though, the senex is open to you. I see that pathway in your future. I see great potential in you. You are right, you are very learned; you just need to learn a little more. Then I will support you.'

Quetzl stood silent. Vespus denied him not because he wasn't worthy, but because of an arcane empirical philosophy. Without a word, he turned and left the pavilion. He marched further south, to the amphitheatre, which had been finished in recent days. Great banners advertised the upcoming Merope Week beginning at the summer solstice. The pictures depicted everything from physical combat to animal fights, promising two weeks of games as well as theatre and music. Across the top of all the banners emblazoned along the very top of the amphitheatre were the words: 'Glory to Merope! Glory to Titus! Glory to Barritus!' Quetzl read these words and questioned where the glory lay in playing games.

CHAPTER 8

Deor shifted in her chair, then shifted again. She wanted to discuss plans, movements, but so far, she'd just waited and waited here in the Great Hall. She and Sam had made their way to the hall earlier, and others had dribbled in since, coming in small groups so as not to raise attention.

'The significance of today cannot be underestimated,' Leon said, opening discussions.

At last, Deor thought.

Leon continued. 'I think the inference is clear that Merope knows about the movement, somehow, and possibly knew about our plans to disrupt the Day of Procurement by hiding the listed children away. Not only that, but it also means they probably have spies operating here in Alcyone and probably here in the Mid Territory, spies who were able to get back to them with information about our plans. Finally, it also means that Merope suspect we have spies implanted over there, because they've fed those spies misinformation about the list and the Day of Procurement plans. That misinformation we relied on to our detriment. The question remaining, then, is what we do about that, and what is our next move?'

Deor stood. 'We have to act. The time for talk has to end; now has to come the time for action.'

Cyrus stepped forward. 'I think first of all we have to limit the spread of information about what our plans are for the time being, so that any future leaks can be contained. From now on, plans do not go beyond the people in this room. No exceptions. I think we go ahead, though, with our plans to free this town, then this territory, by driving the patrollers out.'

Deor smacked her hands down on the table. 'We have to mount a rescue mission to get Sage and the others. That has to be the first move. This has to stop now, this theft of our children. We must find a way to rescue them.'

'Look, Deor,' Leon said, 'of course we want to work out a way to get Sage back. And others if we can. Of course we do. But we have to be practical. If we just storm up the Merope Road through the Asman valley and hightail it to Titus, we'll be shot by the first patrollers we see.'

Deor nodded. 'Yes, I know that. I'm not suggesting a full offensive against Titus, but there have to be other options. We have to act.'

Leon thought for a moment. 'Yes, I think there might be—other options, that is. I have brought something that perhaps we can use.'

Leon produced a map and laid it out on the table. It showed the entire continent with the Asman Range neatly bisecting the land from north to south, Alcyone to the west of the range, Merope to the east. It showed all five territories of Alcyone: the Southern, the Mid Territory, the Mid North, the Coastal and the Northern. Deor studied it closely. Maps were hard to come by these days. Where the Alcyone River started at the high point of the Asman Range at the Southern Mountain, the River Merope also began. At the northern end of Merope lay their capital, Titus, a large circle on the map. Taygete sat near the top of the Northern, Alcyone's capital, though it had been shut down by Merope. Yet another thing.

'Titus is the beating heart of Merope,' Dolus said, also studying the map. 'The roads leading out of there are the veins that connect it to the towns further south. All roads lead to Titus.'

Deor's eyes found it like a magnet. 'It must be enormous.'

'It is,' Dolus said. 'Our spies have given us maps of Merope and of Titus. We understand it fairly well.'

'And that's where the children are taken?' she asked. 'To Titus?'

Dolus nodded. 'Our information is that the girls who are procured are taken to Titus. They're held there until Merope's annual week of celebrations. All the wealthiest people from all across Merope come to Titus for that week to go to parties, functions, events and so on. The girls are auctioned off over the course of a few days. Those families needing or wanting a new servant come and buy the one they find most appealing. The girls are displayed like products in a merchant's window. The buyers inspect them all, talk to them, assess them and make their choice on who they want to bid for. It's one of the highlights of the week for them all. Merope Week is all about showing the superiority and the glory of Merope, and what better way to illustrate that than to sell the very children of the enemy you are crushing.'

Deor looked at Dolus. Sage would be standing in a cell being inspected for purchase. The same sorrow and rage from the town square bubbled up inside her. 'They are sold as slaves …'

Leon nodded. 'Yes, servants technically, but there's no substantive difference. They are owned by the family who purchases them, for life. Usually, they're branded with the symbol that represents that family. Then, if they escape, all of Merope knows who they belong to. It is slavery.'

Anger continued to rise up within Deor. She'd ignored the reality of the procurement in the past, but no more. Sage had been driven away in a cage. Merope had forced her hand. She knew what she had to do. 'We have to rescue them,' she said. 'We have to go to Titus somehow for that week and get them back.'

Eve rose from her spot on the side and came to sit next to Deor. 'It's not that easy,' Eve said. 'You know we can't just head into Titus and attempt to take them back by force. We need to plan another way.'

'Well, then,' Deor said, 'we form an army of our own; we cross into Merope in the north, here, where the Asman mountains end, and it's directly east to Titus. We invade Titus by force of numbers and take the girls back.'

Cyrus shook his head. 'That's impractical. We do need an organised army, and this is something we're trying to begin to do among the five territories, but there's no way we can get that done in enough time to invade Titus before Merope Week. It just cannot happen in time. Plus, even if we did have a trained army ready to go, would they even be able to infiltrate all the way into the inner sanctum of Titus? Possibly not, and we would lose a lot of lives in the process. It may well come to war with Merope one day, but that day is not today.'

'In my territory, the Coastal Territory,' Dolus said, 'we've been training our young men and women to fight. And I've spent a little time in the Northern Territory organising with them to train as well. Secret locations, secret training. That's one of the reasons I'm here in the Mid with you now. Leon is tasked with repeating the process here. We will build an army, but it will take time.'

Deor pointed to the Mid North Territory on the map. 'What about here? Are they training? Have you been there?' The few times she and Sam had snuck over the border into the Mid North, she'd noticed that the hills were more barren there, the land harder. Not a good place to hunt.

Dolus drew a deep breath and put his hand to his forehead. 'The Mid North is problematic. They are resistant to outsiders and resistant to change. Life is hard there. They have no access to the Alcyone River and no access to a coastline. The hills are more barren, and the plains are desolate. Producing food is difficult as a result. Added to that, their northeastern border is the closest point to Titus. As such, they have had to deal with a greater presence of patrollers than anyone else. As we all know, the invasion began in the Mid North. They didn't attack our capital; instead, they conquered the Mid North first and invaded every other territory from there, spreading out. The Mid Northerners have felt distrustful of the other territories since that time. They perhaps feel not enough was done to help protect them when the invasion came. In that, they are probably right. Alcyone didn't anticipate such an invasion. Our leaders in our capital, Taygete, were too slow to act. '

All her life, Deor had lived cut off from the territories around her, not just physically but informationally. She essentially lived on an island in the Mid Territory, separated from the rest of Alcyone.

'The point is,' Cyrus said, 'we are building towards being able to resist, but we can't do it yet. Not on a mass scale. We need to free one territory, then work on others. But that requires coordination of effort between all the territories, which is the focus of our work right now.'

'We cannot sit by and do nothing, though!' Deor said.

'We can't just let Sage and the others be sold off as slaves. We have to do something!'

Leon nodded. 'Yes, Deor, we do. But raising an army right now is not the thing to do. However, I do have one idea.'

'Leon …' Cyrus interrupted.

'Just hear me out,' Leon said. 'It is a dangerous idea, and I wouldn't ask anyone to do it if they didn't want to. They would have to volunteer.'

Deor sat up. 'What is it?' At least this beats the denials offered so far.

'It's to take a small party of people, only a handful at most, and sneak into Titus through back ways, little-known ways, to try to liberate some of those girls taken.'

Cyrus shook his head. 'Leon, it's a suicide mission.'

'It may not be. Not with a small party, aiming to liberate a small number of the girls. We may be able to do that.'

'I'll go,' Deor said, fuelled by determination. She had to.

Cyrus threw his head back in dismay. 'Deor, you cannot; it will mean your death when you're discovered.'

'I'll go with her,' Sam, silent until now, said. 'I'll make sure she's protected. As best I can.'

Cyrus threw his hands up. 'Great! Just great! Three of my children in one day!'

'Dad …' Deor began as diplomatically as she could, 'Sage has been taken. I will not stand by and allow that. I would die to get her back.' She would die for her sister, if it came to it. Living her life knowing that Sage was being held as a slave was worse than death anyway.

Cyrus sighed deeply, his head in his hands. 'I know, I know you would. That's the problem.'

'You won't lose us,' Deor said. 'And you haven't lost Sage. We will get her back.'

'How would we do this?' Sam asked, consulting the map. 'Would we head north and cut across the top of the Asman mountains, then try to sneak unnoticed into Titus from that direction? That way we'd avoid the Merope Road.'

Leon shook his head. 'No, I don't think we can do it that way. It's far too open; there are towns along the Western Road out of Titus. You'd be recognised as an outsider, and that would be the end of it. Plus, you'd have to cross through the Mid North and into the Northern. That's very risky with patrollers at the borders.'

'There are other ways to get this done,' Eve said, her voice thoughtful and measured. 'I've spent much time in the South. I know them well. They can help.'

Sam frowned in confusion. 'I thought the South was uninhabited.'

'It is, sort of,' Eve said. 'But it's actually not. Let's just say there's no Alcyonans down there … The people down there, well, they're not like us. They stay away from strangers, especially Meropan ones. They haven't built towns out on the plains like we have here in the Mid, or along the Alcyone River Delta like in the Northern, or along the coast like in your territory, Dolus, but that's not to say they haven't built. They just go about it differently down there, and I think they could help.'

'So we head south?' Deor asked. 'That's taking us further away from Titus, though.'

'Yes, it is, but it may be the safest way. It's much further, but I think it could be much safer. I could take you down into the South to some people who live in the hills at the southern end of the Asman Range. The Meropans don't know these people exist, and that's how they like to keep it. I think you've experienced a little of their magic already.'

Deor nodded. 'The jakelope veils.'

'Yes, the jakelope veils. That's one of many magical things they've managed to accomplish. Cyrus,' Eve said, turning to him, 'I propose that I lead Deor and Sam into the South and introduce them to the people down there. They will help us, and they know more than just how to weave jakel hair. There's a lot they can do to assist us, including advice on navigating the southern parts of Merope. There are trails where a person can go unseen. The Scarred Lands have paths that Meropans will not tread.'

Eve pointed out the Scarred Lands on the map before continuing. 'They can go unseen through the Scarred Lands to the Merope Range beyond, and then head north through that range. They may have to trek high to avoid seeing anyone, but they can come out at the end of that range and will have covered a lot of ground, hopefully unseen.'

Leon nodded, then pointed to a town just to the west of the northern end of the Merope Range. 'This town is called Remit. It's a trading town that offers an advantageous position in the middle of the northern part of Merope. People from Titus to the north, the towns to the east of them in the Merope Delta, those to the west of them closer to the Asman Range, and those from further south all go there to trade. It's a busy place, the central trading hub for all of Merope, and with all the travellers passing through, it's the perfect place to hide. We have several spies in that town and a safe house. Deor and Sam could head directly to it from the Merope Range. Our operatives there can help them out with supplies and merchant clothes, and from there, it's a straight journey north to Titus along the Remit Road.'

'And then what?' Cyrus asked. 'They just barge into the capital and take the girls back? How does that part work?'

Leon shrugged. 'I don't know. For that part of the journey, you'd be on your own. Our operatives in Remit can help you, but they won't go with you to Titus, as their work cannot be uncovered.'

Sam spoke up. 'We'll have to work that part out when we get there, Deor and I together. We've evaded our share of patrollers in our time. We can dodge a few more.'

'Yes, but Sam, this isn't evading some half-pickled rogue in the Asman hills,' Cyrus said. 'This is Titus, their capital. This is Merope Week. They'll have their best patrollers everywhere.'

'Then we'll need to be careful,' Sam said. 'But we will get Sage back, and as many of the others that we can gather.'

Dolus, strangely quiet by his standards, stood. 'I'll go with you,' he said, turning to Deor. 'That is, if you'll have me.'

Deor turned to Dolus. They'd only known each other for a few days, but here he was offering to put himself at great risk for her cause. She still didn't have him figured out yet, but this offer humbled her. 'I will,' she said. 'Thank you for your help. You're risking your life to save my sister. I won't forget that.'

Sam smiled and shook Dolus' hand. 'Thank you, Dolus.'

'So that's settled then,' Deor said. 'A rescue party of three it is.'

'I would like to go too,' Alexi said from the corner.

'Alexi …' Deor said, ignoring the obvious irony in trying to stop Alexi when Cyrus couldn't stop her.

'No,' Cyrus said bluntly, stopping Deor from having to confront that issue. 'You can't. You're too young, and the journey is too dangerous. I am not letting all three of my remaining children risk their lives.'

Leon came around the table and put his hand on Alexi's shoulder. Down here, in his element, confidence and assuredness exuded from him. 'Alexi, your father told me you were very brave when the patrollers came to take your sister away this morning. That is a noble quality. However, this is not your journey to make. Your father is right; you are too young for this. However, I will take you under my wing and begin training you myself. As Dolus said, we're training our young men and women to fight, and you can begin that training. I will mentor you personally. And Sam, Deor, you'll know your brother is protected, not just by Cyrus, but by me as well.' Leon turned to Cyrus to seek approval for this request.

'Thank you, Leon,' Cyrus said.

Alexi nodded his reluctant agreement.

Deor nodded at Leon. 'Thank you.'

Eve stood. 'It's settled, then. In the morning, we'll set out. We'll meet here at dawn, just the four of us. Go home and pack light. Your journey begins at first light.'

'I can't say I like it,' Cyrus said.

Eve chuckled. 'Did they give you a choice?'

Cyrus shook his head. 'It would seem not. More grey hairs for me it is, then.'

The crew dispersed. Deor walked with Sam towards the northern exit of the Great Hall. Eve walked with them. 'I will see you both in the morning,' she said, stopping to go into one of the rooms. 'Make sure you get plenty of rest. You have a long journey ahead.'

Eve walked into the room. Inside, the stranger with the long earthy-blond hair that Deor had seen on the first day in the Great Hall sat, waiting for her. Eve took a seat opposite, and they began a close conversation.

Absentmindedly, Deor touched the birthmark on her shoulder.

'What is it?' Sam asked.

'I don't know …'

CHAPTER 9

Deor scratched her head and looked out into the morning. Dark. The sun wouldn't rise for a while yet. Still, time to go. She lifted her pack onto her back. It didn't contain much—some light clothes and provisions, and some of the remaining bread that Sage had baked. She slung her spears over her back as well: four of them, all handmade. Finally, she patted her pocket. Can't leave home without Mini.

Cyrus and Alexi came to the front garden to say goodbye. 'Be careful, Deor,' Cyrus said, 'and you too, Sam. Do not take unnecessary risks. Make sure you both get home alive.'

'We will,' Deor said, trying to push down her rising nerves. 'And when we get to Remit, we'll send word.'

'Make sure you do, and hopefully we'll have some updates for you then too.'

The family members said their goodbyes, and Deor and Sam turned their backs away from home. Leaving a tearful Cyrus and a worried Alexi, Deor and Sam started the journey to the Minerva cave entrance. They moved quickly and made it there before dawn. Eve and Dolus were already waiting for them.

'Sleep in, did we?' Dolus asked, grinning.

'It's good you're here early,' Eve said. 'I saw patrollers not far from here, to the north; the sooner we put distance between us and them, the better. Let's go right away. We head for the Alcyone River. It cuts away from the mountain range not far south of here. There's a watchman at the Garden Dock there with a boat for us.'

'Okay, let's go,' Deor said, re-shouldering her pack.

The troop of four started on their journey, mostly in silence. That seemed appropriate, given their mission. Eve led them further into and up the mountain until they found a path that headed south. The forest here, near home, was still dry. Dead leaves crunched under Deor's feet. She trod lightly and tried to avoid them, the legacy of a lifetime of avoiding patrollers.

As they walked, Deor reflected on the events of the previous day. It had all been such a whirlwind. They'd been having a beautiful breakfast, sharing a special moment that Sage had created, then the bludgeoning intrusion of the patrollers—and by extension, Merope—shattered it. The look on Sage's face when the patroller slung her over his shoulder like a sack of grain, and as Sage screamed Deor's name for help, felt tattooed on her soul. She had to get her back.

'Do you remember when she was born, Sam?' Deor asked, breaking the silence at last.

Sam smiled. 'Yes, I do, when they both were.'

'She was just so ready for this world. She came out, and those bright eyes of hers sparkled, and she looked around at the world as if to say, "Okay, I'm here now, at last; let's get going already!"'

Sam chuckled. 'Yeah, she always knew what she wanted, didn't she? From day one. She has always been keen to get on with life.'

Deor nodded. 'Yes, with everything, from her schoolwork to the garden, to cooking, to wanting to learn how to hunt. She's smart, Sam, so smart and so funny. She has your number too!'

'Ha!' Sam grinned. 'Maybe sometimes she does … She certainly thinks she does, anyway!'

'And now she's in a cage. Trapped in a cage, alone, in a foreign place. We cannot lose her, Sam.'

'I know, Dee, I know. We will get her back.' Sadness tinged Sam's voice. He didn't wear his emotions openly, but Deor could always hear them in his voice.

'In one way, it was a good thing she was so young when Mum was killed,' Deor said, staring at the ground in front of her as she walked on.

'What were you doing in the square that day, anyway?' Sam asked.

The memory flowed into Deor's mind, like the ocean into a coastal cave. Eight years old; her mum wasn't at home; she wanted to find her. Protesting. She didn't know what that word meant. She just wanted Mum to come home. Cyrus was busy in the garden. The square was just up the street.

'I snuck out,' she said. 'To find Mum. I got to the square just as one of the men spat in a patroller's face. They were all chained to the courthouse door. Then the patroller shot the man in the head. It was so loud. So loud. And then, it was so quiet. Mum turned and saw me. Just as the other patrollers raised their guns, she looked at me. She whispered my name. That was the last thing she did. Again, I'm glad Sage was too young to know.'

Deor took on a maternal role for Sage from then on. She became more than her older sister. She put herself up for

Sage as the mother Sage needed. When Sage turned twelve, Deor took her away for two nights. They camped down by the Alcyone River and spent time together painting, a hobby they both enjoyed. They painted portraits of each other, and when they returned home, they hung their portraits on the wall of their room. Deor took Sage hunting and discovered that spears were never going to be Sage's thing. She'd nearly speared her own foot when she tried to throw one.

Deor spoke to Sage then about the woman she wanted to become. She didn't know then about the past lives they'd led, but as she looked back now, it was clear that Sage was influenced by the innate knowledge she'd gained in her past lives. She was ready to live, ready to fulfil her potential. Sage wanted to learn about medicine and learn more about gardening, about herbs and plants and their usefulness, not just for cooking but also for medicine. Maybe this was a common theme in Sage's past lives.

'She's an old soul,' Deor said to herself.

'An old soul?' Sam asked. 'How do you mean?'

'Oh, you can see it in her eyes. She has been here before, many times. She is wise, much wiser than a normal thirteen-year-old.'

'That's often a very good way to tell,' Eve said from in front of them. 'When you meet someone who has wisdom, not just intelligence but wisdom beyond intelligence, then that's a sign that they've lived many lives before, especially if they're young and they have that wisdom. Some of the people born are new souls. This might be their first life, or they might've only had a few lives before this one, and you can see it in them. They lack depth beyond their outer layer. You can look into their eyes and not see much beyond that outer layer. You can learn a lot from a person's eyes. When you know what you're looking for.'

'Sage is not one of those people,' Deor said. 'She has wisdom and depth. Yes, she is definitely a very old soul. It would be very interesting to know about the lives she has lived before. And I feel bad for the life she didn't get to live in her most recent one, on Nebra, as Sofi. Her life was taken from her at a young age by the war, by Remus. They will not take that from her again.'

Silence fell, their footsteps on the earth the only sound from the travellers. Deor's heart ached for her sister, scared, alone in a cage somewhere in Merope. With every fibre of her *bakh,* she had to get Sage back. This was one of the things she was on this Earth to do—to protect her sister.

Sam broke the silence. 'So what's it all like?'

What on earth did he mean?

Eve turned with a curious smile on her face. 'What's what like, Sam?'

Sam scrunched his face up, trying to find the right words. 'You know, the whole reincarnation thing. What's it all like?'

'Well,' Eve said slowly, 'you don't really know it's happened. You're just born. You, too, are reincarnated, remember, Sam.'

'Yeah, I don't mean that. I mean knowing you are, or knowing others are, or sensing they are or whatever. You said you can tell a lot from a person's eyes, for example. What did you mean?'

Eve paused. 'How close are you and your sister, Sam?'

'Dee? We're extremely close. We always have been. Ever since she was—oh ...'

Eve nodded. 'You know how you just click with some people right away, like you've always known them? Chances are, you have. You know how there are others you absolutely do not gel with at all from the get-go? As though there's beef between you, and you just don't know it? Chances are, there was.'

'Wait, wait, wait … so I didn't like my teacher, right, at school. Final year. Well, not the final year, but the final year for me anyway. We just didn't get on, right? You're saying we had issues in past lives?'

Eve laughed. 'Not necessarily. Not everyone you have friction with is going to be past-life related. Your teacher might've just been not a very nice person. And not everyone you get along with was bonded with you in a past life either. They might just be a good person you resonate with. However, we do travel through lives together. You reincarnate with your people, usually. Not always, but usually. And you may not recognise them, but you sense it, somewhere in your *bakh*.'

'Family … They feel like family,' Deor added. 'That's why we've always been so close, Sam.'

'That's right,' Eve said, 'they do. But it goes the other way too. We reincarnate with our people, but we also reincarnate with the people with whom we have to set things right. They could be family, or they may not be. But often one of our challenges in life—among others—is to set right a wrong of the past.'

'The destruction of Nebra,' Deor said, her head bowed.

'Well,' Eve replied, 'that's not really what I mean. That happened; you just had a part in it, rightly or wrongly. Personal wrongs are the ones we must personally set right, first and foremost.'

They walked on a while longer, entering the last part of the mountain range in the Mid Territory and getting close to the southern border. Deor and Sam didn't go down that far south due to the potential for patrollers to be in the area. The gap in the mountain range left an easy spot to cross between the two countries. It was usually patrolled.

'I figure we can get there in a day and a half,' Eve said. 'We'll make it most of the way today and camp where we find somewhere safe and secluded tonight, then we should be able to get to the Southern Mountain tomorrow, around the middle of the day.'

'That's where we're headed? The Southern Mountain?' Sam asked.

'Yes, that's where we're headed. It's the furthest mountain south in the Asman Mountain Range. The Alcyone River and River Merope both begin there. And the people I want you to meet live there. The summit is the highest point in the Asman Range, and on a clear day, you can make out the entire range, all the way up to its northern end.'

'And you think the Southerners will be able to help us?' Deor asked.

'Yes, Deor, I do. In fact, I know they can. I've already contacted them about it.'

Soon enough, they reached the foot of the mountain. Two mountains loomed ahead: the Twin Peaks, almost identical to one another. These two mountains marked the beginning of the Southern Territory. The Alcyone River plotted its course through the gap between them, coming down from its source in the far south. Ahead, the river turned west and snaked away northwest into the distance, towards the Coastal Territory. Deor had never ventured further south than this.

'The Gap of the Peaks,' Eve said, indicating the gap between the two mountains, through which the river flowed. 'Once we enter that gap, we are in the Southern Territory. From there, everything is different. Pay attention to your senses, and pay attention to your surroundings. We're leaving your world behind now and entering theirs.'

'Their world?' Deor asked. Eve made the South sound

very mysterious.

'Yes, the people we call the Southerners, though that's not their real name. You're going to see a lot of different things soon.'

Deor turned and looked back to the North into her territory. In the distance, the mountain peaks rose up near her town. The sun had risen in the east enough to cast light across their top. A pang of longing came to her as she looked at her home.

'The Garden Dock isn't far from here,' Eve said. 'It's on the eastern bank of the river inside the gap. Let's hurry on.'

They turned and headed for the river and the gap between the peaks. Ahead was a stretch of flat, open land between them and the river. In the distance, on the east bank of the river, Deor could just make out the Garden Dock.

'Let's move quickly across this flatland,' Dolus said. 'I'm wary of being out in the open like this.'

They moved hastily towards the river and the Garden Dock. Absentmindedly, Deor touched the birthmark on her shoulder.

'You feel it too,' Eve said. 'We're not alone.'

Suddenly, voices shouted at them from the east. Patrollers, five of them, presumably monitoring the border between Merope and Alcyone.

'Stay there and do not move any further!' one patroller yelled.

'We can't let them question us,' Eve said. 'They'll know who we are. From the movement. We'll be imprisoned or killed.'

'We have to go now!' Sam said quickly. 'Head for the dock!'

Adrenaline surged through Deor. Her senses heightened. The dock was several hundred metres away, and they were out in the open like ducks on a lake, waiting to be picked off. 'You three go!' Eve yelled. 'I'll hold them up here!'

'No!' Deor yelled. 'I'm not leaving you! Run with me!'

While running with Eve, Deor pulled a spear from the sling on her back. It was light but strong and elegantly built. She turned to look at the patrollers. They were gaining ground. Shots cracked through the air, but they didn't hit their targets from that distance. Still, the patrollers were closing in.

Sam turned and fired an arrow at the pursuing patrollers. With great accuracy, he hit one in the leg. That patroller doubled over and fell, incapacitated. Two other younger patrollers were making good ground, though; they'd closed to within fifty metres of Eve and Deor. Deor had to do something, or they would catch Eve.

'Keep going, Eve!' she yelled, turning to face the patrollers. She targeted the one at the front, aimed quickly and threw her spear. It headed for him at great speed, but at the last moment, he veered to his right and tumbled out of its way, narrowly avoiding it plunging into his chest. He fired as he moved but fell, off balance, and missed wildly. The patroller directly behind had no time to react. The spear thundered into his shoulder, taking him to the ground. Deor took her chance as the first patroller got himself up. She turned and sprinted after Eve and the others. Hopefully, she'd bought Eve enough time to make it to the boat.

Sam and Dolus made it to the dock, and the boat was there waiting. Eve was still fifty metres from it but closing. Deor was catching her, but the fast patroller was still chasing her. He fired again, but Deor changed direction, and the bullet fizzed close past her ear.

Sam and Dolus got into the boat and held their hands out for Eve and Deor. Deor noticed a strange-looking man disappear into the forest beyond the riverbank. She only saw him for a moment before he vanished like a ghost into the trees.

Deor caught up to Eve mere metres from the boat, but the patroller was only thirty metres behind them. He stopped, aimed at Deor and fired just as she and Eve reached the boat. As they leaped in, the bullet plunged into Deor's left arm.

Sam and Dolus began rowing, setting the boat in motion. Without missing a beat, Deor pulled a second spear from her sling and threw it at the patroller. It moved far too quickly for him to react and plunged into his heart, killing him instantly.

'I am Lore reborn!' she screamed, rage like a tidal wave rising up inside her as the final two patrollers caught up to their fallen compatriot. 'You tell them Lore is coming! And I will have my vengeance! I will have my vengeance!'

CHAPTER 10

Deor collapsed into the boat, the pain overtaking her as the adrenaline subsided. Eve tended to her while Dolus and Sam rowed.

'We need to get the bullet out,' Deor said. Her left arm throbbed, soaked with blood. With her right arm, she reached into her pocket and retrieved Mini. 'Use this,' she said, giving it to Eve. 'Cut my sleeve away, and let's see how bad it is.'

Eve cut away the blood-soaked sleeve from Deor's arm, revealing a bloody hole where the bullet had gone in. She examined the other side of Deor's arm, but there was no other wound. 'It didn't come out,' she said. 'We're going to have to find it. I'm going to have to dig it out. But first, let's clean it up.'

Eve gathered water in her hands from the flowing river, rinsed it over Deor's wound and wiped away the blood that had spread down her arm. After gently cleaning the wound, she again picked up Mini and then held the knife in the rushing waters, cleaning the blade as Sam and Dolus rowed on.

'There is no easy way to do this,' Eve said, holding Deor's hand. 'It's going to hurt a lot, but if you can stay as still as possible, I'll try to get it out as quickly as I can.'

Deor nodded, and Dolus and Sam watched on as they rowed.

Eve held Deor's arm to keep it steady, and gently, with her fingers, she pushed at the edges of the bullet hole to see how deeply the bullet had pierced. 'It's deep,' she said, 'but not too deep to reach. I'm going to try to dig it out now, Deor. I hope it's still in one piece. I know it will be hard, but try to relax your arm as much as you can.'

Deor nodded and looked away, closing her eyes. She tried to let her arm go loose, but the pain and tension didn't help. Eve inserted the blade into Deor's wound. Immediately, an intense lightning bolt of pain surged through Deor's body. She gritted her teeth to stop herself from screaming. As the blade went deeper into the wound, the pain increased, until suddenly Deor felt a flash of white light come over her. Her head spun, and she passed out, losing all sense of where she was and who she was.

A moment later, a vision appeared before her eyes. She was Lore, seeing Lore's memory triggered by the pain. She was on Nebra with a young man. She knew the young man was Julius. Lore was angry at Julius, furious with him.

'You did this!' Lore screamed at Julius, pushing him back. 'You caused this! How could you do this to us? To all of us?'

Julius didn't respond. He'd betrayed her somehow.

Before she could see more, the vision ended, and Deor found herself back in the boat. Her arm still throbbed with pain, but the lightning bolts through her body had subsided. Sweat flooded her face.

However, Eve held a bullet in her hands, a smile of satisfaction on her face. 'I think we got the whole thing,' she said, examining it. 'Though I'm no expert on these new types of weapons.'

Deor sat against the back of the boat and looked at her bullet wound. It was still bleeding, but Eve had done a remarkable job of removing the bullet without widening the wound. 'Thank you, Eve,' she said, relief washing over her.

'You're welcome, my friend. Now sit still, I'm going to treat it again with the water from the river. I'll clean it, then wrap it so the bleeding stops, and you can begin to heal.' Eve cupped her hands and gathered more water from the river, then bathed Deor's wound. 'The waters of the river in this part of the country are very restorative. They have strong healing properties, so your wound will heal quickly and, hopefully, will mend fully.'

For several minutes, while Dolus and Sam continued to row, Eve used the river water to clean and treat Deor's wound. Even though they rowed upstream towards the river's source, the boat glided effortlessly along and sliced through the water without disturbance. There seemed to be almost no friction between the boat and the water.

'Maybe I'm super strong, Eve,' Sam said, 'but this whole rowing-upstream thing is ridiculously easy!'

Eve laughed. 'I told you things are different here.'

Eve took a piece of cloth from her kit and wiped the blood from Deor's arm. Deor took the chance to examine the wound again. The bleeding had nearly stopped, and the wound was very clean. It already looked a little smaller, as though it had begun to close over, but surely she was imagining it.

'You're not imagining that,' Eve said, reading the expression on Deor's face. 'It is healing already. I told you, the waters in this part of the river have strong powers. We'll wrap the wound now, then clean it again later and re-wrap it.' Eve wrapped the cloth tightly around Deor's arm, compressing the wound together.

Deor felt the blood pumping from her heart to her left arm as her body fought to repair itself. Her head felt heavy on her shoulders, as though it wanted to roll off to one side. Exhausted, she sat back in the boat, closed her eyes and breathed deeply. In just a few moments, Deor was asleep.

She woke to a bump. Sam and Dolus had rowed the boat to the shore and were getting out. The day had gotten warmer. Quite a bit of time had passed. 'How long have I been asleep?' she asked and climbed out of the boat.

'A few hours,' Eve said. 'Your body needed it to help fix that wound.'

Deor inspected the cloth wrapped around her wound. It had bled, but not much, only small amounts localised to her wound. She moved her arm around, and the pain was much less. 'My arm feels so much better!'

Eve smiled. 'Yes, it's looking a lot better. We'll take a proper look at it later. For now, let's sit in the shade here and have some food and water.'

They took shelter under a large tree on the riverbank. 'This tree we're under,' Eve said as they sat down, 'is called a Gliding Oak tree. As I explained to the boys while you were asleep, the boat is made from one of them. Their wood is spectacularly strong, but the people who live here are also able to imbue it with a lightness, a buoyancy, that makes it glide on top of the water, like it were flying.'

Deor smiled. 'That explains it. So it wasn't because Sam is super strong. Your girlfriends would be disappointed.'

Sam groaned. 'Don't you start too …'

The forest was warmer here. The carpet of dry leaves was gone, and a thick layer of grass, healthy even covered by a canopy of trees, replaced it. It was very different from Deor's home in the Mid Territory. She touched the grass; it felt alive, as though it had a pulse. Everything seemed more alive here, and there were more noises. A gradual hum vibrated in the air around them at all times, and strange bird calls came to Deor on the breeze, sounds she'd not heard at home. And the atmosphere was wetter while being hotter. All of this contributed to the forest feeling like a large living being.

'The forest is very different here,' Deor said to Eve.

'Yes, it is, and it'll get more so as we progress. Everything is different in this part of the world. You'll see things you haven't seen before.'

'How far do you think we've come?' Sam asked.

'About a quarter of the distance,' Eve replied. 'You and Dolus have rowed a long way. We're now well into the Southern Territory, in one of the inhabited parts. This area is known as the Northwood.'

Sam looked around with a stunned expression. 'Inhabited? What do you mean?'

Eve laughed. 'You haven't noticed anyone?'

'No, I haven't,' Sam said. 'There's been no one to notice!'

Eve chuckled. 'Well, they've noticed you.'

Deor looked around, trying to see signs of anyone. She heard something like a sound of whispering, but was it the breeze in the trees? Her mind could be playing tricks on her. She thought she saw eyes staring at her from next to a tree in her peripheral vision, but when she turned to look, no one was there. Someone appeared in a tree up ahead, watching them, but a moment later, they were gone, leaving Deor wondering if anyone had been there at all. Still, the sounds of whispering persisted through the trees.

'Don't worry,' Sam said, 'I hear it too. You're not going mad.'

'Where are they?' Deor asked. 'Where do they live?'

Eve thought before responding. 'Deor, do you remember how I told you that all people on Alcyone and Merope were reborn here from Nebra and Remus?'

'Yes.'

'Well, that is true, but the Southerners are an exception, of sorts. They're also reborn from Nebra, but they were a different people there. Do you remember anything about them on Nebra?'

Deor thought, trying to remember. Nebra was a big planet, and there were many different cultures. However, they were all the same beings, all human. Except … except there was something else. She pushed further into her memory, trying to get to it. Then a name came to her. 'The Alphym. There was a people on Nebra called the Alphym.'

Eve smiled. 'You got it. They evolved separately to the rest of Nebra, another type of intelligent being, and they kept out of Nebran affairs. They started being reborn here on Earth, leaving Nebra, when they saw that the end was coming. As each Alphym passed over and their *bakh* went to the afterlife, they chose to be reborn here instead of Nebra.'

'But they were more of a myth,' Deor said. 'People never saw them.'

Eve nodded. 'That's right. Long before the war, they were prevalent in their lands and interacted with the rest of Nebra. The Alphym had a relationship with our kind, with humans, but when they saw the inevitable end, they gradually withdrew.'

'How long ago did they start doing that?' Deor asked.

'One thousand years before the war began. They've been being reborn here since then and continuing their culture here. They live a very long life, nearly immortal, but even they couldn't survive what was coming to Nebra. Gradually, fewer and fewer of them chose rebirth on Nebra, until at the end, when the war began, all we had was rumours of the Alphym. No one saw them any longer. They'd all departed. Here, they again choose to keep out of our affairs. They've resumed their old ways of life, in tune with the living world around them, in tune with the mystical and magical parts of our beings.'

'How do you know them?' Deor asked. She'd thought the South was uninhabited. However, there'd always been whispers, tales told to her as a child, about the ghosts that dwelled there. Strange beings in a strange forest. That's why no one wished to journey there.

'I spent a lot of time with them when I was younger, around the age Alexi and Sage are now,' Eve replied. 'As a child, the seeing with which I was born was troubling for me. I wasn't able to control what I saw or when I saw it. Visions of past lives tormented me, not just as Pythus, but before that, and before that, and before that. I was haunted by visions of the future, of fires and floods, and I had no way to stop them. As I became a young woman, my abilities grew stronger, and I struggled to cope with what I could see. One of their elders, an oracle, had sensed me, so she sought me out and brought me into their community. She taught me not only how to control and manage my abilities, but also how to heighten them as well, and how to fine tune them. I lived with them for ten years, and while I was with them, they taught me their way of life so we'd better understand them, and I think with the hope that this time around, they wouldn't be destroyed by the affairs of humans.'

'Where do they live?' Sam asked. 'I've seen no signs of habitation anywhere.'

Eve laughed in reply. 'You'll find out tomorrow.'

The whispering all around them continued. Deor looked around at the living forest in wonder. The trees moved gently back and forth, seeming to react to one another, or to some omnipresent song that only they could hear. The water in the river flowed as if it were one large body sliding through the cavity in the land it had cut. The insects hummed as one, a monotone sound that seemed to echo the hum of the universe itself. Birds called to one another in strange and varied languages that only they understood, back and forth with one another throughout the forest. All of it seemed to resonate with one living force. If she reached out, she could nearly touch it; one force which flowed through everything in the forest, breathing life into and through everything. The feeling was intoxicating. Deor felt peaceful and connected and vibrant all at the same time, as though she, too, were plugged into this eternal life force that flowed through the forest.

You can feel it, Eve said, though Deor realised Eve hadn't said any words out loud. Deor heard it only in her mind. She turned to look at Eve, who was still looking at her.

Yes, Deor thought, *I can feel it.*

Eve nodded her reply. 'However, if we want to get there tomorrow, we need to keep going today,' she said aloud. 'Sam, Dolus, are you up for more rowing?'

A grin spread across Dolus' face. 'I am if strongman here is.'

'Good!' Eve said. 'Everyone fill your flasks with the river water and drink deeply. It will help you heal, Deor, and it will help your muscles not tire out as well, boys.'

Deor walked to the riverbank, filled her flask and poured some water over her head to cool herself down. In these warm, wet conditions, her dark hair felt hotter than it normally did. She rinsed water through it and let it fall down her back, her natural curls bouncing on her back in the warm air. Out of the corner of her eye, she noticed Dolus watching her admiringly.

For the love of Pleid, she did not need that right now.

'You just get yourself ready to row, beach boy,' Sam said, pushing Dolus towards the boat. He'd noticed it too. Dolus laughed and did as he was told.

They set off again up the Alcyone River, heading south towards the Southern Mountain. Again, the boat glided on top of the water easily and gracefully. The rowing seemed effortless. Sam shook his head in amazement. 'Eve, I know you said the Southerners—'

'The Alphym,' Eve interrupted.

'—the Alphym, yes,' Sam corrected. 'I know you said the Alphym built these from Gliding Oak trees, but when I last went to school—and granted that was only for a few years—there was a little thing called gravity, and the way I remember it working is if four people sat in a boat, the boat did not float above the water. And yet I look over the side here, and the boat barely seems to touch the surface. How is this happening?'

Eve smiled. 'Yes, the Gliding Oak tree does produce remarkably strong, elegant and light timber, but you're right, it doesn't have the ability to defy gravity. The Alphym are a race imbued with magic, Sam; they build their boats and whisper a spell into the wood. That's how the boat is able to travel as it does. This enables them, when necessary, to travel vast distances very quickly.'

Sam shook his head slightly. 'So basically, we're rowing a magic boat.'

Dolus laughed. 'Didn't you always want a magical boat when you were a boy, Sam? I always wanted a magical rod.'

Deor laughed. 'I bet you did!'

Eve blushed.

'I was a keen fisherman as a boy!' Dolus said. 'I'm from the Coastal Territory, remember! I am a very good fisherman!'

They rowed on and made good headway up the river. Deor noticed a change in the forest. The trees became taller, of a different type. The thick, heavyset Gliding Oak trees gave way to a tall species of fir, not as thick at the base but far taller, reaching beyond sight into the canopy above. Different bird sounds came to her here, more distinctly sharp and high pitched, seeming to match the trees. The water turned a slightly deeper shade of blue as they rowed. Sam and Dolus rowed effortlessly, and the sound of the water rushing by underneath the boat was soothing, hypnotic. Deor felt deeply relaxed.

'This is the Firwood,' Eve said, breaking the rhythm of the silence. 'So named for the type of trees here. These fir trees are found nowhere else on our continent. The Firwood has its own animals, which also exist nowhere else. Some of the Alphym live here; you may see some of them as we pass. This is also the home of the jakelopes. They climb these tall trees to make their nests and weave their jakel hair up in its branches. The Alphym who live here respect the jakelopes. The creatures allow the Alphym to use their webs when they're finished with them, typically when their young are big enough to leave the nest.'

Deor studied the forest on each side of the boat and looked up into the trees. The branches were too high up to give her any chance of seeing a jakelope, though her mind raced at the possibility of a metre-long insect crawling up the straight trunk. Suddenly, up ahead, she noticed two small children sitting on the bank. 'Eve!' she whispered.

'Yes,' Eve said, smiling, 'they are curious about you. They heard you coming and came down to the bank.'

The two children watched their approach. Their eyes were a striking brown and their hair deep blond—not light blond or beach blond like Dolus', but an earthy blond that seemed to echo the colour of their countryside.

Deor's gaze locked with one of them.

'Hi there, kids!' Sam called out as their boat approached.

The children looked at him and smiled back, then one of them moved his right hand slightly, and they vanished.

'Ha!' Eve laughed loudly.

'What was that?' Sam asked.

'They were having some fun with you,' Eve said. 'They had a jakel hair veil to hide themselves.'

'How do you know they had a jakel veil?' Sam asked.

Eve turned back to where the Alphym children had been. 'Because I can still see them. And I can see that they're laughing, amused by the look on your face.'

Sam shook his head and laughed. 'We're being made to look foolish by little children, Dolus. This does not bode well for when we meet the adults ...'

They rowed on for a while longer, and Deor tried to rest, until eventually the forest changed again. The fir trees gave way to even larger trees, redwoods bigger than any trees Deor had seen before. She marvelled at the size of them. They had to be ancient. Their trunks were at least twenty metres wide, and they shot up far into the sky, creating a canopy that seemed to go up forever. So complete and immense was it that it felt as if they were rowing underneath a world whose sky itself was the tree canopy. There were fewer sounds, fewer birds, or they were higher up and couldn't be heard.

'The forest here is beautiful,' Deor said. 'The trunks are wider than our house, Sam.'

Sam nodded. 'Yeah, and probably have fewer termites too.'

'We'll stop up here very soon,' Eve said. 'We're into the final part of the forest, the Alphwood. This is where the majority of the Alphym live, in this forest and the Southern

Mountain. There's a cave nearby where we can camp.'

Dolus and Sam rowed the boat to shore at a small beach in the river, then got out and pulled it up onto the grass.

'We can leave the boat here for the night,' Eve said. 'It will be quite safe. The Alphym know this is one of their own. They'll already know we're here and will leave the boat alone for us to use again tomorrow.'

Eve led them up the hill a little, away from the river, to a clearing bordered by a cave that went back into the mountain behind it. The crew crossed to the cave, put their belongings inside and made camp for the night.

Deor felt tired again. Her body was using a lot of energy to heal the wound in her arm, and she felt mentally spent after the events that morning. But the rustling sounds from the breeze outside swaying the redwood branches far above made the perfect accompaniment for Deor to fall into a deep and peaceful sleep.

CHAPTER II

Lore paced the room. How could this be? The attack on Nebra had been two days ago. Her parents were dead. She and her brother were presumptive co-pharit, and now it appeared they had a breach in their security. A spy. Someone on the Nebran inside who had fed security codes to the Remusan military, enabling the ships to bypass security and slip onto Nebra undetected, cloaked, fully armed and ready to strike. Someone on Nebra had fed these codes to them, and she had to find out who.

The commander of the military entered the room. He saluted Lore. 'It looks like the codes were fed from one location, the day before the attacks,' he said. 'We have discovered that whoever did this hacked the systems, bypassing the security checks so they could retrieve the codes. They could only do it the day before because codes are randomised each day for the following day. They had a small window only, and they knew this. This means they knew our system, knew the rules in place. This means they are very likely Nebran and very likely Nebran military. In short, someone has betrayed us from within.'

Lore banged her fist on the desk. 'When can we get a name?'

'We're working on it and should be able to pinpoint it very soon. We're getting close on the location, and from there we'll have a name. In the meantime, ships are preparing for battle. We can have an armada dispatched within hours. We're just waiting on your order.'

Lore continued pacing the room in thought. 'More than twenty cities across Nebra,' she said. 'Tens of thousands dead, maybe more. Thousands still missing, unaccounted for. Unprovoked. Why?'

'I don't know the why,' the general replied. 'But I know the what. It is an act of war. I think there's only one relevant response to such an act.'

Lore sighed. 'I know … But I just can't shake the feeling that full-scale war will not end well for anyone …'

The vision dissipated as Deor began to wake. They'd shifted in recent days from the attack to this part of her memory, the discovery that Nebra had been betrayed by someone on the inside, by a Nebran. The anger Lore felt about that was also lined with regret that this situation was so avoidable. They were due to the actions of one person betraying Nebra. 'Julius …' she muttered.

Eve, awake next to her, sat up. 'Yes, Julius. You've seen that?'

'He betrayed Nebra,' Deor said. 'He is the reason the war started.'

Eve nodded. 'He did. He was a spy, working for Remus. He'd infiltrated the Nebran military as a teenager.'

'He was called something after that. What was it? Julius the Betrayer. He got away, back to Remus, and he was labelled Julius the Betrayer. Julius the Deceiver. But he was never caught.'

Eve nodded again. 'Yes, that's all true. As your mind opens to these past memories, you'll remember more things like that. You may find that other memories come into your mind when you're awake. More of your mind is opening itself up to the memories of when you were Lore.'

'I saw him before he left. I couldn't believe he could've done it. I think that's why I didn't turn him in. I should have.'

Eve shook her head. 'There's no point thinking that way now. You cannot change the past, and this is one of the reasons we generally don't remember past lives: so that we don't live a life filled with regrets, or stress, carried over from them.'

Deor nodded. 'I guess we can only make the best of the life we have now.'

Refreshed after a deep sleep, she got up and surveyed the forest. These woods had a very recuperative property about them. It could have been day or night, though; she wouldn't be able to tell the difference. The vast canopy of the Alphwood produced a perpetual twilight, neither day nor night, the enormous trees providing complete cover from the outside world. Deor felt great peace.

Remembering her arm, Deor unwrapped her bandage. She stared in shock. It was clean, the wound gone. All that remained was a small red dot where the bullet had entered, nothing else. 'My arm has healed completely,' she said.

Eve smiled. 'I'm glad. The Alphym magic is very strong.'

Dolus and Sam were rising as well. Sam came over to inspect her arm. 'That looks incredible!' he said. 'And you know what the best bit is?'

'What's that?'

'It means you can row today, Dee!' He laughed.

Deor laughed back. 'Oh, I think I'm feeling a relapse! The soreness is returning!'

They quickly got organised and had some food and drink, but Eve was keen to be on their way again. 'We have a couple of hours of rowing before we can stop, then a hike,' she said. 'The sooner we get going, the sooner we're done.'

They headed back down through the giant redwoods. The branches far above swayed ever so slightly in the breeze coming in from outside the forest. At the river, their boat lay waiting for them. 'We'll take first shift,' Eve said, taking an oar and handing the other to Deor. 'Show you boys how rowing is supposed to be done.'

Eve and Deor set the boat off, with Sam and Dolus seated at the other end. The boat was soon again slicing through the water gracefully and lightly.

'This is the life, Sam,' Dolus said, putting his feet up on the side of the boat and lying back to stare at the canopy of trees. 'Relaxing on a magic boat being rowed up the river. Does anyone have any grapes they can feed me? I feel like an emperor.'

Deor laughed while Eve just shook her head. 'Don't get too cosy,' she said. 'You'll be taking the second shift soon enough.'

They rowed for about an hour, surrounded by the enormous redwoods, then stopped briefly for some water. Eve and Deor swapped seats with Sam and Dolus, who took over the rowing for the final leg.

'Only about an hour to go, I estimate,' Eve said, 'and we'll be at the Southern Mountain. We've come nearly all the way down the Asman Range now.'

After another hour, the boat came to the bottom of a series of steep rapids. Sam and Dolus stopped rowing. On the eastern bank of the river was a dock, similar to the Garden Dock.

'This, my friends, is the end of the line for us,' Eve said, 'at least in the boat. These are the Southern Rapids, falling as they do at the foot of the Southern Mountain. They come down with all the force of gravity from high up the mountain, and it's where boats stop.'

Five or so different rapids crashed down the last part of the mountain into the river. There were no rapids like this in the Mid Territory. Rowing down them could be fun.

Sam and Dolus steered the boat over to the dock. They all got out, and Eve tied the boat to the dock. Suddenly, seemingly from out of nowhere, a young man appeared between them. Tall and fair-skinned, he had the same earthy blond hair as the children they'd seen the previous day. His eyes were the same deep brown.

Eve spoke to him in a language none of the other three recognised, then nodded her head in acknowledgment and thanks. The young Alphym man did the same. A moment later, he turned and was gone, disappearing like a ghost into the woods.

'Welcome to the Southern Mountain,' Eve said, indicating with her hand the enormous mountain that loomed in front of them. 'Home of the Alphym, and the largest mountain on this continent. Now we begin the hike. We follow this track up the mountain to about two thirds of the way up. It'll take about four hours.'

'Where are we headed to?' Sam asked.

Eve stopped and listened. 'Can you hear that?' The group listened with her. 'That dull roar, can you hear it?'

'Faintly,' Deor said. It sounded like a distant wind, but more than that. Like a crashing sound, far away.

'It'll become less faint, don't worry. That's where we're headed. The Falls of Gladhym.'

Sam's face contorted in confusion. 'A waterfall?'

'More than just that,' Eve said. 'You'll see when we

get there.'

The weather had warmed up, though from within the great canopy of the redwoods, Deor couldn't tell what the weather was like above. Sweat stung her eyes as they walked. The air was wetter here.

'I hope all this trekking is worth our while,' Dolus said to Sam.

Sam nodded. 'Me too. Though it's hard to complain about it when Eve has twenty years on us, and Deor was shot yesterday, and still they're leading the hike.'

'Not a manly look …' Dolus laughed.

After a while hiking up the mountain, they found a sheltered clearing in which to take a rest. Deor had refilled her flask from the river before setting off, and the water helped to keep her energised. They were, however, low on food.

'I don't know what we can and can't eat in these woods,' Deor said as they rested. 'There're a lot of plants I don't recognise. I wouldn't want to guess as to what we can eat and what is poisonous.'

'No, and you don't need to try to work it out,' Eve said. 'The Alphym have cultivated these woods and will provide for us.'

'What are they like, the Alphym?' Dolus asked.

Eve thought before responding. 'They're very old souls. And they carry the wisdom of their many lives on many worlds with them in this life. They've seen much and learned much and have seen enough of humans to know to be wary. For example, if the Meropans knew of the existence of the Alphym, I daresay their existence would be under threat. So they take precautions. Trust has to be earned. Thankfully for us, I've earned their trust, and they're supportive of our mission. You'll find them welcoming, generous and gracious hosts.'

They set off again soon after. Deor was keen to get to the top, meet the Alphym and continue on their journey. She looked at the track ahead. It headed straight up the Southern Mountain and looked quite steep. It would be tough going.

'Follow me, and we'll be there soon enough,' Eve said. 'You'll know when we get there.'

The roar of the falls had been growing steadily louder since they set out and continued to do so as they walked on. Deor heard it quite clearly now, a constant roar in the background. Following Eve, Deor made her way steadily up the mountain track. The path looked very well worn, the track clearly delineated from the grass and undergrowth of the mountain. How many thousands of Alphym had worn this track in and over how many years?

Eventually, the path led to a plateau with trees marking the end of the woods. The roar from the falls, even louder now, crashed across the landscape. Deor walked through the trees and out into the open air beyond. She looked at what lay ahead and gasped.

Ahead of her, a flat of grass stretched out to an enormous lake filled with clear blue water. The lake bank curled away on both sides until it rejoined itself somewhere behind an enormous cascading waterfall. The water poured down from the mountain, which rose high up beyond it, and the sun shone down from the clear blue sky, making the spray from the water sparkle as it hit the lake. It reminded Deor of the sparkle of her Minerva gem in the sunlight. She still wore it around her neck, hidden under her clothes. On both sides of the lake, grasslands stretched out several hundred metres, gently sloping down towards where the woods began again. Dozens of horses grazed on the grasslands on both sides of the lake or drank from its waters. Others ran in herds along its sides.

'It's beautiful …' Deor whispered. She didn't have the words to describe just how beautiful it was, though. Life in the Mid Territory was a life of hunting, of scratching and scrapping, and here was paradise.

Eve nodded. 'Welcome to the Falls of Gladhym, home of the Alphym.'

About halfway around the bank, to their right, a large bridge spanned an outlet. On the eastern side of the lake, to their left, an identical bridge crossed a similar outlet. Eve led them towards it.

'These falls have been here for tens of thousands of years,' she said. 'At least. Even when most of the known world was covered in ice, there was a lake here and falls. Seasonal rains fall on the mountain, which feeds the waterfall and the lake. The Alcyone River begins here from that outlet on the west bank of the lake, and the River Merope also begins here from this outlet on the eastern side.'

'Both rivers begin here?' Sam asked.

'Yes, they do,' Eve said. 'They have the same source: the Southern Mountain and the Falls of Gladhym. Both nations fed from the same source, both nations drinking the same water.'

As they walked on, the horses lifted their heads and regarded them with curiosity. Some came closer to see who they were, and some walked alongside them. They had no fear of the humans.

'Hello,' Deor said to one beautiful black horse, who nuzzled at her face. She patted his head carefully. She'd not had much experience with horses, but he snorted his satisfaction and galloped away.

'These are the Akkadym, the horses of the Alphym,' Eve

said. 'They live in these planes and woods, and the Alphym ride them when they need to travel.'

'They don't look like the horses you sometimes see the patrollers using,' Sam said.

'No, they don't,' said Eve. 'These horses have their freedom. The ones the patrollers use have been subjugated. For an Alphym to ride an Akkadym horse, the Akkadym must agree, or the Alphym will not be permitted to ride. It's a union, not a subjugation.'

'We know a bit about subjugation,' Deor said. It felt foreign to think of the patrollers in such a place as this.

They reached the bridge on the eastern side of the bank. Eve led them to the middle, where they stopped. The waters of the lake flowed through the outlet beneath them—the beginning of the River Merope. It cut a channel through the grasslands and into the woods beyond, where it disappeared from their view. Beyond that, over the top of the woods, they could see the Southern Mountain sloping down and away into the valley beyond it. Standing on the bridge and looking to the northeast, they could see Merope stretching away in the distance.

'There's Merope.' Eve pointed. 'At least, the southern part of it. We can't see it, but we're looking in the direction of Titus, the capital of Merope, far in the distance.'

Deor strained to see as far as she could into Merope, but it was no use. The furthest thing she could see was a large dark shadow over the land off to the east. It covered a vast amount of ground and disappeared beyond view.

'That's the Scarred Lands,' Eve said, picking up on where Deor was looking. 'That's where your journey through Merope must begin, across there, then through the Merope Range and on to the road to Remit. You'll start out tomorrow.'

A sense of foreboding came over Deor. When sitting in the Great Hall two days earlier, this mission had seemed accomplishable, with these places just small areas on a map. Walk through the Scarred Lands, along the mountain range, across a road into a town, and then up to Titus. Now, as she stared out at the seemingly endless stretch of country in front of her, with the ominous dark shadow of the Scarred Lands looming in the distance, she wondered how they could possibly achieve this mission. Part of her just wanted to go home, to turn around and go back to the Mid Territory, but then she remembered Sage, who right now must be sitting somewhere in a cage, scared and alone. Thinking of Sage strengthened her resolve, and she again vowed inwardly to get her sister back, and exact revenge upon Merope for everything they had done.

Eve looked at her with a thoughtful expression. 'Let's keep going,' she said, then led them across the bridge and on around the lake. With each step the falls grew louder until the roar was so loud they had to shout to be heard. The spray from the water pouring over the edge of the mountain carried on the breeze and drifted across Deor's face, cooling her down in the warm sun.

'Follow me along this track!' Eve yelled, indicating a track ahead that veered away from the lake bank towards some large rocks sitting closer to the mountainside. They walked behind them and followed the track on, winding around rocks towards the falls, before it turned into the mountainside. Deor followed Eve as the track wound into the hill, heading up as well as in. Up and around, they continued on, winding into the mountain, then suddenly as the path flattened out, they passed through a thin veil of misty water, like the gentlest mist of rain pushed by a breeze. Deor passed through it, and again she gasped.

In front of her, beautifully lit somehow from the sunlight outside, lay an incredible underground city inside the mountain. Grasslands led to lakes within a large park in its centre. Dozens and dozens of Alphym relaxed or walked or played in these parklands in the sunlight. A path led around both sides of the park, and several cut through it. Beyond the side paths, the land rose gently up and away, with streets winding through it. Beautiful arched timber homes, made from the Alphwood forest redwoods, adorned those streets. Intricately carved and built, each home seemed to flow into the next one, giving a sense of harmony and completeness to the city. The streets wound off into the distant hillside on each side.

Beyond the park at the other end stood several taller buildings grouped together in a circle in the middle of the city. They looked to be made of some sort of stone, a light and cool colour that Deor didn't recognise. She looked up and saw the mountain ascending high above her. The inside of the top of the Southern Mountain was hollow!

'Is this …' Deor said to Eve. How could this be?

Eve smiled and nodded. 'Yes, it is. This is the inside of the Southern Mountain. I told you it was the home of the Alphym; well, it's actually their literal home. All this time, they've hidden in plain sight. We can all see the Southern Mountain looming in the sky, but we never knew we were looking straight at their home. They've lived in this city inside the mountain for well over a thousand years.'

'Incredible!' Dolus said. 'And no one knows about it …'

'Exactly,' Eve said, 'no one knows about it. And they want to keep it that way.'

'How does it work?' Deor asked. 'How is it lit from outside?' Light streamed in, but she couldn't see where it

141

came from.

'That's part of the genius. Sunlight feeds into here from many shafts in the mountain, all cut at intervals around the mountain to track the sun as it crosses the sky over the course of the day. Water rushing down the mountain from above goes to the falls, but some comes through the rocks into rivulets and brooks that feed down into the lakes inside.'

'Shafts cut into the mountain top, huh?' Sam said, a wry smile on his face. 'Now where have I seen that before?'

Eve smiled. 'That's right. Where do you think I got the idea? When your father and I first formed the movement, our first order of business was to form a headquarters. The Great Hall took inspiration from the city of Gladhym. We had help from the Alphym to build it.'

Some of the Alphym had begun to take notice of their presence. They'd drawn the gaze of several in the park. 'Should we be worried?' Deor asked.

Eve shook her head. 'No. If we were strangers, then, yes, we should be worried. We'd probably already have a dozen arrows trained on us by now. But they know who I am, and they knew we were coming, so they'll leave us be. However, we should keep going; we need to find our hosts.'

Eve led them along the path that wound around the park. They passed several groups of Alphym, some children, many adults. They were generally tall, usually with the earthy, copper-toned blond hair that Deor had seen on the children of the Firwood. Some took an interest in them and looked at them with curiosity. One younger Alphym, with long hair past his shoulders, paid particular interest to them and discussed them with two of his friends. Deor recognised him as the man she'd seen at the Great Hall yesterday, and on the first day she'd been there. He'd been in discussions with Eve. He nodded to

Deor as she passed by.

They came to the far side of the park and walked down some steps to a slightly lower level. The steps were made of the same light, cool-coloured stone as the central buildings to which they led. Eve led them along the path between two of the buildings and into the courtyard within. Seven stone buildings, all around ten metres high, sat in a circle around the central feature, a pool in which the water moved gently, fed from some unseen spring. A building on the far side had an open pergola facing the pool.

Deor stared at the rippling waters in the pool. They swirled rhythmically and made the slightest whispering sound as they did. It felt hypnotic, and as she stared, she felt herself being mentally drawn into it, as if she were sinking down into the waters, losing her sense of self. Images appeared in front of her, in her mind but seemingly also in front of her, as though she were there. She saw fire on the mountains scorching the Asman Mountain Range, the Earth cracked through Alcyone and Merope, and the skies filled with darkness and devastation throughout the land.

And then, she was free, back in the Southern Mountain. Eve had her hand on Deor's arm. 'It doesn't pay to look into the Reflection Pool if you're not ready for what you might see,' she said.

'What was it I saw?' Deor asked. 'Was that a vision of the future?'

'The Reflection Pool shows you what may come to pass,' Eve said. 'Nothing is certain, not ever. People's actions change future events, and people's actions are always their choice to make. We are never destined to do a certain thing; we have the ability to choose. However, the Reflection Pool shows visions of the way the future may be.'

Three Alphym had arrived and stood by the pool. Eve walked towards them.

One of them, a smaller and older woman, smiled at Eve, radiating kindness and warmth. 'Welcome back, Alphym daughter Eve,' the woman said, embracing her. 'It has been many years since I saw you in person.'

'Thank you, Mother Moorilim,' Eve said. 'It has indeed been many years, and I have aged those many years, while you have not. You look as well and as youthful as when you first brought me here.'

Moorilim chuckled. 'I may not have aged much outwardly, but we all age within, even the Alphym. Just much more slowly than humans.'

'Mother Moorilim,' Eve said, 'Oracle of the Alphym, these are the people I told you about. This is Deor, and Sammu, and Dolus. I have brought them here to receive your help.'

Moorilim looked at Deor, and Deor heard her voice clearly inside her head. *Welcome, daughter Deor. Welcome, Lore reborn. The Alphym greet you as a friend.*

Deor bowed her head slowly and reverently. 'Thank you for welcoming us to your home. We are humbled to have been invited to such a beautiful place.'

Moorilim smiled and nodded. 'May I introduce you to the high king and queen of the Alphym, Örn and Ästrid. They are very wise and will advise you on your path ahead.'

Deor bowed her head to the high king and queen. She did her best to convey her humility, but she was unused to greeting royalty. They both stood quite tall, both with the same earthy blond hair as their compatriots, and both had deep brown eyes that seemed to echo the majesty of the mountain in which they stood. Deor raised her head, and when she looked into their eyes, it felt like looking up at the night sky, so deep were their gazes. Both the king and queen smiled at her, seeming to read what she was thinking.

Not quite as far and wide as space. Deor heard a female voice in her head; it came from High Queen Ästrid. *But we have seen a lot, Lore of Nebra reborn.*

High King Örn moved forward and led them away. 'Come,' he said, 'we will sit and eat. You must be tired from your journey.'

They walked into one of the seven buildings that bordered the courtyard. Within sat a large redwood table, ornately decorated with beautifully carved images of horses, the Akkadym, along its sides. The light streaming in from above danced on the edges of the table, and the horses seemed to gallop along and around its edges.

The high king and queen sat in two chairs next to one another at the head of the table. The others took seats on either side. Food had been prepared and laid out on the table: some fruits and breads, olives and oils. Large jugs of water sat in the middle with a plate and full glass at each seat. Deor's stomach grumbled in anticipation.

Thirsty from the heat and the journey, Deor drank from the glass in front of her. The water flowed through her body, soothing and rejuvenating muscles and bones alike. Her mind cleared and felt refreshed, like waking after a deep sleep. 'Is this the same water as in the river?' she asked.

High King Örn smiled and nodded. 'All the water in Alphym territory is the same water. It flows from the top of our mountain above into the lakes within the mountain and the falls outside, then down into the twin rivers, which you call the River Merope and the Alcyone River. We have our own names for them. All of the water in all of our territory is imbued with the magic of the Alphym. These drinks are also infused with the juices of some citrus that we grow here. They will refresh your mind and heal your body. I encourage you to drink deeply and become well. Help yourselves to the food you see in front of you also. It will also nourish your body and soothe your aches and pains.'

Deor dipped a piece of the bread in the oil provided. It had a light floral scent. She took a bite of the bread, and a wave of satisfaction surged through her body. The oil had a depth of flavour she'd never experienced before, dark and complex flavours that made her think of the colour ochre, but at the same time a light floral note she could smell and which danced over the top of the deep, complex flavour. The bread itself was crunchy on the outside and velvety soft in the middle. She remembered the bread that Sage had made for them a few days earlier. She remembered dipping that bread into the remnants of their stew from the night before and tasting how delicious it was. That had been delicious, but Sage would have been in awe if she'd tasted this.

Sam and Dolus both tried the fruit, types that Deor had never seen before. Juice dripped down Sam's chin as he gorged on pieces of a large melon. For some time, the four travellers ate in silence, filling their stomachs and quenching their thirst.

'No wonder you guys live forever with food like this!' Sam said, breaking the silence.

Deor laughed, and a little piece of bread flew out of her mouth. It landed on the table, right in front of High Queen Ästrid. An awkward silence came over the room.

'My Pleid,' Dolus said. 'You can take her anywhere but out …'

The high queen smiled and brushed the piece of food away. 'It's fine,' she said. 'I'm glad you are enjoying the food. And we don't live forever, Sammu, but we do live a very long time, as we did on Nebra. But we had to leave there when we saw the end of days coming.'

'We have been here for over a thousand years now,' Örn said. 'Earth is now our home, as Nebra was before it. We have great hopes that humans won't do to Earth what they did to Nebra and Remus. This planet is young, at least in terms of its ability to be inhabited by humans. It's in a new era now, one of rebirth and growth. We recognised that and have made our home here, as have the humans from Nebra and Remus. However, we do not want Earth to just be the next staging ground for your ancient battle. Something needs to change this time around. Lore could not make that change happen on Nebra; perhaps Deor can now on Earth.'

'I don't know what I can do to change things right now,' Deor said. 'My life has been lived dominated by Merope, by those who were from Remus. They've resumed the battle with us here on Earth, though it's no battle; it's one-sided. They enslave us for their own growth. I don't want a war, but I'll fight to gain our freedom from Merope.'

'And somewhere in between those two we hope lies the answer,' Örn said. 'We will help you on this mission to rescue your sister, but we will not assist in the waging of war on this planet if it comes to that.'

'All we ask for is whatever help you can give us on this mission,' Deor said. 'We don't know the way through the Scarred Lands, much less Merope itself.'

'So you will take the way through those lands,' Ästrid said. 'Our people do not venture in there, but we can advise you on how to get through.'

Dolus sat forward. 'What's in those lands? What happened in there?'

Ästrid turned to him. 'Nothing is in there now, not living

anyway. Much that is not living dwells there, though. That's what you must worry about when travelling through the Scarred Lands, the dead who dwell there.'

'The dead who dwell there?' Dolus asked.

Ästrid nodded. 'Yes. They are unable to cross over, unable to be reborn, trapped there by the trauma of what happened to them. They cannot let go of the lives they lost, and until they do, they will remain trapped in those dead lands.'

'There's something you need to know,' Örn said. 'Alcyone is not the only place on this world that Nebrans have been reborn. When you began coming here, you settled in Alcyone, and also in those lands that are now called the Scarred Lands. Initially, that was where most of you were reborn, making towns and settlements. Before long, though, the battle began again. As Merope grew, they settled their capital in the north, and the first emperor of Titus, Titavius, invaded the Nebrans to the south and waged war on them. They fought back, and a long battle ensued. After many months of fighting, both sides were weary, so Titavius did something that should have made him go down in infamy, but instead has ensured he is revered as a hero and conqueror by Meropans. He ordered the scorching of the ground. New Meropan troops set up a perimeter around all of the Nebrans in those lands to keep them inside their settlements, and in the space of one day and one night, the Meropan soldiers set fire to the entire area. It was the height of summer, and with hot southerly winds, the fires spread quickly and burned everything in their path. As the fires raged, many Nebrans tried to escape to avoid being scorched, but the Meropan soldiers did not allow it. Any fleeing Nebrans were killed as they came out of the blaze. None escaped; all were killed trying or burned alive, all by the orders of Titavius.

'He personally came down to oversee the operation, and after ten days of burning, when the fires eventually died out, he surveyed the silent, blackened landscape and smiled. They were all dead. Every last Nebran reborn. "As they burned on Nebra, so too now they burn on Earth," he said, his boots crunching on the blackened ground.

'They renamed their capital Titus in his honour. Now, animals will not go into the Scarred Lands. The place is cursed by what happened. Only the ghosts of the dead dwell there, unable to move on.'

Silence fell like a dark cloud over the room. Deor felt an immense sadness, something beyond that which comes from hearing terrible news, something that came from deeper within herself, from the part of her that still longed for Nebra, from the part of her that was still Lore.

'There's another thing you should know, Deor and Sam,' Ästrid said. 'Your parents on Nebra, when you were Lore and Zephir, were among those who had come to Earth to be reborn again. They were the leaders of this new Nebran civilisation on Earth, as they had been on Nebra, and they were two of the Nebrans who perished in that blaze. Like the others, their ghosts roam those lands still, unable to move on.'

Deor sat silently, trying to process this information.

Eve put an arm around her shoulders in support.

'We will help you journey through those lands, though,' Örn said. 'We'll give you food for your journey and some things that may come in handy. Tonight, you can rest, and in the morning, we will meet with you again and bid you farewell. Three of our riders will ride you to the edge of the Scarred Lands, and there send you on your journey. Our riders will not enter, though, and neither will their horses. But what we give you will hopefully help you get through.'

The high king and queen rose from their seats, and the others did the same. 'Moorilim will take you to your lodgings for the night,' Örn said. 'Rest well; it will be the last good night of rest you have for a long time.'

Moorilim led them out of the chamber and away down a path towards some other houses, similar to the ones they'd seen earlier. The energy had drained out of Deor. The travelling had caught up with her, but the weight of the news she'd just heard also pressed on her. Merope would not be stopped. They were bent on the destruction of everything Nebran. The Emperor Titavius had destroyed the first wave of Nebrans, and Emperor Barritus was a direct descendant of Titavius. He was enslaving her wave of Nebrans in Alcyone. She felt sure that he, too, would like to burn the ground on which they walked.

CHAPTER 12

The barest sliver of light came into Zephir's cell, just enough for him to recognise that it was morning. He'd slept badly, but this was to be expected since he had no bed, no chair even, only the ground. His body ached all over, not just from sitting on the ground for many hours, but from the battle, and from the fight that resulted in him being in this cell. Again, he chastised himself for getting caught. He'd fallen into a Remusan trap set by the traitor Julius—whom he'd been pursuing. His entire crew had been taken prisoner and locked in the cells aboard Julius' ship.

They'd been following Julius on the outer edges of Remusan space in stealth mode, cloaked, and he thought they'd not been detected. They waited for Julius to leave Remusan space, at which point they planned to engage and demand that he surrender and face the Nebran authorities for the war crimes he'd committed. Julius' ship had been badly damaged in an altercation with another Nebran vessel two days prior, and Zeph was confident they didn't have the firepower or manpower to put up a fight against his ship.

The previous morning, Julius had finally left Remusan

space, headed—it seemed—for a trading outpost in neutral space, where they could get supplies and equipment to fix their ship. Remus was too many days' journey for them to limp back home. They had to head to the outpost first. When they crossed into neutral space, Zeph dropped the cloak on his vessel and appeared beside them. Immediately, though, Julius' ship fired on Zeph's, and they had much more firepower than Zeph had realised. With the element of surprise on their side, Julius inflicted heavy damage to Zeph's ship very quickly. He lost all defences, his weapons systems were destroyed, and they were dead in the water with no options to fight or flee.

Julius' crew mobilised quickly and boarded Zeph's ship, taking everyone on board prisoner. It'd been a trap. Julius had lured them into thinking his ship was vulnerable when it wasn't. He knew about their cloak. He'd really done a number on Nebra as a spy if he had obtained that type of information. It didn't bode well for the other Nebran vessels that would attempt to use cloaks.

'Stupid …' Zeph said to himself in the cell. 'I should have known he would.'

More light came into his cell. Guards opened the outside doors, and someone walked in. Zeph's eyes adjusted to the change of light so he could see who it was.

Julius entered. 'Stand up,' he ordered.

'Julius,' Zeph said. 'End this. Let me and my people go back to Nebra.'

In one swift motion, Julius raised his left hand, pointed his weapon at Zephir's head and fired. 'It is ended,' he said, as Zeph's lifeless body slumped to the ground.

Deor woke in fright. How was she able to see this memory? She hadn't been there when Zeph died, but Lore had known her brother had died this way at the hands of Julius: Julius the Betrayer, Julius the Deceiver. What did it mean for her now, though, and for Sam? She'd had this dream a few times but hadn't brought it up with her brother. What beneficial purpose would it serve? She felt conflicted, at once feeling hurt and pain for the loss of Zeph, but also grateful for having Sam with her. She wanted to protect him from a similar fate. Could things be different this time around? Could she protect him, as he always sought to protect her?

Deor rose. Eve was up, and Sam and Dolus were emerging from their quarters as well.

'Do you ever sleep, Eve?' Deor asked.

Eve smiled in reply. 'I sleep enough. There is a lot to ponder in these times, my friend. Especially today.'

'You're leaving us today,' Deor said.

'In a manner of speaking. However, you three are actually leaving me. I'll stay here with the Alphym for a while before I head back to the Mid Territory to help your father and Leon with the movement. I cannot come with you to Titus. This is something you three must do on your own. But know that Mother Moorilim will be following your journey also, from afar. There is much she can see in this world.'

'The Reflection Pool?' Deor asked. Moorilim was a powerful oracle; just how far did those powers extend?

Eve nodded. 'Yes, the Reflection Pool. She can use that to see things that may come to pass, but also to see what is coming to pass right now. She'll be watching your progress.'

'And what about you, Eve? Will you be able to follow us? Will you be able to see how we are?'

Eve thought for a moment before replying. 'I can, yes. Not

as much as Mother Moorilim, but I can see some things, yes. I'll have a strong sense of how you're going and where you are.'

'Can you see whether we'll succeed?' Deor asked. 'Can you see that in our future?'

'I would be lying if I said I could see it,' Eve replied. 'But at the same time, I cannot see the alternative, either. It's unclear to me how this will play out. Remember I told you yesterday, events are not pre-determined. People are free to make their own choices and cut the path of their future accordingly. No one is destined to repeat past mistakes; we are all given the chance to correct them.'

'Past mistakes?' Sam asked as he and Dolus joined Eve and Deor at the small table at which they sat. 'Do you mean from lives gone by?'

'Yes. That's exactly what I mean. We aren't reborn just to have another life with no meaning or goal. There is always a goal, always some hurdle or obstacle that the person reborn must face and overcome. Lore has been reborn as Deor; what past mistakes Lore made that Deor must correct is only something that Deor can uncover. What's certain is that there are things in this life that Deor needs to do in order to put to bed the mistakes of Lore's past, and she will be given her chance to do this. It is the same for you, Sam, and for you, Dolus. What those things are, only you can discover.'

Eve turned to Sam. 'You're the only one here who hasn't had a vision of their past life with me. I took Deor through it back at the Great Hall, and I've done the same for Dolus. Did you want to see your past life on Nebra to help you gain some answers?'

Sam thought for a moment before responding. 'No. I don't think I do. Dee has told me that I was also her brother on Nebra, that she and I were co-pharit after our parents' deaths, and we were both involved in the war against Remus. And I know how that war ended: both planets were destroyed. That's enough for me to know. I don't see what benefit I'd get by seeing more of it. It won't help me in this life. It won't help me to get Sage back for us, and I can't see how it will help when we try to win our independence from Merope.'

'You are very wise, Sam,' Eve said. 'And as I've said to Deor in the past, this is why we generally cannot remember our past lives, so that we can focus on this one, and what we need to do in this life, without being distracted by what happened in previous ones.'

'One thing I do wonder, though,' Sam said, 'and have wondered since we left the base, the day Dee had her vision: you said then that intelligent life spreads through the universe by being reborn onto new planets. Are you saying that this is happening on other planets as well? People being reborn there, having previously been on another world?'

'Yes, this is happening all throughout the universe, as far and as wide as it goes. Wherever there is a world that has developed to a point where it can sustain intelligent life, like Earth now has, people will reincarnate there and continue the spread of intelligent life. This is how intelligent life evolves, through rebirth on new worlds. The story of civilisation on Earth is just beginning now with the arrival of Nebrans and Remusans.'

'And Alphym,' Moorilim added, having just appeared in the room.

Deor jumped, which made Moorilim and Eve laugh.

'Oh, Deor,' Eve said, 'you should know that the Alphym are very good at making themselves unseen. In fact, for us humans, they only allow us to see them when they want to be seen.'

'This is correct,' Moorilim said. 'But for now, we will be seen, as the high king and queen wish to see you before you go.'

Moorilim led them back to the hall they'd been in the previous evening. Light still streamed into the room, illuminating the ornate horses on the large table. Again, they seemed to gallop around its edges.

'How do they do that?' Deor asked Eve.

Eve just smiled in reply.

Food had again been laid out on the table along with jugs of fresh water. Other supplies were stacked at one end, and five spears leaned against a wall. Deor walked over to them.

High King Örn joined her. 'I thought you may be interested in those. They're a gift for you, made from the same wood as the boat in which you arrived here. They're light, but strong, and will travel much further and faster than the spears you have in your sling. The tips are made from metals we create from the rock of this mountain, melded onto the wood so they become as one piece. The tips are the strongest metals within our power to create. They will pierce anything. The spears are imbued with the same spells as the boats we use, so you can trust them to fly straight and fast.'

Deor picked one up. Though slightly larger than the others, it was still incredibly light, and the wood seemed to shape itself to her palm. In the tip was a cavity: a small diamond-shaped hole. 'What is this for?' she asked.

The high king answered her, but in her mind only. *You wear something valuable around your neck.* Instinctively, her fingers reached for the Minerva gem underneath her clothes. *However, I do not think you realise how valuable it is. There may come a time when you need more power than the spear can bring alone. Put your gem into that spear before you throw it. Then trust your arm.*

Deor turned to the high king. 'Thank you. This is very generous of you.'

High Queen Ästrid joined them. 'There is something else we have for you, Deor.' In her hand she held a small piece of wood, smaller than a pencil and half as thin, plain in colour with no markings on it. She offered it to Deor. 'Take this, and wrap your hand around it.'

Deor took the small baton and did as requested.

Ästrid placed her hands over Deor's enclosed hand, leaned in close, whispered four words Deor didn't understand, then blew gently on Deor's hand. The breath of the high queen drifted over Deor's hand and between her fingers, sliding underneath to the baton she held inside. The baton grew warmer, and it seemed to hum and vibrate within her hand. Then it stopped, and the wood grew cool again.

'There,' the high queen said, 'it is bonded to you now. It will only work for you from now on, and for eternity. Keep it safe and away from others.'

'What is it?' Deor asked.

'Open your hand, then rub your thumb along it in one swift movement, and you will see.'

Deor slowly opened her hand and inspected the baton. It looked like a well-polished small piece of wood. She ran her thumb along the length of it as instructed, and a veil sprung from the wood and bound itself to Deor, covering her from head to toe. Deor could see the veil, but she could also see through it. The high queen stood in front of her, still smiling at her.

'Where is she?' Sam asked, looking for Deor. 'Where did she go?'

The high queen turned to Sam. 'Oh, she's still there.' She

pointed at Deor.

Deor tried to feel the veil but couldn't.

'She has been covered by a jakelope veil,' the high queen continued. 'She is invisible now to all but the Alphym and herself.'

Deor ran her thumb back down the baton again, and instantly the veil vanished, drawn back inside the wood.

Sam took a step back in shock. 'Maybe warn us before you're going to do that!'

Deor laughed. 'This could come in very handy!'

'You are on a rescue mission,' the high queen said, 'and they require stealth and secrecy. You may find it very handy. A word of warning, though: be judicious when you use it. If you are forever disappearing and reappearing, people will get wind of something being not right, and may seek to remove from you the means of your disappearance. Use it only when it is absolutely necessary.'

Deor nodded and thanked the high queen again.

'There is much food and drink laid out for you on the table,' the high queen said. 'Eat and drink, and fill your packs with bread for the journey. There is also a small jar each to take of sustym. This is a paste we make from foods we grow here in the mountain. It is concentrated; a small amount can sustain you for many hours on its own. When the bread you carry runs out, the paste can sustain you.'

They turned to the food and loaded some into their bags. Deor had grown in strength, and the longer she stayed here, the stronger and healthier she would become. But she longed to see her sister again and felt glad to be getting ready to leave. Two Alphym men and one woman appeared at the end of the room: the three from yesterday, including the one she'd seen at the Great Hall.

'Deor, Sam and Dolus; this is Rohanë, Aafjë and Claude,' the high king said.

The three Alphym nodded their greeting. Rohanë held Deor's gaze with a contemplative look. He'd looked at her the same way in the Great Hall.

'Gee, I feel for Claude a bit,' Sam whispered to Dolus. 'Everyone else here has these complex and magical names, and he just got plain old Claude!'

'Ssh!' Dolus whispered. 'They have amazing hearing!'

'Actually,' said Claude, stepping forward, 'in our tongue, the name Claude means strength, both physically and mentally. It is a very proud name. The name Sam means something entirely different, though …'

Deor laughed.

Sam looked guiltily at the floor. 'I didn't mean anything by it. I'm sorry, Claude,' he said. 'I was just having a little joke …'

'It's fine,' Claude said. 'We Alphym have a sense of humour too, don't worry. In fact, Sam, I think this means that you should ride with me. I can tell you more about Alphym names and their origins.'

'Oh, wonderful …' Sam said.

'Rohanë, Aafjë and Claude will take you to the edge of the Scarred Lands,' the high king said. 'Their Akkadym horses await you in the Great Field in front of the falls. They will ride you swiftly and safely, but that is as far as they will go.'

'Come,' Rohanë said, 'it's time for us to leave.'

Deor turned to Eve and embraced her. 'Eve, my friend, thank you for everything you've done for me, and for us, these past many days. Please look after my father and Alexi when you get back home. I will see you again; I know I will.'

Eve nodded. 'Stay safe, Deor. Remember, you were Lore, but you are now Deor. Your story is not written, my friend. It is for you to write. I will see you again in our home territory.'

Deor held Eve in the embrace. She'd only known her for a few days, but the bond between them was deep. She felt sadness deep within her that they had to part. 'I wish I had more time with you,' Deor said, a tear coming from her green eye.

'Me too, Deor,' Eve said. 'Me too.'

Rohanë, Aafjë and Claude led the group out of the hall and towards the city. Deor had loaded the five spears into her sling, but they seemed to take up almost no room, and added almost no weight to her back. With food in their packs and their flasks full of the Alphym water, they wound their way around the park and out beyond the falls into the Great Field, where the Akkadym grazed. Three of the horses cantered up to the three Alphym.

'These are the Akkadym with which we've bonded,' Rohanë said. 'When we bond, we bond for life. This is Arion. He is my horse. I am his rider. Deor, you may ride with me.' Rohanë slipped effortlessly onto Arion's back. They used no saddles, no stirrups, no spurs, no whips, no tools of men at all to urge the horse on.

'How do I get up?' Deor asked. She'd never sat on a horse before.

'Here.' Rohanë held out an arm. 'Take my arm with your arm, and push yourself up, swing your leg over the other side of him, then hold onto me.'

On her first tentative attempt, Deor didn't push herself off the ground enough and landed on her feet again. For the second attempt, she pushed off harder, and Rohanë pulled her up with his hand. She swung her leg successfully over Arion's back and clutched at Rohanë to keep from falling. He held her, and she stayed on top. Arion adjusted his back legs to balance her.

'There you go!' Rohanë chuckled. 'You're a natural! Now make sure to hold on tight when we ride! He is very, very fast!'

After watching Deor, Dolus and Sam managed to clamber their way onto the back of their respective horses. Dolus rode with Aafjë, and Sam with Claude.

Sam playfully slapped Claude on the shoulder. 'Let the adventure begin!'

He had barely gotten the words out, though, when—with merely a word from the three Alphym riders—the horses lunged into action. At high speed, they sprinted towards the forest, straight for the trees.

'What the Pleid!' Dolus yelled as he hung onto Aafjë for dear life. 'We're going to crash!'

Aafjë laughed, her long, earth-toned blonde hair streaming out behind her in the wind. 'Don't worry!' she called out. 'We know what we're doing!'

They reached the tree line and seemed about to thunder straight into the trees, but at the last moment the horses veered right and galloped between two giant trees and down a previously unseen path. Without slowing, they charged down this path in single file, Arion leading the way. The horses were sure of foot, and the Alphym riders balanced perfectly on their backs.

Deor hung on as tightly as she could.

Sam closed his eyes for long periods of time and whispered prayers to Pleid. Claude grinned and shook his head.

After what seemed like a long time, but was measurable in minutes, the horses came to the bottom of the mountain range and cantered out onto the flatlands beyond. They had arrived in Merope, but down in the very southwest of the country. Ahead of them, in the distance, lay the Scarred Lands. Deor could barely make out the beginning of it, a line of darkness on the horizon. Dread rose in her stomach.

'We're in Meropan territory now,' Rohanë said as they surveyed the land ahead. 'But there is no one here. They don't come down this far. The River Merope heads northeast from here, and in the distance is the southernmost of the Meropan towns, a river town called Tavius. If you go there, you'll be recognised as an outsider, and you'll be captured. That's as far south as Meropans go, though, and they avoid the Scarred Lands. That's why this is the only path open to you. We'll take you as far as the southern entrance to the Scarred Lands, and there we will leave you.'

Without a word, the three riders took off again. Holding on was a little easier this time as the horses were on flat ground at last. They ran so smoothly, so easily, that Deor didn't feel as though she could fall off. Arion had a rhythm and grace that made his galloping seem more like swimming through air. The riders sped across the plains at speeds Deor had never encountered before, though it felt as though they merely glided.

'You know, I saw you in the Great Hall,' she said to Rohanë as they rode.

Rohanë laughed. 'I saw you too, Deor!'

'What were you doing there?' Deor had to speak loudly to be heard over the sound of the air rushing past them.

'I was there to see Eve. We have business with her, and with your father, from time to time.'

'What kind of business?'

Rohanë paused. 'Let's just say that not all Alphym think we should stay out of the affairs of humans.'

The blackness of the Scarred Lands grew as they drew closer. Deor felt torn. She wanted to get there and get through it so she could find Sage and rescue her, but she felt an immense dread of going into these lands full of the dead who couldn't pass over, full of spirits, possibly the spirits of her parents on Nebra.

Eventually, the horses pulled up, seemingly without direction from the riders. The Scarred Lands stretched out in front of them, a dark landscape that extended north as far as they could see.

Rohanë slid off his horse and helped Deor down. The other riders did the same. They'd stopped at the beginning of a narrow road that led into the Scarred Lands. It led to a forest of burned and blackened trees within, but Deor couldn't see where it went after that, nor make out the land beyond.

'This is the old road,' Rohanë said. 'When the Nebrans first came here, they built settlements along this road. It runs through all the Scarred Lands out to their northern border. If you follow this road, you can get through and out the other side. You won't find any Meropans in there—it's safe from them—but you may find the spirits of the dead, especially during the night. I advise keeping a watch at night, and definitely do not leave the road during the dark hours. If you get lost at night, you will never be found. You'll end up with the dead, and your spirit will wander those lands with them from then on.'

They gathered their possessions and looked at the road ahead. 'If you have any doubts,' Claude said, 'now is the time to express them. This is the last chance you have to turn back. Once you go into the Scarred Lands, you cannot turn back; you have to continue on until you either perish in there or make it through.'

'I'm going on,' Deor said.

Sam looked at her, worry spread across his face, but also

determination. 'I'm going too.'

Dolus glanced at them both. 'Well, you're both mad; that's clear. But we've come this far, so let's do it. It'll be fun, I'm sure.'

Deor laughed, which made Dolus grin and Sam smile. For a second, they shared a moment of levity and pleasantness, but it was only a moment. The Scarred Lands loomed large, both physically and mentally.

'Good luck, Deor, Sam, Dolus,' Rohanë said. 'It was nice to meet you, if only for a brief time. Good luck with your quest. Moorilim will be watching, and we will find out from her how you're faring. There is one thing I would like to say to you, though: our high king and queen do not want the Alphym to get involved in the affairs of humans, but not all of us think that way. If we can find a way to help you on your quest, we will. If things seem to be too much—if you feel as though you have no way out—don't despair. Don't lose hope.'

The riders mounted their horses, and within a moment they were gone, the horses thundering away into the distance towards the Southern Mountain. Deor watched them go, then turned to face the road ahead. Together, they walked the short distance to the edge of the Scarred Lands. Deor looked at the blackened ground ahead of her. The grass at her feet was green, and just ahead it was grey and black, a clear delineation between the land inside and outside. The charred earth stretched away ahead and on both sides.

'They really did scorch the earth here, didn't they?' Deor said. 'You can almost see the Meropan soldiers standing here, forcing the people back in, holding their line. The earth is black from here on as far as I can see.'

A low grey cloud overshadowed the entire landscape. Ahead, on the right of the path, stood a blackened tree, and further on from that, the beginnings of a forest, which loomed up over the path. The trees had no leaves, though. Their blackened limbs shot out over the path and joined with scorched tree limbs on the other side, each side grabbing at the branches from the other side, forming an arch above the road. In that tunnel, there was only darkness. Deor shuddered and looked at Sam. He wore a look of dread on his face.

Without a word, they stepped onto the path and into the Scarred Lands. They walked down the path, past the first scorched tree and to the edge of the forest. Deor pushed some of the reaching branches out of her way and looked ahead. The tunnel formed by the forest seemed to go ahead endlessly in near-complete darkness. With a deep sigh, she walked on, followed by the others. Their journey through the Scarred Lands had begun.

CHAPTER 13

Deor trudged on, trying to ignore her weariness. They'd been on this path for a day and a half. Yesterday had been a long trek through the blackened forest. Little light got through those gnarled trees, making it seem as though they walked through a dark tunnel, seemingly forever. Though there'd been just enough light by which to see, it had been difficult to keep their feet. Tree roots sometimes jutted up from the path and tripped them over, as did unseen potholes. The walk through the scorched forest had taken most of their first day, and they had all come through it with scratches from the branches and cuts and bruises from falling over along the way.

They stopped for a rest halfway through that first day and ate a little food, though none of them felt very hungry in that place. 'How far do you think we've come?' Sam had asked, his voice low in the oppressive quiet.

'I studied a map of this place,' Dolus said, 'this morning before we ate. The high king gave it to me.'

Dolus pulled the map from his pack, but it was hard to see in the dim light. 'From what I could tell this morning,' he said, tracing his finger along the path, 'the path cuts directly through this forest, then sometime after the forest ends, it turns northeast, heading more or less directly to the northern border. That's where we come out of this place, and we head into the mountain range. It looks as though there's some sort of old town ahead of us, once we clear this forest.'

'How long does the forest go on?' Deor asked. She wished to see some light, anything other than the darkness of this forest.

'It's hard to tell, but I think we should get through to the other side today.'

They had trekked on for most of the previous day, and their spirits lifted a little when they emerged from the forest, though what lay ahead didn't promise any improvement. For kilometre after kilometre ahead, the path wound on. After they'd cleared the forest, they walked past the ruins of farmhouses and the occasional devastated settlement, but mainly through desolate, blackened land.

They slept restlessly that night, taking turns as lookout, and blessedly, they'd been left alone, not seeing or hearing anything. They continued on early the next morning, though it was hard to tell day from twilight in the Scarred Lands. An eerie pall of darkness hung over the land, dimming the light, even during the day.

Now, after a day and a half, they stood less than halfway through the Scarred Lands, and what Deor saw ahead troubled her. In the distance, where the path led, lay the ruins of a large town or a small city. A deeper darkness hung over it, as though something dark from inside the place was spreading out and stopping any light from coming in. The city was grey and black, the buildings scorched shells. Deor felt a sense of foreboding as they approached it.

'What is this place?' Sam asked.

'The high king told me about this,' Dolus said. 'This is the capital they set up, the new society, the Nebrans. They called it Celano. For one hundred years, they lived in these parts before they were attacked by Merope. This was becoming a thriving capital, servicing towns spread out to the east, west and north of it.'

'I don't like the look of it.' Deor touched the birthmark on her shoulder, noticing this time that she did so. 'I feel a strong sense of … something, more than just dread. This place seems to pulse with misery.'

Two giant obelisks marked the gateway to the small city. Deor examined them. 'Look at these,' she said. 'They bear the insignia of Nebra.' It seemed that the reborn Nebrans wanted reminders of their previous lives when they built new ones here on Earth.

Each obelisk was embossed with the two-moons insignia, but the blaze had scorched the stones black like everything else around them. Deor put her hand on the insignia on one of the obelisks, and a pulse of energy surged through her body.

The landscape in front of her changed. Fire rolled through it, engulfing buildings and houses that collapsed before her eyes. People screamed. In every direction they fell out of buildings or lay dead in the streets, burned alive. Nearby, a mother huddled over her child, protecting it from the blaze, but both were blackened corpses. It had been her final act in life.

Deor jerked her hand off the obelisk, and the vision stopped, but it remained in her mind. Celano had been torched as Nebra had been. 'They were all sent to hell.' Deor's voice quivered. 'Just as we burned on Nebra, so they did here. History repeated itself.'

She looked ahead at the path they had to follow. There was

no way around the city without leaving the path and heading east or west, and they didn't know what lay in those directions.

'Well, we have to keep going north,' Dolus said, voicing what she was thinking. 'We can't leave the Scarred Lands to the west; we'll come out near their towns, and to the east are mountains, impenetrable until we get further north. We have to keep going.'

Deor nodded and looked at Sam. He nodded as well, and they walked through the gateway into the torched city of Celano. Where the mother had lain, protecting her child, an outline was marked on the ground, blacker than the surrounding area, as though their spirits had been burned into the ground itself. The path led them past other similar spots, roughly shaped like bodies—the darkened silhouettes of the dead.

'Let's just stick to this main path. It should cut straight through the city and get us out the other side,' Dolus said. His voice seemed muffled by the heaviness in the city.

Footsteps sounded from a building on their right. Deor stopped and motioned the others to do the same. The footsteps came again: unmistakeably, the sound of slow footsteps on a timber floor.

'There's ... there's no one who lives here, right?' Sam asked.

Now footsteps came from close by on their left, on the street. Deor quickly turned, but no one was there.

'Leave ...' a voice hissed at them.

Fear pierced Deor's heart like a blade. The voice came from all around them.

'Leave now...'

Deor looked around. She could hear footsteps and whispered voices coming from all directions. In the building to her right, a woman looked out a window at her, and her spectral body floated closer to the window. 'Look!' Deor cried out.

Sam and Dolus turned and saw the ghostly spectre of a woman with a burned face, her eyes filled with rage, blazing at them with fiery hatred. Deor looked to the left and saw others in the buildings there, and more appeared on all sides. The ghosts of the dead had been woken.

'Leave …' the voice repeated, but now it was a hundred voices, all hissing at them. The voices rolled around, surrounding them. 'Now … Or die …'

'Run!' Sam yelled.

Deor needed no further encouragement. The three of them set off, sprinting as fast as they could down the road. They couldn't see where it ended, and many more buildings flanked each side. More spirits appeared around them, and then even more. Deor glanced back. The spirits were following them, hundreds of the dead closing in on them from behind, and those from the buildings surrounded them on each side.

Ahead in the distance, she saw the end of the city, where two obelisks marked the northern gate. For a fleeting moment, she had a clear view of those obelisks, but then dozens of the dead rose from the ground in front of them, blocking the way.

They stopped running. They had to. Spirits of the dead, their faces burned and angry, surrounded them. They hovered above the ground, their bodies blackened by the fire, but eerily transparent. Their clothes were tattered rags. Burned and shredded, they hung in pieces from their spectral forms. Everywhere Deor looked, eyes blazed back at her from the faces of those who had been burned here.

'Now you will die …' the voices hissed, coming from all directions. The spirits advanced towards them.

'Stop!' Deor yelled.

The dead halted.

'You will let us pass! I am the warrior of Nebra, Lore reborn, and I command you to let us pass!'

No sound or movement came from the dead. Deor stood still, facing them, waiting for a response. Then, slowly at first, then gaining in strength, laughter rippled through them. Not joyful laughter, but sinister, mocking, deriding laughter.

As the laughter subsided, one voice spoke to them from the spirits. 'Nebra is dead to us …' the voice hissed. 'Lore is dead to us … You will be dead with us …'

The spirits advanced again, closing in from all sides. Deor breathed deeply and shut her eyes. In her mind she could see Nebra. She could see herself as Lore. The visions she'd been getting since she first met Eve had become frequent, and now she knew a lot of what Lore had done. She'd been the warrior of Nebra, leading the battle against Remus on her own after Zephir was killed. She'd turned the tide of a war that had looked set to destroy Nebra and had kept her people alive until eventually the forces of war overpowered both planets. She'd given all of her life, and her death, for Nebra and the Nebran people. It was not going to be in vain. She felt a power surge through her body.

'Stop!' she screamed, opening her eyes. Her voice came out deeper, raspier, and her eyes flashed, empowered with the spirit of Lore.

Sam turned to look at her, stunned.

Dolus stared, eyes wide.

Deor looked around at the gathered spirits and stood up to her full height. She held their enraged gaze and roared, 'I am Lore, warrior of Nebra, and as your sole pharit, I command you to let us pass!'

Her words echoed throughout the capital, bouncing

off walls and carrying down the side streets. The dead again stopped advancing. Silence fell upon them. At length, some whispering could be heard, but Deor couldn't make out any words. One spirit floated forward from the group and approached Deor, coming close enough to touch. Deor looked into her eyes, eyes that burned with rage born out of what the Meropans had done to them and what the Remusans had done to Nebra.

'If you truly are Lore reborn,' she hissed, reaching towards Deor, 'then you will know who I am …'

The ghost touched Deor's shoulder on her two-moons birthmark. Light flashed before Deor's eyes, and she was again on Nebra, on Two Moons' Day, the day of the attack, in her villa in the morning. The attack hadn't happened yet. She sat with her mother, Ada. The vision only lasted a moment, then she was back on Earth with the spirit of her Nebran mother staring into her eyes.

'Yes,' Deor said, relief washing over her, 'you were my mother, Ada. You and Octus were co-pharit of Nebra before you were killed. Remus killed you, and they attacked you again here on Earth, and they killed you again. They are bent on destroying Nebra yet again, and I am here on Earth to stop them.'

'Yes, Lore,' the spirit said. The rage in her eyes subsided a little. 'I was your mother, Ada.' The spirit smiled at Deor, the love she had for Lore as Ada returning to her, even in death. It was shaded, though, by the pain of her memories. 'They burned us on Nebra,' Ada continued, 'and they burned us on Earth. We cannot leave here until we have our revenge …'

'You will have no revenge from beyond the grave,' Deor said carefully, 'but if you let us pass, I will fight for your revenge, and perhaps by the time this is all done, you will get your peace. Grant us safe passage through your lands, and you have my word I will fight for your revenge and your peace.'

Murmurs spread throughout the spirits gathered around them. Deor looked at some of their faces. All of them bore countenances burned with rage, anger and hatred, but most of all what was scorched into them wasn't fire, but pain. Not the pain of the fire that killed them, but a much greater pain—the pain of loss: loss of Nebra, loss of Earth, loss of their civilisation. Deor understood what they needed, and in that moment came to a realisation about her own pain: it wasn't just the world on which they'd lived that had been destroyed, or their civilisation on Earth, here at Celano—it was the destruction of their right to live at all. The pain they felt was because Remus and Merope sought to destroy their very existence, to rob them of the right to live. And now, trapped here by death, for these spirits, Merope had achieved that.

'You are right to be angry!' Deor yelled. 'You are right to feel pain! Remus and Merope have robbed you of your right to exist, and now you are trapped here, unable to pass on, unable to exist again. I know your anger; I know your pain! They took Nebra from me too, and now they try to take Alcyone from us! We Nebrans are building a new society again, here on Earth, like you did, but now Merope is crushing us, and if we do not change it, they will again burn us and again destroy our right to exist! I—Lore reborn as Deor—will fight to push them back and restore our right to exist, for all Nebrans on Earth, and for you! Let us pass, and I will fight to get you your peace, so that you may pass on and be reborn again, here on Earth! You must let us pass!'

Silence from the spirits. A dreadful pause hung in the air. The faces of the dead still stared at Deor, Sam and Dolus, still scorched by pain, but then they began to dissipate. The dead retreated back to the places where they'd died, back to the buildings and the ground on which they were now trapped. As Deor watched, they all slipped away, except the spirit of her mother from Nebra, Ada. After just a few moments, only she remained with them.

'You will have free passage through our lands, daughter Lore,' Ada said. 'But you must not delay; you must not linger. We are not the only dead who dwell still in these lands.' The spirit of Ada also retreated back to the buildings and faded from view, leaving her words echoing in Deor's mind. All of a sudden, they were alone again in the scorched city.

'We should go,' Sam said, and they strode on without delay.

It seemed strange for the city to be empty now, considering what they'd just experienced. The buildings, just burned-out shells again, showed no signs of life. And no footsteps or voices could be heard. The dead rested again in Celano.

At the northern end of the city, they came to the two obelisks marking the gateway, burned black like the ones at the southern end. Deor resisted the temptation to touch the two-moons insignia embossed on them.

They emerged from the city and saw the landscape ahead for the first time. The path turned northeast, towards the northernmost point of the Scarred Lands, which lay well beyond their sight. Deor looked ahead at the path stretching out in front of them, leading into the dark distance and disappearing beyond view.

'Well, we know what we have to do,' she said.

For a long time, as they walked on, they saw nothing but blackened farmland, any evidence of crops long gone. Occasionally, they spotted the remains of livestock, such as musk-ox bones, near the path. No birds of prey picked at these long-forgotten carcasses.

The farmland stretched on for many kilometres, and hour after hour they trudged on, their legs becoming wearier and their conversation more sporadic. In such a dire and grim landscape, conversation felt pointless. They had a shared goal: to leave this place, and that could only be done by walking, and walking, and walking—nothing else.

Eventually, the day began to wane, and the darkness in the landscape deepened as somewhere above them—beyond the endless grey cloud that hung over the land—the sun began to set.

They came to a large open area where the ground seemed darker. Emptiness stretched out on either side of them, but this wasn't farmland; it was something else. Human bones lay scattered near the path and away from it, strewn about on the ground like the remnants of a giant's feast.

'What is this place?' Dolus asked, his voice sounding small in the vast emptiness.

'I don't know,' Deor said, barely whispering.

They walked on a little further, but found more of the same. An enormous plain stretched out on all sides.

The sense of foreboding Deor had outside Celano returned. 'I don't like it here,' she said.

'Neither do I,' Sam said. 'But we're not going to be able to see the path much longer. We can't keep going on today. There's a clump of trees ahead; we can make camp there.'

They headed for the small clump of trees just off the path and set up camp in a clearing. Sam lit a small fire, and they had some food, though Deor didn't feel like eating.

'What do you think this place is?' Sam asked.

Dolus shook his head. 'I don't know, but it's like a giant cemetery, a graveyard.'

Deor sat on the ground near the fire, but she couldn't get

comfortable. She shuffled around, but to no avail. Something jutted up from beneath the topsoil. She felt around in the dirt and brushed the top layer away with her hands.

'What have you got there?' Dolus asked.

'I don't know,' she said, continuing to brush soil away. Something solid lay underneath. The end of a hilt made of some sort of bone emerged from the dirt. She'd been sitting on top of it, where a little corner stuck out of the ground. She brushed more soil away, then pulled on the hilt, and out from beneath the ground came a long sword with a strong steel blade. Deor held it in her hand; it felt light but balanced. She touched the blade lightly; amazingly, it was still sharp.

'Why was a sword buried here?' Sam asked.

Deor examined the hilt. It bore the two-moons insignia. 'Because this was a battleground. This is a blade made by the Celanites. This entire field is an ancient battleground. They must have fought the Meropans here. Before the emperor scorched the land, they fought a great battle, leading him to decide to end it by burning them all. This was the site of that battle.'

The land became nearly fully dark. Deor looked out across the plain. Bones lay scattered in every direction. 'There must be thousands and thousands of dead here,' she said. 'Celanites and Meropans alike.'

'This place is cursed,' Dolus said quietly in the still night air. 'I don't think any of us will get much sleep tonight.'

'No, we won't,' Sam said. 'But we have to try. You two should get some rest. I can take first watch. I'll wake one of you in a few hours.'

Dolus and Deor found places near the fire to lie down. Deor kept her newfound sword by her side. Just in case. Neither wanted to be far from the fire, nor from their companions.

Sam sat with his back to the fire, keeping lookout. Sleep wasn't going to come easily.

'Still awake?' Dolus whispered after a while.

'I don't feel like I'll ever sleep again,' Deor said.

'Pretty hard to sleep in a place like this.'

'It's not just that. For me, it's the dreams. Nearly every night now, I dream of Nebra and Lore. Usually, it ends in fire and destruction, whether in the war or at the end of it all.'

'Nearly every night?' Dolus asked.

'Yes,' Deor said wearily. 'Sometimes, I wish I didn't know. About Lore, Nebra, the whole thing. Sometimes, I wonder if maybe it would've been easier just to live life in ignorance, hunt game, try to avoid the patrollers. But that would be taking the easy way out. Avoiding life and avoiding whatever challenges life has for me. I was Lore. I burned on Nebra; we all did. And I have to be a part of putting a stop to it this time around.'

Silence fell for a little while. Deor stared at the sky, but could see no stars. The view of Pleid from the Southern Mountain had been exquisite, the universe laid out like a map in front of her, but here in the Scarred Lands she could only see darkness.

Sleep still didn't come. 'What about you, Dolus?' she eventually asked. 'Do you dream of Nebra? Of your past life?'

Dolus paused before responding. 'Yes, I do. Not every night, but I get the dreams too. Ever since I had a regression with Eve, a little while ago. Before that, flashes, horrible flashes. But I never knew what they meant. I do now.'

They both fell silent again. Deor didn't feel it was her place to pry further about Dolus' experience on Nebra.

Later, Deor woke to strange sounds, unaware she'd slept. Sitting up, she looked over to Sam. He was standing but seemed to be in some sort of trance. Then she saw why: four figures with swords surrounded him. Their spectral forms wore military uniforms that hung off them, tattered, fragmented rags that bore the insignia of Merope—an eagle surrounded by flames. Deor knew that insignia well. The patrollers wore it on their uniforms. Sam floated above the ground, suspended in the air by the four figures.

'Sam!' she called out.

Slowly, his head turned towards her, revealing an expression of horror frozen onto his face, his eyes rolled back in his head. His hand slowly reached out towards her, but otherwise he couldn't move.

'Sam!' Dolus called out, now also awake.

The four spectral Meropans turned to Deor and Dolus. Their faces were cut and haggard from the ancient battle, but they had malicious grins on their faces. One of them pointed his sword at Sam's throat. 'The Nebran will die …' he hissed.

They each had a hand on Sam's arms, and they silently moved away from the camp, into the field and away into the darkness, carrying him with them.

'Sam!' Deor yelled, picking up the Nebran sword and running after them. 'Sam, wake up!'

'Deor, wait!' Dolus called, but Deor paid no attention.

She ran off into the darkness, chasing the figures, all the while tripping and stumbling on the bones of the dead. She ran wildly after them, away from the camp, only faintly able to make out their forms.

'Sam!' she yelled. 'Sam, fight them! Stop them!'

But they were faster than her and getting further away into the darkness. She kept running, unable to see where her feet were landing, and eventually realised she couldn't see them at all anymore. Desperately, she scanned ahead as she stumbled on, searching for some light or sign of them, but the darkness had swallowed them. Suddenly, her foot struck a hollow in the ground, tripping her. She fell face first onto the hard dirt, her sword twisting dangerously in her hand as she did. Her head thumped hard into the ground as she fell, and she blacked out, face down in the dirt surrounded by the bones of the dead.

CHAPTER 14

Barritus sat in his private lounge on the third floor of their villa. He sipped tea, though it was late in the day and he would have preferred wine. The tea came from the southernmost town in Merope, a river town called Tavius. It had been named after his great ancestor Titavius and the glorious victory he'd achieved near there. The air was warmer down there, so the tea grew stronger flavours, more robust than the teas from Alcyone his daughter enjoyed. Hers came from the north of that country and were lighter in flavour, more delicate. Barritus didn't care much for delicate things. He preferred strength.

Barritus thought often about his great ancestor, Titavius, and now looked with fondness—and respect—at the statue of him that adorned his lounge. Titavius had built Titus, made it what it was today, and Barritus' life's work was to continue what Titavius had begun all those many years ago. For the glory of Merope.

Out of his southern window, he looked down towards the amphitheatre they'd finished building just the week before. Its towering walls dominated the skyline. It would be opened in

Merope Week and would be named the Titavian, also after his ancestor. Barritus had games planned, contests and feats of bravery, but he needed something more to really excite the people and to reinforce the dominance of Titus and of himself as emperor.

A knock came at the door. 'Come,' Barritus said. He was expecting it. Vespus entered the room with a bottle of wine. 'Ah, good,' Barritus said. 'Much better than the tea.'

Vespus nodded his agreement and took the wine to the sideboard, where glasses sat at the ready. 'I've been saving one or two of these,' he said, 'for when the time seemed right. They are, of course, from my private vineyard, and I keep the best ones aside, Emperor. This one is aged ten years; it should be perfect.' Vespus decanted the wine into a moon-shaped jug and allowed it to sit.

'A special occasion?' Barritus asked.

'Well, perhaps not a special occasion, but a commemorative time, sir. Merope Week draws close, and the Day of Procurement was a success. The procured girls arrived in the city earlier today and have been placed in the new cells underneath the amphitheatre, and most of all, the harvest from the Northern Territory has come in. We have much livestock to house and produce to distribute, as well as a large distribution of Minerva gems from the Mid Territory. The empire is wealthy, sir, and healthy. We grow fat off the stock of the enemy and rich from their gems.'

'And from the Coastal and the Mid North?' Barritus asked. He'd been emperor a long time and knew that keeping the empire fed was a key part of maintaining his power. The harvest was a very important part of that.

'From the Coastal Territory there is fish, but not as much as usual. The patrollers stationed in the outposts must be fed, of course.'

'Overfed, more like it,' Barritus said. 'I fear without constant checkups they grow fat and weak, soft in the belly and the mind. And what of the Mid North?'

Vespus paused to pour two glasses of wine and handed one to Barritus before responding. 'Not much comes from the Mid North, sir. There're some cattle; that's about all we can get from there.'

'And the people?'

'The people in the Mid North remain angry, sir. They are angry, and they stay that way. They live a stony, dirt-based existence. There is no water. The land is bare. The cattle they drive walk many kilometres looking for sustenance. They are angry at the rest of Alcyone for leaving them to die, not just during the invasion, but now.'

'Good,' Barritus said.

'They feel that their neighbours in the north grow fat on the bounty delivered by the Alcyone River,' Vespus continued, 'and what they harvest from the coast, and that they in the Mid North see none of these benefits. They feel that those in the Coastal Territory live a life of luxury on the water, fishing and eating, and that those in the Mid Territory hunt all the game in the mountains and grow food by the river. They are angry at all of them. They have no river and no coast. They are isolated, sir, landlocked, surrounded on three sides by other territories who do nothing for them, and to the east by the mountains. They are angry at everyone, sir.'

Barritus snorted. 'Very good. That anger will come in handy when we need it. See to it that the patrollers maintain the disconnect between each of the territories. Especially the Mid North. More than ever, we cannot allow contact with them. With contact comes planning; with planning comes resistance. Each territory must remain isolated from the others, their own border-based prison. Only with that disconnect in place can we maintain our dominion over them.'

Vespus took a sip of his wine and swirled his glass thoughtfully.

'What is it?' Barritus asked.

'Well, it's probably nothing at this stage, sir,' Vespus said, a note of caution in his voice. 'But there are murmurs from the outposts, from our spies, murmurs about a secret resistance growing in number across the territories.'

'What do the murmurs say?' Barritus snapped.

'The rumours are of underground bases and talk of training young men to form an army.'

'How many people are involved? Which territories?'

Vespus shrugged. 'It's hard to tell. We assume they have hidden bases in which they are planning, recruiting and possibly training, but we haven't found any yet. From what we hear, though, it began in the Mid Territory, and has also gained traction in the Coastal Territory. We've stepped up the presence of patrollers in both. We did have one piece of luck, though. We have identified who we think is the leader in the Mid, a man by the name of Cyrus.'

'Have you captured him?' Barritus asked.

'We did something even better, My Lord. We procured his thirteen-year-old daughter. Her name is Sage.'

'You have his daughter? Well, that is interesting. This is something I can work with ...' the emperor said thoughtfully. 'What of the Northern Territory, though? And the Mid North? Are they forming any pockets of resistance?'

'Our intelligence states that those in the Mid North would more likely fight against the other territories than with them,' Vespus said. 'That is how deep their anger runs. We haven't heard any rumours about the Northern, though. That territory is reasonably content because of the rich farmland they enjoy. Our patroller presence is less obvious there.'

'Yes.' Barritus nodded. 'That was my plan. Keep the North happy. If they're happy, they'll keep farming and won't see the need to fight. And the patrollers keep their capital, Taygete, locked down. All the while, we isolate the Mid North and keep them angry with everyone else, especially the North.'

'Rather brilliant, sir,' Vespus said. 'We take most of their produce in the North, but still leave them with some, and it is good food, grown as it is on the river delta. Their capital remains locked down. None can enter. We will not allow central organisation by allowing them to rebuild that city. All their citizens in that territory work the land or the coast for us. I hear their teas and preserves are especially enjoyed by a member of your household, sir.'

Barritus grunted. 'Yes. Arieitis. Alcyone this, Alcyone that. It's all I hear about.'

'It would be wise to stamp that out, sir. No good can come from humanising the enemy. They are a slave race for us; their lives are about the service they provide to Titus and Merope, nothing more. Your great ancestor Titavius knew who they were.'

'As do I!' the emperor barked. 'Do you think I have not had the visions? Seen who they are? Who they were? Filthy Nebrans, haunting us, like ghosts drifting across the universe to be reborn here as well. Titavius had the right idea; burn them in their homes, scorch the earth! Raze them to the ground! You know who I was on Remus, Vespus. You know of what I am capable.'

Vespus' hand trembled ever so slightly. 'Yes, My Lord, I do. And I would never question the strength of your commitment to the cause, sir. Never. I just fear that at times some of our citizens begin to forget who the Alcyonans are and what they represent. As we grow fat on the bounty we take from them, some of our people begin to entertain overly generous thoughts, overly liberal ideas. Some of the young discuss the occupation of Alcyone as though it were not the right thing to do. These schools of thought need to be stamped out. That is what I mean, sir.'

Barritus didn't respond. He walked to the southern window and again looked down the strata towards the Titavian amphitheatre. Schools of pro-Alcyonan thought springing up in Titus had the potential to poison the thoughts of others, to take root like a weed and spread. When the Nebrans in the south had resisted the will of Merope, Titavius burned them to the ground. He needed to do the same: burn to the ground those in his own ranks who would spread pro-Alcyonan thoughts. The seeds of dissent had to be crushed.

'The young discuss it openly, you say?' he asked.

Vespus sipped his wine and thought for a moment. 'I am not sure that they discuss it openly, as such,' he said eventually. 'But I do hear that there are pockets, you might say, small groups who get together to discuss such things. The university is such a place where ideas like that foment.'

'Left unchecked, those ideas will spread,' Barritus said.

'Yes, My Lord, they will. And such ideas threaten to undermine the belief in the glory of Titus and Merope. Just the other morning, I said the same to your son, Quetzl: the people need to know their place and remain in it.'

'Perhaps we grow too fat off the plunder we take from Alcyone,' Barritus said. The people had become soft. 'Perhaps our people need reminding that they grow fat and healthy because of the glory of Titus, not in spite of it.'

'Yes, My Lord, I believe such a reminder is always timely.'

Barritus smiled. 'And I think I know the perfect way to remind them. Vespus, you are going to the university.'

CHAPTER 15

Sage sat in her cell with three other girls. They'd only arrived in the city that afternoon, and it was now very dark outside, late at night. Two of the girls were crying, and the other sat ashen-faced, staring away into some distance only she could see. The crying annoyed Sage; it interrupted her. She was trying to listen to the guards.

'Can you keep it down?' she said, a little gruffly.

One of the crying girls turned to her. 'Oh, sorry for being sad …' she said sarcastically.

Sage rolled her eyes. What a little princess.

'I suppose this is your idea of a holiday, is it?' the girl continued. 'Judging by your rags, I imagine you're from the Mid. This is probably a step up in quality for you, this prison cell. Not for me. I was perfectly happy in the North. I had a life ahead of me.'

'None of us have lives ahead of us while we're occupied by Merope,' Sage quickly replied. She thought of her older sister; she was probably directly quoting her. 'We just have the illusion of a life they grant us.' Now she was definitely directly quoting her.

'Well, my illusion was one I enjoyed. And I don't want to be here a second longer. Where are you two from?' she asked, turning to the other girls.

The other girl who'd been crying was blonde and tanned. 'I'm from the Coastal,' she said between tears.

'And you?' the first girl asked, this time to the girl who hadn't said anything. 'You don't talk much. Where are you from?'

The other girl didn't reply; she just turned and gave the first girl a cold, hard stare. Why wouldn't the princess just shut up?

'Mid North by the look of you,' the princess said. 'You hate the world, hate all of us, don't you? Hate us in the North. And you should too. You know why? Because we're better than you.'

'Cut that out,' Sage said sharply. 'She doesn't have to reply to you. You have no right to judge her either. And just because you're from the North doesn't mean you're better than any of us here. That kind of rubbish attitude is what makes Merope think they're better than us. If you think that way, you're no better than them. Northern, Coastal, Mid North, Mid—we're all Alcyonans, and we're all supposed to be on the same side.'

A guard appeared outside their cell. He swayed like a tree in a liquor-laden breeze. Intoxicated. 'You're all very bloody chirpy in here, aren't you? What are you all so chirpy about?'

None of the girls answered. Sage held his lopsided stare.

He looked her up and down. 'You're a cute one, curly tops,' he said, leering. 'Aren't you? Hey? I think I might take you somewhere with me for a little while.'

Fear spread through Sage, but she breathed deeply and slowly, something Deor had taught her, and she pushed the fear away.

The guard fumbled for his keys to the cell. He found them in his pocket, then dropped them in the dirt. He wobbled as he leaned down, and after fumbling in the dirt, he picked them up. 'Let's get you out of here and take you somewhere a little bit more private,' he said to Sage.

Sage watched him closely as he opened the lock, then tucked the keys back into his pocket. The guard opened the door, lurched over to Sage and took her by the arm. 'You other three stay quiet!' he said as he led her out of the cell. He closed the door again and locked it, returning the keys to his pocket.

Many cells lined the passageway, and by the sounds of crying coming from them, many dozens of girls were locked up here. The guard, reeking of liquor, led Sage away, down the passageway to a small room at the end. He opened the door and pushed Sage inside. The room had a desk and a bed—the guards' quarters when on duty.

The guard groped at Sage's shoulders. 'You are a pretty little thing, aren't you?'

Sage wriggled out of his grasp and walked to the other side of the desk. 'Are you sure you want to do that? I'm just a kid. Perhaps we could just talk. I'm a good listener.'

'A good listener, huh?' The guard chuckled. 'I suppose there's not much else to do out in the territories but talk and listen.'

Sage shrugged. 'Maybe not. But I'm sure Merope is a much more exciting place than Alcyone. You must have lots of exciting adventures and things you could tell me about. Could you tell me some things? Do you have kids of your own? Do they go on adventures in Merope?'

The guard's mood changed a little. He sat in the chair at the desk and poured himself a strong-smelling drink from a flask he kept in his jacket. 'Kids, yeah,' he said after a long draw from his cup. 'One about your age too, a daughter, like you. Well, not like you. She's not a mountain rat, after all. But she's your age.'

'And what does she do for fun in Merope?' Sage asked.

The guard took another swig from his cup. 'Goes to school. She's very smart. Much smarter than I was. I didn't go to school for long. Joined the military. I fought in the invasion!' he said proudly. 'That was a long time ago now, a long time.'

The guard refilled his glass, took another swig and looked thoughtfully into space for a moment. 'I was a much younger man then. Much younger. Full of hopes and dreams. I wanted to become a general one day. Imagine that … General Argia! Has quite a ring to it. Still, those days are gone. I'll never make general now. I'm just a lowly guard.' He took another swig from his cup, then refilled it again.

Sage smelled how strong it was from where she stood a couple of metres away. He had large bags under his eyes, his nose seemed swollen, and his eyes were blurry and pointed in slightly different directions.

'Well, maybe you still could make general one day,' she said. 'You could wake up tomorrow, fresh after a good night's sleep, full of ambition again, and go to your commander and ask to be promoted.'

'Promoted …' He nodded. 'Promoted, that would be good …'

'And your wife and your daughter, they'd be so proud,' Sage said. 'Your friends would call you the general.'

The guard chuckled, and his eyelids closed.

'Sometimes all we need is a really good night's sleep,' Sage said softly, 'and we feel better in the morning about things. Everyone feels better after a sleep, don't you think? A nice, long, deep sleep … We always feel better after a deep sleep …'

'Yes.' The guard's head drooped, his eyes closing. He murmured something unintelligible, and his head sank further.

'Just relax …' Sage used her most soothing voice, one she used when she talked to the plants and vegetables in the garden back home. Home—that felt an eternity away. She shut it out of her mind—for now—to concentrate on the guard. 'Relax … you can have a rest now …'

The guard nodded off, chin on his chest, eyes closed tight. A moment later, a deep snore came from his nose. Success.

She waited for a few moments while the guard continued to snore. When she thought it was safe, she very softly tiptoed across the room. She waited for him to let out another snore, and as he did, she gently slid the keyring out of his pocket, quickly cupping the keys with her left hand to stop them jangling. The guard breathed out, but didn't wake. Sage found the key he'd used for her cell, slid it off the ring and slipped it into her pocket while the guard continued to snore.

'What? No, that's my …' the guard said, his head rising.

Adrenaline rushed through Sage's body, but when she looked at the guard's face, she could see he was just mumbling in his sleep. A moment later, his head nodded back down to his chest, and he let out another snore, and as he did, Sage slid the remaining keys on the keyring back into his pocket. She dared not slide them in too far in case he woke, but she slid them in just enough that they wouldn't fall out—she hoped not, anyway.

Very quietly, Sage tiptoed towards the door.

The guard breathed out, a whistling sound coming from his bulbous nose, then as he breathed in again, he let out a loud snore followed by a rumbling exhalation from his behind. The smell assaulted her like a mugger, but Sage took the opportunity to open the door the smallest amount and slip outside. As he exhaled and whistled out his nose again, she closed the door, then paused outside for a moment to be sure he was still asleep.

But no snore came. Panic threatened to rise in Sage. Had he woken? Was he about to open the door and grab her? What could she do to get away? She looked around but couldn't see a way out. She had to choose where to run, but which way? Then she heard a snore, long and loud, from within the room. She breathed out a sigh of relief.

Ensuring that the key was safely hidden away in a pocket, she made her way back to her cell. Two of the three girls had fallen asleep. The girl from the Mid North was awake. She looked up as Sage appeared and watched silently as Sage used the key to open the cell door and let herself in, then locked it again. She found a vacant corner of the room, sat down and looked across at the girl from the Mid North. Sage showed her the key, then put her finger to her lips in a soundless 'Ssh' as she slipped the key into her pocket. The girl watched her with a stony countenance, but after a moment the stoniness broke a little, and she gave Sage a small smile.

Sage tucked her knees up to her chest and tried to stay warm. Hopefully, the guard wouldn't notice his key was gone and wouldn't remember their encounter. What was she going to do with it now, though?

CHAPTER 16

The next morning, the sun rose early—and so did Quetzl. He took breakfast in the dining room before anyone else had risen and was out of the house as quickly as he could be. He had people to see.

The sun shone bright and warm. Quetzl felt the summer solstice coming with the lengthening of each passing day, and he had things to do. With Vespus denying his application to enter the elections for the senex, Quetzl needed to earn an income. He'd been lecturing in law, science and mathematics at the university for the past year, but hadn't applied to extend his tenure for the upcoming year, since he'd assumed a path in politics awaited him.

'Vespus!' he muttered to himself as he strode east towards the university. 'How dare he stand in my way!'

Not many stood in Quetzl's way, certainly not intentionally. This morning, as he again strode with purpose towards his destination, women and small children alike scattered when they saw him coming. Quetzl smiled at this.

He made his way quickly to the university grounds and strode across the courtyard and common green. A lot more people were around now, and there was a demonstration going on. People were holding up signs, pro-Alcyone in nature.

'End the occupation!' read one.

'Freedom for Alcyone!' read another.

'There are two eyes in Invasion!' read another, perplexingly.

Quetzl gave them barely a glance as he walked past. He had no time or inclination for the pro-Alcyonan movement. His fields were much more important—science, law, mathematics, philosophy, history. These were the foundations of knowledge; the pro-Alcyonan movement was just a political issue. In the back of his mind, he was aware that if he did one day join the senex, he would need to turn his mind more keenly to political issues such as this one. However, today was not that day.

'Professor Quetzl!' one protester said, attempting to gain Quetzl's attention and hand him a pamphlet.

'Out of my way!' Quetzl barked, brushing off the pamphlet and scattering the pile the protester carried to the ground. He continued on towards the main building in search of Professor Arcad. He marched inside and headed straight for the professor's office.

'Professor Arcad,' he said, walking in without knocking. 'I must speak with you at once.'

The professor looked up from his study, surprised to be interrupted. 'By all means, Professor Quetzl. Have a seat.'

'I prefer to stand. Perhaps you have heard, Vespus has denied my application to be on the electoral ballot for the upcoming senex elections. He stands as a roadblock on my political path, with no valid reason!'

'Yes,' Arcad said, 'I had heard. I presume you are here to ask about extending your tenure?'

'Yes, Professor, I am. I would like a twelve-month extension, if that is acceptable. I am happy to lecture in anything from mathematics to science to law.'

'Well,' Arcad said, 'this is problematic. When I did not receive your application for extension, and you informed me that you were seeking election to the senex, I offered your law, mathematics and science classes to someone else.'

Quetzl fumed. 'To whom did you offer them?'

'Professor Demeritus.'

'Demeritus!' Anger rose inside Quetzl's large frame and threatened to burst out. 'He's inept! Barely fit to lecture pottery! He would be more suited to teaching dance to children, such that he minces! And you offered him law, mathematics and science?'

'Well, you did miss the deadline,' Arcad said, 'and I do need to keep this university running and in order.'

'Well, what else can you offer me?' Quetzl asked, shaking his head.

'In your area of expertise—' Arcad started to say.

'All areas are my area of expertise!' Quetzl interrupted.

'I can only offer you history,' Arcad finished. 'We have not filled that position yet. It is yours if you want it.'

Quetzl thought, but only for a moment. 'Fine,' he said, 'I'll take history. But let it be known that I pity those students taking mathematics, science and law this year! I pity them! Let it be known!' Quetzl spun on his heel and marched out of the room, leaving Professor Arcad's door open. He strode out of the building and back into the main courtyard, but he stopped as soon as he arrived.

In the square, patrollers were attacking the protesters, and Vespus watched on. The patrollers loaded the protesters into cages and began driving them away with oxen. The procured girls from Alcyone had come in the same way the previous day.

'What is going on here, Vespus?' Quetzl asked, his bluster

momentarily overtaken by confusion.

'Oh, hello, Master Quetzl,' Vespus said casually. 'These protesters are being taken away to be locked in the cells of the amphitheatre by orders of your father, the emperor.'

'What are they being locked up for?' Quetzl asked.

'For incitement and treason,' Vespus replied. 'The emperor plans on making an example out of them in the games.'

'In the games? What does he plan to do with them in the games?'

The hint of a smile cracked the stony mask of Vespus' face. 'They are to be brought into the arena, Master Quetzl, and made an example of. The emperor will not suffer sedition. Empires erode when their foundations are unstable, and these people, Master Quetzl, are instability itself.'

Quetzl looked down at the pile of pamphlets he'd knocked away minutes earlier. They lay scattered on the ground, now spattered with blood. In stunned silence, Quetzl watched the protesters being driven away from the university. Just where did the real instability lie?

CHAPTER 17

Deor gradually woke. Her head throbbed with pain. She lay in the midst of the plain, surrounded by the bones of the dead. Gingerly, she sat up, but the blood drained from her head, and she collapsed back to the ground. She vomited up the scant remains of food in her stomach and struggled to keep conscious.

She lay still, breathing as slowly as she could, trying to settle the nausea. The cold breeze helped a little, one benefit of the lifelessness of this place and the eternal grey cloud overhead. Eventually, she sat up again. Her head was still foggy, but a little improved. The remnants of the battle that had been fought here lay scattered in all directions. Bones, some discarded weapons, shards of steel and pieces of wood. The cold wind blew dirt onto her face, where it stuck to the sweat and saliva.

Deor looked in the direction in which she'd been running, where her brother had been taken, but she saw no clue ahead as to where he'd gone. Behind her, in the distance, she could just make out the clump of trees beneath which they'd camped. She tried to get her bearings from the sun, but the grey cloud hung overhead, draped like an enormous cloak, blocking out the sky. Her head still pounded, but she had an idea.

Deor picked up the sword she'd found, which lay on the ground where she'd fallen, and swept aside the bones to form a clear area. Using the point of the sword, she drew an arrow in the dirt, pointing in the direction that Sam had been taken. Then she turned, again located the clump of trees, and with the arrow behind her and the trees ahead, Deor walked slowly towards the trees, sweeping a path before her with the blade.

'If there is no path out here to follow,' she said to herself, 'then I will just have to make my own.' She paused after every step and carefully swept away all the bones and debris that lay in front of her or to the side, forming a clear path as she did so. It was painstakingly slow. Still, she began her trek back to what she hoped was their campsite. Step by step, sweep by sweep, Deor inched her way back. As she got closer, she grew in confidence that she was on the right track. Eventually, she got close enough to see that it was indeed their campsite; however, no one was there. Her heart sank. Had Dolus tried to find her? Where was he?

Deor walked to the extinguished campfire and looked around. Her belongings were still there, but Dolus' and Sam's were gone. She looked around for any clues as to where Dolus had gone. On the far side of the fire, where Sam had encountered the spectres of the Meropan soldiers, many shuffled footprints marked the dirt. Where Dolus had lain, the ground was smooth, but at the edge of the camp, several bones had been arranged, not scattered, but placed. It had to be Dolus.

'It's an arrow,' she said to herself, her voice tiny and hoarse. She looked along the path of the arrow and saw that Dolus had continued along the road. It was the right thing to do. If she could find Sam, and find him alive, then they'd know they just needed to relocate the road in order to find Dolus again.

Deor packed her things, including her newfound sword, and turned away from the camp. The road down which Dolus had headed stretched ahead into the distance. She tried to remember the image of the map that he'd shown her, but that had been in the forest, and there hadn't been much light. It seemed to have headed off fairly straight in a general northeasterly direction. She looked at the path she'd swept to the campsite. It headed away diagonally compared to the road, generally east, she calculated, though nothing from the sky gave her any clue to confirm that.

Deor followed the path she'd swept back to where she'd fallen the night before. Nausea remained her companion, and her head still throbbed, but she had to go on. She located the arrow she'd drawn in the dirt and looked to her left to see if she could see the road, but it was already out of sight. She tried to remember the angle at which her path had skewed off from the road, so she could work out which way to head when she eventually needed to find it again.

Deor swallowed a mouthful of water, tasting dirt and blood, and with one last look behind her, to re-orient herself, she set off east again further into the plain. She tried to find something in the distance to head towards, so she could head in a straight line, but it was difficult to find anything. The plain ahead was flat and empty with no distinguishing features onto which she could latch, and darkness sank everywhere around her.

Determinedly, Deor walked on, fixing herself to a general point on the horizon where she thought the spectres had dragged Sam the previous night.

She walked on for an hour, and eventually the bones

and scattered remains of the battle dissipated, then stopped altogether. 'This must be the end of the battle,' she said to herself, her voice lonely in the emptiness.

She looked north. No sign of the road or any structures. Ahead of her lay trees, not thick like the forest through which they'd passed, but a woodland. She couldn't see far into it, though, thanks to the blanket of darkness across the land.

With one final look around her, and no other clues as to Sam's path, Deor headed into the woods. She tried to keep her direction roughly east, at least as easterly as possible, but the woods made it harder to ensure that. She walked on, getting deeper into the woods, not sure if she was on the right track. She could only cling to the hope that the spectres had continued on this way. Occasionally, she called out Sam's name, but all she got in reply was her own echo, dulled by the trees, her voice inconsequential in the oppressive, endless grey.

After a while, the ground rose, and she headed up a hill, the forest rising with it. She decided to follow it to its top, where perhaps there would be a clearing from which she could look down at the surrounding lands. Her legs burned as she pressed up the hill. Her muscles were sore, and her head still ached. She had some of the Alphym water remaining, and that brought a little relief.

Eventually, she came to the top of the hill and stopped in surprise. Ahead of her, in the middle of a clearing, stood a stone fort. She scanned the area but saw no signs of life.

'Hello?' she called out, carefully walking around the outer edge of the clearing to survey the fort from all sides. 'Sam? Can you hear me?'

No response.

On the far side of the clearing, she found the entrance to the fort—a doorway. The remains of a wooden door lay in pieces on the ground outside, and etched into the stone above the archway was the two-moons insignia. A Celanite fort. Painted over the top of this insignia, though, was the eagle and flame insignia of Merope.

'Hello?' she called out again and entered the fort.

Skeletons of long-dead soldiers lay where they had been killed on the ground in the entrance hall. The Meropans had breached the fort and spared no one.

Deor walked further into the hall, trying to avoid the bones of the dead. She heard something: a grunt, small only, but definitely there. Where did it come from? 'Sam? Sam, are you here?'

She waited for a response, and after an agonising wait, she again heard it. From her left, in the darkness, came a grunt of pain and discomfort. 'Sam?' She headed to that side of the hall and saw him. Sam, strung up, his hands and feet tied to the wall on each side of him, hung up to die like an animal being drained of its blood.

Deor rushed to Sam. He was barely conscious, barely alive, his skin as pale as death and nearly cold to the touch. Working quickly, she used her sword to cut his bonds, first his feet, then his hands. As she cut the final one, he fell off the wall, but she caught him as he fell and brought him to the ground.

'The Nebrans will die ...' a voice hissed from behind her.

Deor spun around and, without thinking, pulled one of the Alphym spears from her kit. Immediately, she threw the spear, and it sank into the chest of one of the four Meropan spectres who stood there.

The spear plunged through its spectral form, and it let out a bone-chilling scream, dissipating into nothingness as it did. The other three spectres advanced on her, but with the same speed, she pulled out another Alphym spear and threw it through one of them, then another, destroying the third. But the fourth spectre lunged at her with a sword. She blocked it with the Celanite sword held in her left hand. The spectre's haunting face came within centimetres of her own. Its dead eyes stared into hers, its mouth twisted into a malevolent grin.

'The Nebrans will die …' it hissed, pushing its sword closer to Deor's face.

Straining, she pushed against it with her own sword while reaching back with her right hand to find another Alphym spear. She grabbed one and plunged it into the spectre's chest. The face of the spectre, mere millimetres from her face, changed instantly. Hatred and anger and fury flooded it as it let out a soul-piercing scream. Its face contorted with pain, and it fell away from Deor, its ghoulish scream fading away as it disappeared into the unknown.

Deor fell onto the ground, her head pounding. She breathed rapidly, her heart racing, still terrified. She only allowed herself a moment to regain her breath, though, before going over to Sam. She felt his pulse; still alive. Barely. Quickly, she gathered up the three spears she'd thrown and dragged Sam out of the fort onto the grass outside.

Deor gave Sam some of her Alphym water in small sips, which he drank involuntarily. She remembered the paste the Alphym had given them back at the Southern Mountain and found it quickly in her bag. She spread some in his mouth, then gave him a little more water.

Deor laid Sam down so he could rest and got up to scan the horizon. She needed to get herself and Sam away from here as swiftly as possible before nightfall came. She couldn't see clearly through the trees, though. Moving quickly, she hunted around the fort for a way up to the top, but she couldn't find one. She'd have to go back inside. Gathering her courage, Deor ran inside. Avoiding the dead Celanites on the floor, she quickly made her way to the staircase at the back of the entrance hall and bounded up it two steps at a time. After three flights, it came out at the top of the fort. She stopped and stared out at the land sweeping away in all directions below.

The view was inspirational and awful in equal measure. How beautiful this land must once have looked from this tower—green farmlands and settlements where now it was all scorched grey and black. Based on where she'd entered the clearing, she had some idea of which direction was east, so she oriented herself that way, then turned to where north must roughly lie. She strained her eyes to scan the distance, trying to see the road, but the scorched land stretched on into the north without any sign of the road. She knew it had to be there somewhere, though, and she had to get there as soon as she could.

Deor raced down the stairs and out into the clearing. Sam looked a little better already, colour returning to his face. His eyelids fluttered.

'Sam,' she said, 'can you hear me?'

Sam muttered and groaned, then opened his eyes. They took a moment to focus. 'Dee,' he said, relief washing over his face. 'I thought I died … I think I might have …'

'You're not dying on me, Brother,' Deor said, smiling at last. 'Not this time.'

Deor helped Sam up. He got unsteadily to his feet, but he could walk. 'Where's Dolus?' he asked.

'It's a long story,' she said. 'But I hope he's on the road. And we have to find it as quickly as we can. We have to get away from these lands before nightfall. Do you think you can walk? Or, even better, run?'

'We always seem to end up running …' He gave her a wan smile.

Deor led Sam to the edge of the clearing and back into the woods, heading in a north-to-northwesterly direction. 'We have to cut back to the road,' she said, 'and I think this may be the shortest path to where I think it must be. If that makes any sense.'

Deor gave Sam more paste and water, after which he regained more of his strength, and they moved more quickly. Deor led the way, and Sam followed, still gingerly, back down the mountain, then eventually out of the woodlands. At the bottom of the hill, the woods gave way to an open expanse of land. They continued on in the same direction, crossing some old creeks and rivers that no longer held water, and passing a couple of burned-out farms. The charred shells of the abandoned farmhouses sat on the landscape, like gravestones marking the deaths of the families who once lived in them.

They travelled in the same direction for a long time before Deor noticed the sky was getting darker, and they still hadn't found the road or seen any sign of it. Ahead of them, though, she could make out a valley.

They stopped for a brief pause. 'We have to get out of the open before it's too dark,' Deor said. 'Let's head for that valley there and see if there's somewhere safe to camp and hide.'

Though she saw nothing, she could hear and sense stirrings in the land around them. As the night drew closer, the dead also drew closer. Her birthmark felt more prominent on her shoulder. She touched it and realised that danger wasn't far away. 'Let's hurry!'

Deor and Sam began to run again, the valley ahead being their target. The temperature fell, and darkness began to spread across the land, the vast cloud above them getting darker with each passing minute. They continued to run, not knowing what lay in the valley but hoping for something that would keep them safe, somewhere to camp and somewhere to hide.

They made it to the edge of the valley and looked down into the gloom of fading light. Below them, the land sloped steeply down to the bottom of the valley several hundred metres away. The other side sloped up and away in a similar manner. Deor strained her eyes, scanning the bottom of the valley. Then she saw it.

'The road!' Deor pointed, excitement bubbling up inside. 'I can see the road!' A thin strip cut through the valley below, heading away into the distance. It had to be it.

She grabbed her brother by the arm and ran again, down the steep descent towards the valley floor. A hiss came from behind. Deor turned and looked. At the top of the ravine stood two spectral figures, standing where she and Sam had stood only moments before.

'Hurry!' Deor pulled out an Alphym spear, and they ran on, trying to be careful on the rocky descent while moving as quickly as they could. Slipping as they went, they made it to the bottom. Ahead of them lay the road, and they ran straight for it. Relief washed over Deor when she finally set foot back on the stony road.

'Where to now?' Sam asked, catching his breath.

Deor looked back to the top of the valley and saw no sign of the spectres above, and, for now, it was clear close to the road. 'Let's keep going, for as long as we can, north on the road. Let's get as far as we can before we can't see any further.'

They continued up the road, walking briskly but carefully. The road was well delineated here in the valley, probably a major route used by the Celanites, and Deor could make it out without too much difficulty, even in the deepening dark.

Eventually, in the distance, she spotted a small light. It seemed to be on the road or near it, but she couldn't tell what it was.

'What is it?' Sam asked. 'Do you think it's a fire?'

'I don't know. But it gives us something to aim at.'

They kept the road underfoot in the now near-total darkness, and the light gradually grew in size as they continued along. When they got close, Deor realised it was a campfire.

She and Sam crept closer to the fire, approaching noiselessly. Someone sat next to it, trying to look out into the night. The figure was hunched over. Sam crept around to one side of the seated figure, and Deor to the other. Though they were both within a couple of metres, the person couldn't see them in the darkness.

'The Nebran will die …' Sam hissed, coming out of the shadows.

Dolus screamed in fright, jumped backwards and nearly landed in the fire.

Deor appeared also, laughing uncontrollably.

'Pleid!' Dolus said, annoyed. 'Why did you do that?'

Laughing, Sam helped Dolus up and brushed off his clothes.

Deor doubled over with laughter. Something about the grimness of the place, the night she'd had last night, the blood, dirt and sweat on her face, and the day she'd had today—fighting Meropan spectres and running for their lives—something about all the things they'd gone through broke apart inside her when her brother Sam played such a funny, childish practical joke. Tears of laughter ran down her face while Dolus looked at them both, annoyed but relieved. Deor let her emotions flood out of her as she cried tears of laughter and relief, surrounded on all sides by complete darkness.

CHAPTER 18

'Sam!' Deor whispered urgently, prodding her brother with her foot. 'Sam, wake up!' She stood on the edge of the campfire, holding an Alphym spear.

A dozen or more spectres of Meropan soldiers approached and formed a line on the edge of the road. Deor waved the spear at them, hoping it would keep them at bay.

On the other side of the fire, Dolus did the same, each facing one side of the valley, guarding against attack. Sam had taken the first shift to rest while Deor and Dolus guarded a side of the road each, but he needed to be woken now.

'Pleid!' Sam said, sitting up.

'The Nebrans will die…' the Meropans hissed as one.

Deor and Dolus brandished the Alphym spears in front of them, trying to stave them off. The spears glowed lightly in the dark of the night, casting some light, and they held the spectres at bay for now. The special powers of the spears held some fear for the spectres.

Sam grabbed a spear and stood, wielding it in the same way. 'What do we do?' he whispered as more of the spectres appeared, more than thirty now on each side of the road.

'They're growing in number; they'll overpower us,' Deor whispered back, unable to hide her alarm. 'We won't have long before they'll attack.'

'Can we make a run for it?' Dolus asked, urgently waving his spear from one spectral form to the next.

'We might have to,' Deor said.

Deep drums began to beat on either side of the road as the number of Meropan soldiers continued to swell. *Baaa-dumm, baaa-dumm, baaa-dumm.* The spectres raised a low chant in time with the drumbeats. 'Reeee-mus, Reeee-mus, Reeee-mus,' they chanted. All around, the chant of Remus sounded, reinforced with the drumbeat. The sound filled the whole valley and grew louder as more and more spectres appeared. 'Reeee-mus, Reeee-mus, Reeee-mus.'

'There's hundreds of them!' Dolus yelled, his voice flooded with fear and panic. 'What do we do? We can't escape!'

The soldiers advanced towards them from both sides of the valley. One reached Dolus and swung its sword at his neck, but Dolus plunged his spear into its heart before it could reach him. Spectres attacked Sam and Deor, and they held them back with the Alphym spears, killing those who got close.

'We can't hold them off for much longer!' Deor yelled, spearing another spectre as Sam next to her did the same. 'There's too many of them!'

The drumbeats increased in volume, and the chants of 'Reeee-mus' amplified as the spectral army swelled. Lines of Meropan spectres spread back as far as Deor could see in both directions. The chant hit full volume, booming through the valley, as the drumbeats deepened and the ground shook.

Then, suddenly, the drums and chants stopped. For a brief moment, there was silence, and the spectres stopped advancing. Deor's rapid breath pushed steam in front of her face. Her heart pounded hard in her chest.

A roaring sound came from further south, growing louder as it drew closer. A cloud seemed to be rolling up the road, a pale grey mass swarming towards them. Meropan soldiers screamed. Deor strained to see through the darkness and made out spirits bearing the two-moons insignia attacking the spectres. The Celanite army had risen to fight them.

In seconds, hundreds of Celanite spirit soldiers engaged the Meropan spectres in battle. The Meropan spectres turned away from the travellers and flooded towards the Celanites. The ancient battle that had occurred further south was being fought yet again, the war reignited.

A voice spoke in Deor's mind—the voice of Ada. *Go, Deor, the Celanites will protect you.*

Deor turned to Sam and Dolus. 'We have to go!' she yelled and frantically gathered her things.

All around them, Meropan spectres screeched as they engaged in battle with the roaring Celanite army, their numbers spilling down the valley.

Keeping their spears in hand to cast some light, Deor ran up the road, with Sam and Dolus following close behind.

The cool light-blue and yellow light cast by the spears was just enough for them to see the road ahead. It shone like the moonlight cast by the two moons on Nebra that Deor had seen in her dreams and visions. Guided by this light, she led them up the road, putting ever more distance between them and the battle.

Once well clear of the battle, they stopped to catch their breath.

'What was that?' asked Sam, alarmed and nervous.

'The Celanites,' Deor said, her breath coming in short hitches. 'The Celanite army rose to defend us, to fight for us.

I heard the voice of Ada in my head.'

'Voices in your head now,' Sam said. 'That's not alarming …'

Deor looked back at the battle in the distance. Shrieks and screams floated up the valley on the wind, but they had not been pursued. The Celanites had done their job, keeping the Meropans at bay.

'We should keep going, though, while we can,' Dolus said. 'We may be able to get clear of these lands tonight.'

Deor nodded. 'Agreed. I don't think any of us will be able to sleep now anyway. Let's put as much space between us and them as we can.'

Keeping close together, they followed the ancient road as it headed steadily northeast. In places, it was hard to make out, but the glow of the Alphym spears helped enough to guide them. They followed it deep into the night for the next several hours, feeling exhausted and in dire need of rest, but not daring to stop.

They passed smaller settlements, some more like towns like Apin. All were burned. At one point, the road crossed a river that headed east, a tributary of the River Merope. On either side of the bridge that crossed it, small towns stood, silent now, razed to the ground. Only the foundations of some houses and buildings remained. The river was dry. Nothing that suggested life remained in the Scarred Lands.

❨❨❨

Eventually, the sky began to grow lighter, and Deor's heart rose a little. She said the first words any of them had spoken for hours: 'I think the dawn is coming.' Her voice came out husky and exhausted. 'We may be able to stop to rest.'

'Look!' Sam said, his voice tired and cracked but with a tinge of excitement. 'Look ahead! The end of the cloud!'

In the distance was blue sky, dark blue in the pre-dawn twilight, a thin strip of it on the horizon beyond the large cloud hanging overhead.

'Green!' Deor exclaimed. 'I can see green! We must be near the end of this place!' She pointed to where, in the distance, just within their field of vision, the earth turned to a dark shade of green.

They pressed on quickly now, energised by the prospect of getting out of the Scarred Lands. The day grew lighter as they got closer to the green land ahead. Legs aching, they walked more quickly until it was just ahead of them, then finally they were there, at the end of the Scarred Lands. Just as at the southern end, there was a clear delineation between the blackened lands and the green grass beyond. The three of them stood together on the path, one step away from leaving it, finally at the end.

'Are you ready?' Deor's voice croaked with exhaustion. 'Let's do it together.'

Together, they took a step forward, crossed over the border and walked onto the path beyond. They all breathed a sigh of relief, then collapsed, exhausted, lying down with their packs, metres beyond the end of the Scarred Lands, in the lush grass of Merope. The warm sun in the east rose above the mountains, bathing them in gentle sunlight, the first they'd seen in many days.

CHAPTER 19

'It's like some evil hand has drawn a line around it,' Deor said, looking back at the land through which they'd just travelled. The previous night seemed more like a dream than reality. They'd rested for a couple of hours and were preparing to move on again. 'Everything inside the line is cursed and dead. Everything outside it, alive and lush.'

'Even the cloud that hangs over it ends here where the scorched earth ends,' Dolus said. 'It's scary just to look at it. No wonder the Meropans never go in there.'

'I hope I never have to go in there ever again,' Deor said. 'But the dead who remain there cannot rest, and I made a promise to the Celanites.'

At last, they turned their backs on the Scarred Lands. Deor looked north through a vast plain of flat land stretching into the distance. To her right, in the east, the Merope Range loomed large.

'Somewhere up there'—Dolus pointed north—'is Titus. Somewhere. But we can't go that way yet. Somewhere over there, to the northwest, is Remit. But we can't go that way either. We have to go there, the other way, along the mountains.'

The Merope Range loomed high above them to the east, steep and stark. Unlike the Asman Range, which was gentler in the Mid Territory, and greener, the Merope Range was blacker and more severe, sharper in its angles and more pointed. Deor looked upon the mountains; how difficult would they be to traverse?

In the distance, at the base of the mountains, she saw something large, like a city wall. 'Do we have any idea what that is?' she asked, pointing.

'None at all,' Dolus said, consulting a map of Merope. 'Your father gave me this. It's based on the latest information we received from our spies, who are in Remit and Titus, but whatever that thing up ahead is, it's not on this map. There isn't supposed to be any town or city down here, just the mountains. There're towns further north, along the trade routes; they head east from Remit all the way to the coast and west to the Asman mountains, but not down here. Whatever this is, it's new and secret.'

'I don't like the look of it.' Deor absentmindedly touched her birthmark.

'Well, I can't see any alternative,' said Dolus, folding the map away. 'We have to go around it to get to the mountains. We can't go south to avoid it, as we'll be back in that black place. If we try to cut straight through to Remit, we're going to hit the river, and we don't know what lies between here and there. We have to head through the mountains; let's just hope we don't come across anyone along the way.'

Resigned to the task ahead, they headed towards the Merope Range, the Scarred Lands kept firmly to their right. Heads down, they headed east as quickly as they could. Deor felt weary and sore but determined to keep going. The day grew hot, the sun climbing higher in the sky, and sweat ran off her brow, stinging her eyes. A steady hum came from insects around them.

The structure grew closer. They were going to have to skirt fairly close to it, as it was only a couple of hundred metres north of the end of the Scarred Lands, and it spread all the way to the base of the mountain range. Whatever it was, a high wall surrounded it on all sides, and a lookout tower stood at each corner.

'Is it a town?' Sam asked as they drew closer.

'The walls bear the eagle and flame,' Deor said quietly, 'the insignia of the Merope military. This is no town …'

A large gate in the south wall opened slowly.

'Get down!' Deor whispered, and they ducked down in the grass to hide.

Through the gates, a patroller led a file of younger patrollers. At first, they headed straight for them, but after a few paces, the head patroller turned eastward, towards the mountain range, and led the young men that way.

'It's a training facility …' Deor whispered.

'And it's enormous,' Sam whispered back, tucking his head lower. 'It's bigger than a town.'

When the trainee patrollers had finished filing out of the big gate, it began to close, but Deor got a glimpse of what lay inside. Several large buildings from which smoke rose, and lines of smaller ones.

'Factories and barracks,' she whispered. 'What do you think they make in the factories? They're building something in there.'

'Weapons would be my guess,' Dolus whispered back. 'It's a Meropan war machine. They're training new patrollers and making large numbers of weapons.'

'We have to get out of here,' Deor said as the last of the

trainees disappeared into the mountains. 'We have to get up the mountain and as far away from them as quickly as we can.'

'How can we do that?' Sam asked, trying to keep his voice low. 'If we head to the mountain, they'll see us!'

'Maybe they will,' Dolus said, 'but maybe they won't. If we can head there quickly and head as high as possible as quickly as possible, then maybe we can avoid them. And if they do see us, they have no reason to suspect we're from Alcyone. As far as they know, we're hiking Meropans.'

Sam shook his head. 'Meropans who just happen to be a long way from any town, hiking in the mountains at the edge of the Scarred Lands? That's going to raise suspicion!'

'What choice do we have?' Dolus said. 'We can't go back; we can't go around the base; we'll be spotted for sure. They'll have guards stationed in those towers. We have no other path. The mountains are our only option!'

'He's right,' Deor said. 'It's the only way we can go. We have to head straight for that mountain ahead and get as high as we can, then maybe we hide out until they finish whatever they're doing.'

'We can't hide out,' Dolus said, 'because if they find us hiding, they'll know something is up. We have to pretend we're hikers, and there's no problem. We're just headed to the mountains to hike. We've come here from Remit and are headed home later.'

'We're a long way from Remit, though, based on that map of yours,' Sam said.

'Yes, we are, but it's the only story we can make stick,' Dolus said. 'In fact, if they do have guards in those towers, then lying here in the grass is going to look extremely suspicious.' He stood and looked down at them. 'Come on, we have to go. Let's make for that mountain and get as high as possible.'

Deor and Sam got to their feet, and they started for the mountain.

'Let's walk in single file,' Dolus said. 'That's what hikers do, I'm told. I'm more a beach person myself. Why can't we ever have to head for the beach? Or a boat? No, it's always the bloody mountains … I hope we get to see a boat again before all this is done.'

Nerves rose in Deor as they approached the mountain. Gunshots went off nearby—the trainees had rifles. They made it to the tree line and started up the slope. The woods were thinner, the trees barer and the slope steeper here than in the Asman Range.

Deor listened to the gunshots, but they weren't getting closer. They stepped into a clearing, and to her left, in the distance, through the trees, she saw the younger patrollers shooting at something—target practice. They were shooting away from her, thankfully. Behind them, on the edge of the clearing, the head patroller stood, monitoring the trainees.

The patroller, perhaps somehow sensing they were there, turned around. His eyes locked with Deor's, and a flash of recognition crossed his face. Deor knew him: the head patroller from the Asman Range, the one who had shot and killed the other patroller when Deor and Sam hid in the cave, and he'd killed Dolus' friend the next day.

'Oh no …' she said, instinctively grabbing Sam's arm.

'Mountain rats!' the patroller mouthed. He pulled his gun and ran towards them.

'Run!' Deor cried and sprinted up the hill. Bullets spat into a tree behind her. She zig-zagged up the hillside, trying to avoid being shot. When she glanced behind her, she saw the head patroller at the edge of the clearing, striding back to his trainees. 'Keep going, fast as you can!' she called out. 'He has thirty trainee patrollers down there, all with guns! They'll be after us in seconds!'

The firing stopped in the woods below. The head patroller was no doubt setting a new task for his trainees: three live targets. Yells and roars came from the trainees below, and the ground shook as they began chasing the trio up the hill. Deor, Sam and Dolus kept running as fast as they could, Deor trying to ignore the fatigue and soreness in her legs. The mountain climb was steep, though, steeper than the Asman Range, and she quickly felt it.

'There!' Sam called, spotting a track. It led further up the mountain and north. They ran along it, getting higher and higher, as bullets spat bark from trees behind them.

'They're gaining!' Dolus yelled. 'Head further up!'

Abandoning the track, they again ran directly up the hill through the woods. They were able to keep enough distance between themselves and the trainees to avoid being shot, though the bullets got closer.

'We're getting close to the top!' Deor yelled. Through the trees, in the distance, she could see the summit. The slope was steep, though, and the summit looked rocky. 'There's not much further we can go! We have to head north!'

Changing direction, they sprinted north across the face of the mountain, keeping the summit to their right. The pursuing patrollers on the path below took more shots as they ran, but the trees blocked the way, and they couldn't get clean shots. Suddenly, Deor realised the ground was about to go down again. They would be going down the far side of the mountain. She came to a sudden stop at the mountains' northern edge. It dropped suddenly and severely below them.

'Higher!' Sam yelled. 'We have to head to the summit!'

Turning right, they ran towards the summit until they

cleared the tree line and saw it, the very top of the mountain. It culminated in a jagged rock line, high and pointed, heading back behind them to the south. They had no way to climb over it and nowhere else to go.

'Look!' Deor said, catching her breath. A dizzying sight lay ahead. Where the summit reached its northern edge at the end of the rock line stood a bridge. However, this was no ordinary bridge, not like the small bridge over the Alcyone River back home, or even the bridges that crossed the outlets on the Southern Mountain; this was a very old bridge, forgotten by time.

'It's our only way!' Deor said, panic lacing her voice.

The bridge was barely wide enough for two people, and it extended out over the gaping valley below, connecting to the summit of the adjoining mountain to the north at least two hundred metres away. Made of timber that had gone black with time, it had no guard rails, nothing to hold on to, nothing to keep them from falling. She ran to the edge of the bridge and looked down at the sheer drop to the valley below. If they fell from this bridge, they fell to certain death.

'We have to take it!' Deor said. 'We have no other way!' She put one foot on the bridge. It creaked and wobbled a little as she touched it, but it seemed solid. She walked quickly out onto the bridge.

Sam and Dolus followed in single file, the bridge wobbling with their motion. Deor overbalanced. She spread her arms out to steady herself and thrust her left foot down ahead of her. A piece of the paling she'd stepped on broke away, sailing down into the abyss below.

'Be careful!' Sam caught her arm and steadied her.

The shouts of the trainee patrollers grew closer, nearing the summit. Deor found her balance again and, getting a feel for the motion of the bridge, hurried across, step by step with her arms stretched out on either side of her. Before long, she could see the end of it just ahead. She took long strides in time with the bridge's motion and jumped the last metre to land on firm ground on the other side. Turning, she helped Sam and Dolus off the bridge.

They looked back. The trainee patrollers had reached the summit of the mountain on the other side of the bridge, and some had begun crossing the bridge in pursuit.

'I have an idea!' Deor said.

Remembering the Southern Mountain, she pulled the largest Alphym spear from her pack, then took the Minerva gem from around her neck and placed it in the spear's cavity. The spear glowed blue and yellow, and a bright light shone from her gem. She raised the spear above her head, feeling a power surge through it and her, and slammed it down into the final paling of the bridge. A loud explosion from the spear shattered the palings at her end and destroyed the bridge. The supports that connected the bridge to the mountain broke away, leaving nothing to hold it up on her side, and the rest of the bridge fell away as a result. Like a wave crossing the valley, the ancient bridge collapsed into the abyss below. Several trainee patrollers screamed as they fell into the valley with it.

Deor stared across the gulf at the head patroller on the other side. His eyes locked on hers, and even at that distance, Deor could see the murder in them. She took her Minerva gem back out of the cavity and hung it around her neck again.

'No big line this time?' Sam teased.

'I've used them all up.' She rolled her eyes and smiled. Even out here in the mountains of Merope, her brother could make her laugh. They only spared a moment, though. The journey was not complete.

'We need to get across this mountain,' Dolus said as they strode on. 'The River Merope bisects this mountain range somewhere in the distance. We have to keep going until we get there.'

Deor looked ahead and braced herself for the journey. The mountain range stretched away into the distance. They had a long hike ahead of them.

CHAPTER 20

By evening, Deor, Sam and Dolus had reached the edge of that part of the range. Deor felt weary and sore from a long day of walking in the hot sun. They stood at the summit of the final mountain and looked down at the River Merope, wide and dark blue in the early evening twilight. It wound its way northeast through the countryside and then through a valley. In the distance in the northeast, where the river finally poured its waters, the sea glinted.

They were all hungry and thirsty, but fortunately they had seen no further sign of the patrollers. However, they'd run out of water, and all they had for food was some Alphym paste. Sam spotted a stream further down, and they made their way towards it. Near the stream, they found a small clearing, filled their flasks, and set up camp for the night, careful not to light too big a fire lest it drew attention.

A rocky outcrop, above which the mountain continued to rise, sat at the eastern end of the clearing. The rocks rose higher than the trees around the clearing, offering a potential view of the terrain below. After setting up the fire, the three of them climbed to the top of the outcrop.

From on top of the rocks, with the sun setting, Deor had a breathtaking view of the countryside of Merope. A small town sat at the bottom of the mountain. Smoke rose from the chimneys, and light shone from the windows of houses dotted along its small streets.

'It kind of reminds me of home,' Deor said. A pang of yearning for home came to her as she thought of Apin. 'Except that the people down there in that town aren't living a life of occupation. The children in those houses go to bed fed and full. They don't worry where their next meal will come from or if they'll have a patroller break down their door in the morning. They're free.'

'It's beautiful countryside,' Sam said. 'It really looks like the Mid. Merope looks just like Alcyone to me. Even, look, in the distance, the Asman Range. You can barely make it out. It looks like home.'

Dolus nodded. 'I think you're right, Sam. In fact, funnily enough, if I've read this map right, your town, Apin, is just on the other side of the range. We're pretty much staring straight at it. This is essentially the Mid Territory of Merope.'

It struck Deor just how alike they were, the two countries. She didn't know what she'd expected to see in the countryside of Merope. Black smoke rising from the engines of war, perhaps; a militarily dominated landscape where men and women toiled endlessly making weapons. If this were fiction, that might be what she'd see. But it was not. They had their war machines at the military camp further south; here, it was just a normal small town in the countryside. Here, Merope looked peaceful and beautiful. She gazed out over the countryside. The setting sun dipped below the Asman Range, the last of its rays bathing the Merope countryside in golden sunlight. To the north of them, the River Merope turned black as evening set in.

❮❮❮

The next morning, the travellers woke early. 'Alphym paste for breakfast, lunch and dinner,' Sam said gloomily. 'Perhaps in Remit we can get a nice meal.'

'I'd literally kill for a steak,' Dolus said.

'Oh yes,' Deor said, her stomach grumbling. 'A steak, cooked over an open fire, a thick broth like the one Sage mixed up for us as sauce, Sam.' A wave of sadness came over her as she thought of her little sister. How was she going? Was she safe?

Deor shouldered her pack and looked determinedly to the north. 'Come on, let's do this,' she said, and they set off down the mountain.

They came out of the mountain at the north to avoid the town at its foothills. When they came out of the woods a few hundred metres north of it, Deor looked back at the town, again struck by how similar it was to her town, except that the houses appeared to be in better condition, more well maintained and generally bigger.

'That town has to have a road that crosses the River Merope,' Dolus said. 'The map indicates as much. Let's head west and find it.'

They walked on, and after a little while came across the road, as the map had shown. It was still early enough for the road to be quiet, so they turned northwards and headed towards the river. It didn't take long before it came into view. At the top of a gentle rise in the land ahead, they saw it, wide and blue, winding east towards the valley between the mountains.

A bridge lay ahead, with patrollers guarding it on either

side. 'That's where we cross,' Dolus said. 'We are travellers from Remit, visiting, and are now headed home.'

'Hopefully, these patrollers haven't been alerted to the presence of three travelling Alcyonans as yet,' Sam said anxiously.

Nerves rose in Deor as they continued on to the bridge. The patrollers held guns, not unlike the ones Deor was used to seeing at home. Fear struck her as they approached. All her life she'd lived in fear of the wrath of the patrollers. At least at home, they had places they could hide; they could get away. If they were found out here to be Alcyonan, there'd be nowhere to hide.

'Good morning,' one of the patrollers said politely. 'Out and about early today?'

'We are,' Dolus said. His voice betrayed nothing of the nerves he must have felt. He seemed completely at ease. 'We are headed back to Remit, keen to get home.'

The patroller nodded at Dolus, then peered closely at Deor and Sam. He looked them up and down suspiciously. Deor tried to remain calm, to not let her face betray the panic that she felt under the surface. 'Names?' he said, still staring at Deor.

'I am Dolus, and this is Deor and Sammu,' Dolus said.

The patroller continued to look at Deor closely, an almost imperceptible nod the only reply he gave Dolus. The silence hung in the air like a wet, thick fog. Deor glanced nervously from one patroller to the other. Should she say something? Or nothing? Or stare or look away?

Eventually, the patroller looked back at Dolus. 'Carry on,' he said, stepping aside to allow them to pass.

'Thank you, sir,' Dolus said casually. How could he remain so casual under such scrutiny?

'For the glory of Merope!' the patroller said formally.

'Always and forever,' Dolus replied.

They walked onto the bridge. It was long, and the River Merope flowed strongly underneath.

'What on earth was that?' Deor whispered as they crossed.

'It's what they say,' Dolus said. 'If a patroller says to you, "For the glory of Merope", you reply with, "Always and forever". It's like a calling card for the Meropans.'

'How did you know that?' she asked.

'I told you we have spies; we get information.'

'You could have shared that information with us earlier,' Deor said.

'I didn't think anything of it,' Dolus said quickly. 'I didn't actually think we'd run into any patrollers. Not sure why they have them guarding a bridge. I haven't been to Merope before, remember. I didn't know what to expect.'

'For the glory of Merope.' Sam impersonated the patroller. 'What a joke.'

'Always and forever,' Dolus said with a smile. 'You mustn't forget that part.'

The guards on the other side of the bridge let them through, and they continued north along the road.

'The Western Road is somewhere up ahead,' Dolus said. 'It'll take us a while to get there.'

They walked on steadily. Deor still felt anxious about the encounter in the mountains the day before. Hopefully, word of their presence wouldn't catch up to them.

Late morning, they found the Western Road and headed west on it towards Remit. They passed many travellers heading east, coming home from Remit, but encountered no issues with them. The Meropan people all just went about their business, leaving them to do the same. Deor moved among them as one of them; it felt foreign.

❨❨❨

Eventually, as the shadows grew longer, Deor saw a town looming in the distance.

They stopped on the side of the road for a rest and to consult the map and took some water and Alphym paste—which had lost its appeal. Deor's mouth salivated thinking about the prospect of real food in Remit.

'We've walked most of the day,' Dolus said, 'and there're no other towns listed on this map. That must be Remit. We're nearly there, finally!'

'What do we do when we get there?' Sam asked.

'Well, I think the first thing is to find something to eat. I'm starving,' Dolus replied. 'Then after that, we find the safe house. I have the address. Alcyonan spies are based there. They'll be able to help us, I'm sure, and give us somewhere to stay for the night.'

Anxious to get there and hungry for food, the trio moved on, shadows lengthening as the day wore on. Deor felt strange. Not tiredness or hunger; something else. Her birthmark felt prominent, worryingly. Did Remit hold some danger? She kept her gaze on it as they walked closer, and suddenly a flash of light came across her mind. She found herself as Lore once more.

'How could you? How could you do this?' Lore demanded, tears on her face.

Julius stared back at her with a blank expression.

Deor returned to herself to find Sam helping her up from the ground. She must have stumbled.

'Are you okay?' he asked. 'What happened?'

'I don't know,' Deor said shakily. Her head spun, and she felt nauseous. 'A vision flashed into my head and took over my senses for a moment.'

A concerned expression spread across Sam's face. 'Do you want to stop for a little?'

'No, I am okay now,' Deor said. 'I think. I just need a little water. Let's keep going. It's probably just exhaustion and hunger.'

They walked on. The town ahead was large, big enough to have a town wall, with gates on the eastern side. The gates were open to all right now, and lots of people moved about inside the walls.

❨❨❨

'Julius!' Lore yelled at his image on the screen in front of her, where he stood in command of a Remusan vessel. 'Do not do this; I implore you! Those ships stand defenceless; we still have time to negotiate peace for both our worlds. Do not jeopardise that!'

'War is upon us, Lore of Nebra,' Julius replied on screen. He had a hardness in his face now, a sternness. His mind was set. 'We will prevail for the glory of Remus!'

The transmission cut out, and Lore watched as his ship fired on a Nebran armada of civilian aid vessels. They exploded in an instant.

❨❨❨

'Deor?' Sam and Dolus both had her by an arm, looks of concern on their faces. 'Deor, are you all right?'

She looked at them groggily, her vision skewed and blurry.

227

After a few seconds, they gradually came into focus.

'Yes,' she eventually said. 'I'm sorry; I don't know what's coming over me. The visions don't often take over like that. Usually they're in a dream or they come as a memory. Something else happened here. I had visions of Nebra, of Julius betraying us, betraying Nebra. They were powerful visions.'

They sat on the side of the road while Deor ate a little of the Alphym paste and had some water. Soon, she felt a little better.

'Eve said I would get visions in dreams or even when waking, but she indicated the ones waking would be more subtle, like memories surfacing from beneath. And when I've had them, it's been like that. Not like this. I don't know what this is, but it's different.'

Sam shook his head. 'That's why it's better not to know, Dee. This can't be healthy; it can't be good for your mind.'

'I'll be okay. They must be coming for some reason. I'm fine now. The town is just ahead; let's get there and get some proper food.'

They pressed on. The visions seemed to have cleared now, and Deor was thankful that they didn't disturb her further. Soon after, they arrived at the town gates, which remained wide open. No patrollers manned the gates. The Meropan traders were free to come and go as they pleased.

The town was bigger than Deor had realised. The Western Road ran straight through the middle of Remit, and merchants had set up stalls on each side of the road. Many side streets branched off the main road, and merchants lined those streets as well. Walking down the main road, Deor marvelled at the colour and variety of what she saw.

'Fish! Fresh fish! Lobster! Shark! Caught this morning in the Meropan sea!' one merchant cried, displaying an impressive array of fish and seafood.

Deor's stomach turned with hunger. She wanted to grab one of the raw fish and devour it whole. 'By Pleid, hunger is turning me into an animal,' she said to herself.

'Spices! Pepper and salt! Ramsons, nettle, chives and mint!' called another, who displayed a wide range of herbs and spices. The merchant caught Deor's eye. 'Miss! Have you ever seen bay laurel this aromatic? Or fennel this rich in flavour? You must have these in your cooking! They are a Meropan delicacy! Your cooking will delight your boyfriend!'

Deor smiled and shook her head.

'Gems! Gems from the Mid Territory of Alcyone! Minerva gems!' another called out. His stall had several shelves of Minerva gems of all sizes.

Deor stopped in her tracks. A wave of anger came over her—her people toiled at great physical cost for those gems, and Merope took them without right. She turned towards the merchant.

'Let's find something to eat,' Dolus said, taking her arm and leading her away from the Minerva gems. 'There must be something down this side street. I can smell the most delicious smells coming from there. Pork, it's killing me; come on!'

They walked down the side street and found several larger, more-permanent shops serving meals inside. Dolus led them to one that advertised roasted pork and goat. The smells wafting from it assaulted their senses.

'Oh Pleid, I am so hungry,' Sam said. They found a table to sit at inside.

'I'll get us some food,' Dolus said. 'Hold the table.'

'Hurry!' Sam said. 'I'm going insane with hunger here!'

Dolus laughed and slipped off to the counter, where others were ordering food.

'I hope he has some money; I only have a little,' Sam said, searching in his pockets.

Deor didn't hear him, though. She felt dizzy again, and her birthmark felt prominent. She shook her head, determined to stay present, and took some water from her flask. Turning, she saw Dolus returning to the table with no food. He was flanked by four patrollers.

'These ones?' one of the patrollers asked.

'Yes, this is them.' Dolus indicated Deor and Sam. 'Alcyonan spies. I've been tracking them on behalf of the Merope Guard for the last several days. They're here to infiltrate Titus and attempt to liberate their sister, who was taken on the Day of Procurement.'

'Dolus!' Deor yelled. A vision began to creep in again. She was Lore, on Nebra, again demanding to know of Julius why he'd betrayed them. 'Oh no …' Realisation flooded her mind. 'I could never see who you were because you weren't from Nebra! You were Julius! Julius the Betrayer!'

'They need to be taken to Titus, at the pleasure of Emperor Barritus,' Dolus continued, ignoring Deor. 'Bring word to Senator Vespus that Agent Dolus has brought these two in. I want to be sure to receive my reward.'

'You were Julius the Betrayer!' Deor said. 'Now you do the same as Dolus! Dolus the Deceiver! How could you?' Anger rose inside her, not just at Dolus but at herself for not discovering earlier who he was. She should have known; she could have stopped him. Just like with Julius.

'For the glory of Merope!' Dolus said to the patrollers.

'Always and forever!' the patrollers replied, then they grabbed Deor and Sam by an arm each and led them out of the shop.

'How could you?' Deor shouted, enraged, as she was

hauled outside. 'Dolus! How could you?'

Sam cursed Dolus repeatedly under his breath and struggled against his captors, but could not get himself free.

The patrollers pushed them onto the street. Meropan traders and merchants looked on in shock.

'Dolus the Deceiver!' Deor yelled as Dolus watched on from the doorway of the shop. He had a piece of meat now and began to eat it.

Deor struggled to get free, but she could not. 'Dolus the Deceiver! Why have you done this?'

Dolus turned away from them, returning to the shop as they were dragged away.

The patrollers took Deor and Sam down the street, away from the shopfronts. At the end, a cage waited, the same type that had taken Sage from home all those days ago. The patrollers manhandled Sam into the cage, then threw Deor inside it after him. Her head hit the bars as she landed. The patrollers locked the cage; the driver urged his oxen forward, and the cage slowly rolled out of Remit and onto the northern road.

CHAPTER 21

rieitis strode to the amphitheatre, not quite with the same bluster as her brother Quetzl a few days earlier. The amphitheatre was opening in two days at the summer solstice and would be named the Titavian on that day, which would also signal the beginning of Merope Week. Her father, Barritus, had given her a role to oversee the man charged with organising the upcoming games, Fuscus.

'He's unreliable,' Barritus had said to her the day prior. 'He slacks off, and if left to his own devices, nothing will get done. I want you to go through every act we have planned, check over all of it and report back to me.'

It was an odd role for her father to give to her, and so late in the planning, but she hadn't questioned it. The games were interesting. Something new, something different.

'Good morning, Arieitis,' Fuscus said in surprise as she walked into the amphitheatre. Ari glanced down at him— literally, as Fuscus was quite short. The size of his girth, however, reflected the laziness her father had mentioned. 'What can I do for the daughter of the emperor today?'

'My father has sent me to … be of assistance to you,' Ari

said, 'in the final days leading up to the games.'

'He wants you to check up on me, make sure everything is in order,' Fuscus said testily. 'The emperor does not trust me.'

'No,' Arieitis said carefully, 'it's not necessarily that. He is just very anxious to ensure that the games run smoothly and successfully. He is very keen to make these games a big event, something that Meropans flock to and rave about afterwards. He wants it to be a grand celebration of our great nation and, as such, wants nothing left to chance.'

'Well,' Fuscus said, 'what would you like to know? What do you want me to show you?'

Ari brought out her notes. 'I have an outline of the events for each day, but there are gaps; I was hoping we could go through the entire schedule of each day, starting with day one, and fill in all these gaps. Then I thought we could inspect the arena and the contestants. Is that what we're calling them? Contestants? Something else?'

Fuscus chuckled. 'Victims, perhaps.'

'Victims?'

Fuscus shrugged. 'Combatants. That's a better term.'

'Okay, combatants,' Arieitis said. 'Then let's start with day one. What's the plan?'

'Come.' Fuscus led Ari towards the arena. 'Each day, there will be a variety of different events, culminating in one grand, main event in the early evening to finish the day in style. The earlier events, in the morning, will be ones that are more family friendly, so children can come to see them also, while the main event will be strictly for the adults. On the first day, we are starting with races between our finest riders, a series of knockout races around the arena, ten laps each. One rider starts on one side of the arena, the other on the other, the first to either catch their opponent or complete their ten laps wins.

Sixteen of our best riders on their best horses, until we are down to the final two. The adults can place wagers on the races. The children can barrack for their heroes. The grand champion will be crowned late morning and rewarded handsomely. The children will also get the chance to meet their heroes after the races, outside the arena. That will give the parents a chance to clear the children out before the afternoon's spectacles begin.'

They stood in the arena as Fuscus described the races. A flag had been erected on each side, and a platform sat above it for an official to stand on to officiate the race. All fairly basic.

'Where are these riders now?' Ari asked.

'Many of them are patrollers, but all are here in the city now in readiness for the games.'

'And they have been briefed on their roles in these races?'

'They have,' Fuscus said.

'What about practice runs?'

'What do you mean?' Fuscus' eyes widened.

'Trial races,' Ari said, 'in the arena, before the big day. So there's, you know, nothing left to chance.'

Fuscus looked thoughtful. 'I hadn't thought of that.'

'Let's get them here tomorrow,' Ari said brusquely, tossing her golden-brown hair back over her shoulder. 'We don't have to do a full run through, but they should at least do a race each, so they know what's expected of them. And get the officials here too, for a proper trial.'

'Yes, okay, I'll organise that today,' Fuscus said, a little stunned.

Just what had Fuscus been doing all this time?

'What are the events in the afternoon and evening?' she asked as they walked a lap of the arena floor.

'There'll be a break after the races,' Fuscus said, his voice more dutiful now. 'This will give people a chance to eat lunch.

We have food vendors organised for the corridors—meats, fruits, wines, especially the wines. The more the adults drink in the afternoon and evening, the better. At a solid markup, of course. Then there will be battles between combatants, warriors armed with swords and shields.'

'Who are these warriors?' Ari asked.

'Slaves recruited for this purpose,' Fuscus said. 'They have been training at a facility run by a retired commander, just outside the city. They will fight one another, and the people will cheer their heroes, sometimes to the death of the other.'

'Have you inspected these slaves and this facility?' Ari asked.

Fuscus paused.

'You haven't?' she asked.

'I have had discussions with the commander. He assures me all is under control. The slaves are motivated. They have the chance to win their freedom in the arena, if they perform well enough during Merope Week.'

'We need to pay a visit to the facility today,' Ari said. 'Nothing can be left to chance. We will go there this afternoon.'

'Okay, but I don't think it's really—'

'It is necessary,' Ari interrupted. 'So there's armed combat, and then what? The main event in the evening?'

'Yes, that's right,' Fuscus said. 'There'll be a break so the spectators can get more food and more drink, especially more drink, before trumpets are sounded to announce the main event.'

They'd made their way around to the part of the arena that showcased the imperial box. 'Your father, and you and your family, will all be seated here,' Fuscus said, 'in the imperial box. The best seats in the house! The spectators will make their way back to their seats, and I, as host and announcer, will announce the presence of your father, Emperor Barritus. The crowd will cheer him on, and he will make a speech.'

'Does he know this?' Ari quickly asked.

Fuscus smiled confidently. 'Oh yes, he certainly does. Your father is very much looking forward to this speech.'

'Why is that?' Ari asked.

'Because this event was specifically designed by him,' Fuscus answered happily. 'It is called "The Scourge of Alcyone".'

'It's what?' What did he mean, *scourge of Alcyone*? What did Alcyone have to do with it?

'Senator Vespus has rounded up several Alcyonan sympathisers,' Fuscus explained. 'They are imprisoned below the arena right now in our holding cells.'

'Meropans?' Ari asked.

'Yes, Meropan citizens, but Alcyonan sympathisers.'

'And what is to happen to them?' She dreaded his answer.

'That's the best part'—Fuscus grinned wickedly—'and the part your father is most pleased with. Wearing only rags, they will be brought into the middle of the arena. They won't know what they're there for. I will announce that they are the enemy, the sympathisers of Alcyone, that they seek to undermine our glorious Merope. They will then be doused with pigs' blood. Drums will beat. Two dozen chanters will chant a war chant, and the crowd will be whipped into a frenzy, then we will release eight starving cave lions. The lions will devour the sympathisers before the crowd's eyes, while the drums continue to beat and the chanters continue to chant. It will be glorious!'

Ari did not reply. She stood still. What had she just heard? Somewhere in her mind, barely acknowledged, she wondered if this was the real reason her father had ordered her to oversee the games. As a warning. As a way to serve notice to her about how Alcyonan sympathisers would be treated from now on.

'I would like to see them,' she eventually said, her voice shaky.

'Of course,' Fuscus said with a grin. He had mistaken her shakiness for excitement. 'Come with me; I will lead on.'

Fuscus led Ari off the arena floor and down into the holding cells below. She hadn't been down here before, and now she saw that there were several corridors of cells. They walked past many cells containing procured girls, who looked out at Fuscus with hatred. Eventually, they came to a cell containing five Meropans, dishevelled and bruised, cut and bloody.

'On your feet!' Fuscus ordered.

Reluctantly, and some with difficulty, they stood.

'These are the sympathisers,' Fuscus said, then turned to face them. 'Filthy, anti-Meropan, low-life, Alcyonan-sympathising dogs!' He spat on their cell floor.

Ari walked closer to their cell, partly to get a better view of them, partly to avoid having to look at Fuscus any longer. 'What did you do,' she asked, 'to be imprisoned here?'

'I tried to give a pamphlet to your brother, Professor Quetzl, advocating for the end of the occupation of Alcyone,' one man said. 'We simply staged a peaceful demonstration to state our belief that the occupation is wrong. We have been imprisoned for nothing more than exercising our right to free speech.'

'Just a demonstration at the university?' Ari asked.

'Yes,' the man said. 'All of a sudden, Senator Vespus and several patrollers attacked us with weapons and locked us up, and here we remain. Meropan citizens, locked up for nothing more than stating our opinion.'

Ari knew she had to choose her words carefully. Her own thoughts and feelings had to remain hidden. 'Thank you,' she said, turning to Fuscus. 'For bringing me down here. I don't need to see these enemies of the state any longer.'

She turned away from Fuscus and made her way quickly back down the corridor, then out of the arena. She barely made it outside before a wave of nausea washed over her. She doubled over and retched violently into a bush.

🌙🌙🌙

In the south of the capital, a cage driven by a patroller rolled through the gates. Deor and Sam sat wearily in it, having not slept on the rough ride north. Regardless of that, Deor sat up as the cage rolled into the city.

'Oh …' she said. 'Sam, it's enormous … it's so much bigger than I ever …' Her thought trailed off.

Terraced houses lined the streets here, far grander than the modest homes in the Mid Territory. Meropans in colourful clothing looked with disdain at them as they rolled by. A large domed temple adorned one street corner. A grand set of steps led up to its entrance, which towered above her. Two enormous statues gazed down over the city below: on one side, Pleid, the familiar and archetypal image of him holding a staff of lightning, looked ominously down upon them. On the other side, a sign indicated the statue of Emperor Titavius wearing the military uniform of Merope, with the eagle and flames on his chest. By placing the two statues in this way, equal in height and on the same level at the top of the steps before the grand temple, Titavius was being depicted as the equal of Pleid.

They drove through a square with an enormous waterfall in its centre. A plaque at the front indicated that it had been erected sixteen years earlier to commemorate Merope's victory over Alcyone. At its top and in the centre stood a statue of the Emperor Barritus, also clad in Merope's military uniform. He gazed upwards and into the distance, towards the west, oriented so he stared towards Alcyone.

The patroller drove them further into the city, and Deor leaned back against the bars of the cage. They turned down one street, which headed east. An enormous amphitheatre came into view. Its walls stretched up towards the sky; stone statues of Pleid, Titavius and Barritus adorned the windows along the second and upper levels. It dominated the sky, soaring high above them. With its perfectly circular walls, it was the most impressive structure she'd ever seen.

'Sam …' she said. 'Look at what they've built. We're so far … how can we ever …'

Sam just shook his head. 'I had no idea either, Dee. This is what they've become. It's so much, so much more …'

A woman stood at the entrance, watching them arrive. When they reached her, she called on the patroller to halt.

He obeyed. 'My Lady Arieitis,' the patroller said respectfully, 'how may I assist the daughter of the emperor?'

'Who are these people, and why are they imprisoned?' Arieitis asked.

'They are Alcyonan spies, miss,' the patroller replied. 'They were captured in Remit and have been brought here to be held at your father's leisure. I was informed they were here to attempt to steal back their sister, taken on the Day of Procurement.'

Arieitis turned to look in the cage. Her eyes met Deor's. 'Well,' she asked, 'are you spies?'

Sam spoke up. 'Not technically …' He did not sound convincing. 'Technically we're … travellers? From Alcyone? Thieves, at a stretch?'

Deor groaned. He wasn't helping.

Arieitis looked at them both thoughtfully, then turned back to the patroller. 'Carry on,' she said, 'and I will bring the news of this to my father on your behalf.'

'Thank you, my lady,' the patroller said. 'And I have also been ordered to inform Senator Vespus that they were brought in by Agent Dolus of the Merope Guard. He will be seeking his reward.'

Arieitis nodded. 'You can leave all that to me,' she said. 'I know Agent Dolus personally.'

The patroller drove them on and into the amphitheatre. They went down a ramp and into an underground section. As her eyes adjusted to the lack of light, Deor saw a small, fat man waiting for them.

'Fuscus,' the patroller said, 'these two are Alcyonan spies. They are to be imprisoned here at the emperor's pleasure.'

Fuscus looked them up and down. 'Mountain rats!' he spat.

Deor shuddered. What a disgusting man. He embodied everything she disliked about Merope: he'd grown fat on the bounty of her land and had nothing but hatred in his eyes.

'Throw them in the cells!' Fuscus cried out, spitting again.

The patroller opened a cell door and, gun in hand, ordered Sam inside.

'Dee,' he said, as the door clanged shut behind him. 'Don't do anything stupid, okay? We'll work this out. Somehow. Just stay alive.'

The patroller then trained his gun on Deor and ordered her out of the cage. With the gun so close, she had no other option but to do as she was told. Battling against every instinct she had to fight against this man, she stepped out of the cage. The patroller grabbed her by the arm and hauled her to a cell further up. She wanted to turn, to punch him, to try to get free, but she fought against those instincts. She'd just be shot. Sam was right. Stay alive.

'Get inside!' the patroller said gruffly as he shoved Deor into an empty cell.

She landed on the ground, and he closed the door behind her.

Fuscus looked her up and down with a leer as she got to her feet. 'You're a cute one, for a filthy, stinking mountain rat, aren't you? I might have some fun with you later.'

The patroller smirked.

Deor stared back at him. 'You try it,' she said, 'and I'll break your fat little legs.'

The patroller immediately opened the cell door and stepped inside, taking a baton from his belt. Deor put her hands up to protect herself, but the patroller struck her with the baton, hard on her head. Everything went black.

CHAPTER 22

Arieitis barged into her father's study, surprising him. Many things bothered her, and many of them conflicted in her mind. She loved Merope, believed in Merope and believed in Titus, but what she had seen today shocked her. She'd always believed that the situation in Alcyone was not ideal, but she'd been told that it was a joint relationship that benefited Alcyone. What was the real story? Feeding sympathisers to cave lions? Alcyonan spies trying to infiltrate the capital? Was this a joint relationship or the beginnings of a war? She knew, though, that whatever conflicts she felt, she couldn't betray her thoughts to her father.

'Arieitis,' Barritus said, looking up from some papers. 'Come in, Daughter. I am surprised to see you so soon. Did you meet with Fuscus?'

'That's what I have come to speak to you about,' she said in a flurry and a fluster. 'Fuscus is *useless!* The games will be a disaster if he is left to manage them! He has vaguely organised events but has seen none of the athletes and practised nothing. He waddles around the stadium, spitting and hissing from his bloated lips, organising nothing and doing nothing. They will be a shambles if he is left in charge.'

'Well, that is why I sent you to check on him,' Barritus said. 'What do you suggest?'

'I suggest you put me in charge, and he can assist me. I will give the orders. He can carry them out and report back to me. We only have two days, including today, until it opens. We have to act now.'

Barritus looked at her thoughtfully. She couldn't read his thoughts, nor interpret his facial expressions. She'd never been able to do that with her father. She loved him and sometimes feared him, but she didn't feel she knew or understood him. They were very different individuals. She had no real idea what he was thinking.

'That could be a very good idea, Daughter,' Barritus eventually said. 'Okay, then, I will put you in charge of organising the games from here out. He will answer to you. Tell him that I have authorised this.'

'Thank you, Father,' she said, relieved. 'There is one other matter, though. There were two new prisoners brought into the holding cells today from Alcyone.'

Barritus sat straighter, his full attention focused on Ari. 'From Alcyone? Who are they? What happened?'

'They're a brother and sister, here to attempt to take back their younger sister, who was taken on the Day of Procurement.'

'Their sister?' Barritus tilted his head, appearing even more interested. 'Did you get her name? Or their names? Or their father's name?'

Ari shook her head. Why the interest in their names? 'No. I did not. But they are being held in the cells, and I need to get back there to keep organising the games. I can find all that out.'

'I will come with you,' Barritus said decisively. 'And we

will get Vespus on the way. How were they captured?'

'Agent Dolus of the Guard captured them in Remit. Presumably, they were headed to Titus from there. I don't know how they got to Remit, though. That's the heart of Merope. They would've had to go through a lot of towns unrecognised to make it there.'

'Not if they came another way,' Barritus said thoughtfully. After a moment, he picked up on something she'd just said. 'Agent Dolus, you say?'

'Yes …' Ari said cautiously.

'Weren't you and he …'

'For a short while …' she said quietly.

(((

A short time later, Arieitis, Barritus and Vespus arrived at the amphitheatre, where they were met by Fuscus.

'Take us to the new Alcyonan prisoners,' Barritus ordered, striding past him. 'And also, from now until after the games, Arieitis is in charge of preparations. You answer to her. Understood?'

'Yes, my lord,' Fuscus said, staring at the ground ahead of him.

'What do you know about the prisoners?' Barritus asked.

'They are brother and sister,' said Fuscus, walking quickly to keep up and directing the group down the correct path. 'From the Mid Territory. Mountain rats. Their names are Deor and Sammu.'

'Here to attempt to take back their sister, I am told?'

'Yes,' Fuscus said, 'though I don't know which one that is. They would not tell me. I beat them both, but they wouldn't give me a name.'

Vespus nodded. 'I'll wager I know which one she is,' he hissed.

Ari's skin went cold as he spoke.

They arrived at Deor's cell. Ari recognised her from earlier, but noted she now had a mark across her face. She had been hit with something.

'On your feet, mountain rat!' Fuscus ordered.

Deor stood.

'That's enough, Fuscus,' Barritus said. 'I'll take it from here. What is your name?'

'My name is Deor,' she said. 'I'm from the Mid Territory of Alcyone. I have broken none of your laws. I have done nothing wrong. Let me go free.'

'Nothing wrong?' Barritus laughed. 'I'll be the judge of that. Why are you soiling Meropan lands with your presence, you and your brother? Why are you here?'

'Our business is our own,' said Deor determinedly.

Ari watched her closely. There was strength in Deor, an inner fire that burned within her and fuelled her.

'Your business is not your own!' Barritus roared. 'Your business is the business of the Meropan Empire! Nothing that you do—nothing—is your own! Do you understand?'

Deor, who until now had not looked at Barritus, turned to look at him. Anger burned in her eyes; it flowed from beneath the surface, from deep within. She stared into Barritus' eyes, and in a voice deeper and full of unwavering courage, said, 'My business is not the business of Merope!'

Deor held Barritus' gaze with her own, and neither spoke for several seconds. Just briefly, Ari saw on her father's face a slight quizzical aspect. Something about Deor surprised him.

'Mountain rat,' Vespus said eventually, breaking the spell, 'we know who you are.'

'You don't know anything about me,' Deor retorted, barely glancing at Vespus.

'Oh, I don't doubt that,' Vespus said. 'However, we know who you are. And your brother. And your sister … Sage.'

A change came over Deor at the sound of that name. Fear and panic washed over her strong and defiant countenance.

'Oh yes'—Vespus smiled and moved closer to the cell— 'we know you are here to try to rescue her. We took her, your sweet little sister, on the Day of Procurement. We took her, and she is now the property of Merope. She belongs to us now. And you know what? In Merope Week, I am going to buy her. She will be my property. She will be mine to do with as I please, and believe me, rat, I will do as I please …'

The fear vanished in Deor, replaced by an uncontrollable, visceral rage, an anger boiling up from deep inside her. With incredible speed, Deor lunged through the bars of the cage and grabbed Vespus by his throat. Screaming, she grabbed him with her right hand and squeezed hard, choking him, but Fuscus smashed her arm with his baton, breaking her hold. She withdrew her arm quickly, holding it in pain.

Vespus held his throat, shocked and hurt. He coughed violently, and fear broke through his usual calm, calculated demeanour.

Ari couldn't help but smile a little.

'My Lord,' Vespus eventually said, when the coughing had subsided. He turned to Barritus, trying to recover his composure. 'I have a suggestion.' The two of them conferred quietly for a few moments.

Barritus eventually nodded in agreement. 'We have decided on your fate, Deor of Alcyone,' Barritus said, the slightest of smiles coming onto his face.

The smile on Ari's face disappeared.

'My fate?' Deor said, still holding her arm in pain. 'You decided my fate a long time ago when you invaded my land!'

The smile on Barritus' face increased. 'Oh yes, we did. At least, in that respect, the fate of your people. You are the tools of Merope. Nothing more. I think you understand that well. I suspect you understand your plight better than most of your people, in fact. However, today we have decided your fate as an individual. You will have your chance to win your freedom.'

'How?' Deor's eyes narrowed with distrust.

'How? In the games, of course. You will get the chance to win your freedom by fighting in the games. You will be the main event of night two. You will fight against your brother, a fight to the death, with the winner gaining their freedom and a return to Alcyone. The loser's dead body will be fed to the cave lions.'

'You're kidding me …' Ari heard the words spoken and assumed Deor had said them. It took her a moment to realise she had said it, but she covered it quickly. 'That is an incredible idea! We will not only show that we are powerful, Father, but that we are also merciful.'

'That's right.' Barritus nodded and smiled at Ari. 'The might and power of Merope is not to be trifled with, and those who would seek to undermine us will be punished, but we can also show mercy. One of these two, either this girl or her brother, will get to go home. After they have killed the other in combat.'

Ari dared not look directly at Deor, but in her peripheral vision, she saw her staring at Barritus in shock, but not responding.

'And don't get any ideas about not fighting,' Vespus said, standing well back from the cell this time, 'because if you refuse to fight, you'll both be slaughtered for our entertainment.'

'Excellent,' Fuscus said, turning to Ari. 'Should I add it to the schedule as the main event for night two?'

'Yes, right away,' said Ari authoritatively. Fuscus began taking some notes. 'And when you've done that, I want you to go to the training camp outside the city, inspect everything, including the slaves who are being trained there. Speak to them, find out if they're actually interested in fighting or if we are going to have a legion of cowards running away from one another. Demand a display of their fighting abilities, a dry run. When you're done with that, visit the riders and get them organised for a practice run here tomorrow. Is all of that clear?'

'Yes, my lady,' said Fuscus dutifully.

Barritus looked on with an approving smile. This was the kind of Meropan her father wanted her to be. She would have to keep the façade up.

'I'll walk you out,' Ari said, guiding her father and Vespus away. Fuscus followed them out of the stadium.

'Keep up the good work in there, Ari,' Barritus said approvingly. 'And you, Fuscus, make sure you follow all her instructions.'

'Yes, my lord,' Fuscus said through gritted teeth.

Barritus and Vespus walked away, leaving Ari and Fuscus alone. 'Well?' Ari asked. 'Don't you have a facility to inspect?'

'Right away, my lady.' His words were obedient, but his expression betrayed him. A man like Fuscus, convinced he is superior just by virtue of being a man, hated having to concede and defer to her. To a man like Fuscus, women were only things to pleasure him, not to give him orders. However, Fuscus was not stupid enough to defy the orders of the emperor's daughter, and he proved that as he turned and headed for the city gate to the south, leaving Ari alone.

She watched the short, fat Fuscus until he walked out of her sight, then she turned and walked back into the amphitheatre. She walked past cell after cell holding girls taken on the Day of Procurement, many of them crying or seemingly about to resume doing so. All of them had a look of misery or despair on their faces. Most of them looked away, frightened or intimidated. The occasional one looked back at her with anger, though, or defiance. One girl, however, stood out to Ari. She watched Ari walk past with a thoughtful look on her face.

It was clear, though, that none of the procured girls wanted to be there. Ari had never seen this aspect of Meropan life before. Her father and the senex propagated the idea that the girls who were taken from Alcyone were getting a better life, that they were happy to be here in Titus, that Merope was doing them a favour. Looking at the faces of these girls now, though, Ari was not convinced of that. She thought of Missy, taken five years ago, who her father had purchased. Was she like this when she was taken? Were they really giving them a better life?

Inevitably, Ari found herself making her way back to Deor's cell. She didn't know anything about her, but she needed to. She felt inside herself that there were things she needed to find out, and that perhaps Deor could give her some answers. She didn't know if Deor would be receptive to a conversation with her, but she had to try.

'Deor,' she said when she arrived at her cell.

Deor looked up from where she sat on the small stone platform that was supposed to pass as a bed. 'What do you want …? Arieitis, is it?' Deor asked.

'Yes, but call me Ari, please. I just want to talk. Will you talk with me for a little? My father and Vespus and Fuscus have all gone now; I thought we could have a conversation.'

Deor looked pointedly at Ari and rose and walked to the bars. Ari did not move away from her, even though Deor had already shown her speed and strength with great purpose. Deor walked all the way up to the bars so that their faces were separated only by those bars. If Deor wanted to, she could easily choke Ari, like she had Vespus. And there was no one around to stop her. She could choke the life right out of her. Right now. Ari was putting her trust in Deor's better nature. However, Deor didn't lunge for Ari; she just studied her eyes, and Ari held Deor's gaze.

'You can learn a lot from a person's eyes,' Deor said. 'When you know what you're looking for.'

'Oh, yes?' Ari said. 'And what are you looking for in my eyes?'

Deor just smiled slightly in reply.

'Why are you here in Titus?' Ari asked.

'You've already heard that,' Deor said, continuing to study Ari's eyes. 'We came here to rescue my sister, Sage. Meropan patrollers took her on the Day of Procurement. She is not Meropan property. She is our sister, and we are here to take her back.'

'I understand that,' Ari said. 'You care for your sister; you do not want any harm to come to her. Do you not think she would have a good life here, though, in Titus? Do you not think she would be looked after? Fed? Housed? Kept in good health?'

'Not if that man Vespus has his way!' Deor said bluntly. 'Did you hear what he said?'

'Yes, well, Vespus is a vile man. A despicable, vile man. But he is a man of great power. We are not all like him, though. I have an Alcyonan woman who attends me; she came to us five years ago; her name is Missy. She is well looked after in our house. She is well fed, has a comfortable room that she shares with one other and even has some free time once a week, every week.'

Deor laughed and shook her head.

'Why do you laugh?' Ari asked. 'I mean it; Missy is well looked after here. I think of her more as my friend than my servant. Is that a bad thing?'

'I laugh because it doesn't matter if she's well looked after! It doesn't matter if she's well fed, or has a nice bed, or has *free time*, or anything else. None of that matters! You know why?'

'Why?' Ari asked, perplexed.

'Because it was not her choice to come here! Because she was taken against her will! Because humans have the right to decide their own fate. I have the right to decide my fate. You have the right to decide yours. The dignity of the human spirit transcends Titus; it transcends Merope; it transcends all the laws your father and that other vile man put into place. I believe, and great societies have been built on this premise, that humans have fundamental rights that exist before and above any human-made laws or rules or ideals. And the right of a person to choose the path of their own life is paramount among those rights. The right to self-determination. It comes first, before anything else. Before laws. Before rules. Before men like your father. Right now, no Alcyonans have the right to determine their path, because we are an invaded and occupied people. Merope, with all its strength and all its might, still has no right to assert its will over the birthright of Alcyonan people to their own self-determination. This invasion is an invasion of what is our right by birth. And your servant? Missy? You therefore had no right to take her, regardless of how well fed she is, or whether she gets *free time*.'

Ari took a step back. No one in Merope had spoken to her like this about these sorts of things. Regardless of whether Merope improved the lives of Alcyonans or otherwise, could they be beyond their rights, as a people, to occupy their territory?

'Merope doesn't recognise that rights exist for the individual,' Ari eventually said. 'We make laws, and people must obey them. As long as they obey them, they are free to do as they please. That is self-determination, is it not?'

'It is the illusion of self-determination,' Deor said. 'Tell me, what would happen if citizens of Titus spoke out against your father or the senex? What would happen to them?'

Ari thought about the Meropans who were being held in another cell, waiting to be fed to cave lions on night one of the games. She knew what happened when people spoke out against the state. 'The illusion of self-determination,' she said to herself, lost in thought.

'While Merope imposes its will on the people, no one is truly free,' Deor continued. 'We are not free in Alcyone, we are—as your father called us—tools of Merope. Nothing more. Used as instruments to mine and grow and capture the fruits and bounty of our land, for the consumption of the ever-expanding Titus and Merope. No choice in what we can do with our lives, no options open to us, no right to keep the things that belong to us by virtue of being Alcyonan. We are allowed to live, in bondage, so long as we keep doing what we are told.'

'It is the same here in Titus …' Ari felt energy drain from her as realisations set in. 'There are Meropans held in another cell for being Alcyonan sympathisers. They are to be slaughtered on night one of the games.'

'So that's what happens when you push back against the will of Merope,' Deor said quietly. 'It seems Alcyonans are not the only ones whose rights have been invaded. While Merope is able to force people to bend to its will, then no one is free, not Alcyonans or Meropans. Everyone is a tool of Titus, a tool of the empire. Whether free or servant, Alcyonan or Meropan: all tools of the powerful few. Food for the immortals.'

Ari felt unsteady on her feet. This is how it really was for the people of Alcyone. The barriers she had erected between herself and the truth tumbled down, shattered by the plain truth in Deor's words. She felt helpless, small against the might of the city she called home. What could she ever do against the power of men like her father and Vespus? Deor was right; the only way that she—or anyone in Titus—survived was by doing what the men in power told them. She had known this in some way all her life.

'Right to self-determination,' Ari said. 'Before law. What did you mean when you said that great societies have been built on those ideals?'

Deor looked at her closely. 'I meant great societies in other places. Not Merope, not Alcyone … I mean on Nebra.' As she spoke, Deor revealed a birthmark in the shape of two moons on her shoulder.

Ari couldn't speak. Her mouth felt dry, as if she could never utter a word again. 'What … what is that?' she eventually asked.

'That is the two moons of Nebra,' Deor replied. 'That is where I came from, before I was here. Have you seen it before?'

Ari felt like the earth shifted under her feet, like she could fall through it if she even moved slightly. Her head spun as well, and she felt like she might fall over. She held one of the bars to steady herself, then slowly reached down, feeling as though she hovered outside of herself watching her own movements. She moved her skirt down slightly, revealing the birthmark on her hip: the same two moons.

CHAPTER 23

Deor stared at the two-moons birthmark on Arieitis' hip. She had felt something, something deep within her; that's why she'd revealed her own birthmark and mentioned Nebra. When she'd first seen Arieitis, she knew something else was under the surface; she'd sensed it. Then, when she'd studied her eyes up close, she knew it. She could see it.

Now, as Arieitis stood before her, no doubt herself feeling a range of emotions, Deor had a flashback to Nebra again. It was brief, but clear, and of their final moments on the last day. They were branding one another with the two-moons symbol. She saw who Arieitis had been. 'Nikita …' Deor whispered.

'Nikita?' Arieitis asked, looking pale. More than that, though, Deor could see that Ari recognised the name, somewhere inside herself.

'Ari,' Deor said, 'do you have any recurring dreams?'

Ari looked afraid of this conversation. Deor knew what she felt, understood her emotions. Ari already knew where Deor was going; Deor could see it in her eyes. Part of Ari did not want to hear this, because she knew that it would upset her entire world view. Her world was about to be flipped over, and Deor felt empathy for that. As much as part of Deor wished she didn't know about her Nebran past, she also knew that she had to know. And Ari would be feeling the same way, Deor was sure of it.

Ari's expression revealed her anxiety. 'I do have recurring dreams. One in particular of fire and destruction. I am in it, with six others, and we're at some place that is burning up. I am there, but it's not me; I am someone else.'

'Nikita …' Deor said.

'Nikita … Yes, that was my name. How do you know this? What was that place?'

'That was Nebra. That was where we lived, and died, before this life. You were a warrior named Nikita.'

'It burned in a war, didn't it …?' Arieitis asked.

'Yes, it burned, and we all died.'

'And you were there in the dream,' Arieitis said. 'I saw you get that brand on your shoulder, the birthmark. I saw it happen. I can see it now in my mind. Another woman gave it to you, and you gave her one, on her forehead. She was an oracle.'

Deor nodded. 'Her name was Pythus, my name was—'

'Lore,' Ari said. 'Your name was Lore. You were our leader.'

'Yes.' Deor nodded again. 'My name was Lore. That was Nebra; that was the life before this.'

'Part of me has always known,' Ari said. Some colour had returned to her face. 'I've always felt that there was something else, something before this, some other time, and that I couldn't quite get to it or remember it. That there was another past, somewhere in my mind. And the dream of fire and destruction on Nebra, that dream was always so real that it didn't feel like a dream.'

'More like a vision or a memory?'

'Yes, like that, more like a memory. Dreams are more fanciful, less real, and they don't stay with you very long unless you write them down straight away. This dream has stayed with me all of my life.'

'Because you lived it,' Deor said, 'because you were there, with me, with the last seven of us. On the final day of Nebra.'

Ari looked down, nodding gently. It was sinking in. She was understanding her past. However, Ari needed one more little push to fully understand.

'Ari,' Deor began gently, 'do you remember who we fought in the war? Who the enemy was?'

Ari looked up. She hadn't considered this. She frowned, trying to remember. 'We fought … the war … It was a long way from here, wasn't it? Another planet. It wasn't here. And we fought … I can't remember.'

'That's okay,' Deor said. 'I'm not an oracle like Pythus; I can't regress you to help you see. But perhaps you'll recognise the name … the war was fought with Remus, after they invaded us.'

'Remus …' Ari's eyes widened as something unlocked in her mind. 'Yes … They invaded. The war went on for years … Both planets perished.'

'That's right, we burned alive while Remus froze. We sent one another to hell. The thing is, Ari, it's beginning all over again. All of us, both Alcyone and Merope, we are all people reborn from Nebra or Remus. Both peoples have come here to start new civilisations, but the past is repeating itself. The invasion of Alcyone—it's all happening again.'

A look of shock spread across Ari's face as the ramifications of this began to sink in. 'Wait,' she said, as she thought it through, 'you're saying that everyone here is reborn from Nebra or Remus? And the war is—so the invasion by

Merope … Meropans are Remusans reborn? And Alcyonans are Nebrans reborn?'

'Yes, for the most part, though you're an exception,' Deor said. 'And there are others. One who betrayed us, an Alcyonan, he was Remusan in his last life.' At the thought of Dolus, anger again rose within Deor. She pushed it down, though, needing to focus on what was happening now.

'Most people probably don't know it, though,' she continued, 'and maybe don't even feel any of it. You felt it and had dreams of it. Others are like that too, but I've been told by Pythus, who in this life is called Eve, that everyone here is reborn from Nebra or Remus.'

The colour drained from Ari's face again as more things began to sink in. 'That means my father …'

'Your father, the emperor. Ari, you have to be ready to confront the fact that he was very likely part of the Remusan forces that destroyed us. Most of the people you know were probably once your enemy. Our enemy.'

'Oh no …' Ari said. 'They won't stop, you know. I hear the things my father and Vespus and others say about Alcyone and your people. They won't stop.'

'I know,' Deor said. 'And that's why we have to do something before Alcyone is completely destroyed. Right now, we are occupied by Merope, but it will only go in one direction from here unless Alcyone can fight back. War may be unavoidable.'

'We need to get you out …' Ari said, thinking more quickly. 'We need to get you out of Merope. You will die here if you stay. They'll make you fight in the arena with your brother, and when you both refuse to fight, they'll kill you. They'll most certainly kill you, Deor.'

'Then help me, Ari,' Deor said. 'Help me get out of here

with my brother Sam. We need to get out of here and we must find our sister. Please, help us do this.'

'Your sister?' Ari asked. 'Of course, your sister. You are here to rescue her! She is here, Deor, in the cells too, she and all the procured girls. They are all here.'

'Sage is here …?' A sliver of hope opened up in Deor's heart. Sage was here in the cells of the amphitheatre. They could get out. With Ari's help, they could escape and try to get home to Alcyone.

'They all are. All the girls who were taken.'

'Then, please, I beg you, Ari, help us. There has to be a way to get us out.'

'If we are to do this,' Ari said, pacing as she thought, 'it has to be soon. The games start the day after tomorrow. It has to be before that, or there're going to be too many people around. And it will have to be done before first light. We can't escape the city in the night, as it will be locked down. All the gates in the city walls are shut each night. We would have to escape before first light and leave through the western gate at dawn.'

Though talking of escape, Arieitis kept saying *we* rather than *you*.

'Yes. Can we do this?' Deor asked.

'We have to. I can't let you stay here. I can't let you be killed.'

'Ari, do you know what you're risking, though?'

Ari gulped. 'Oh, don't worry, I know who they are. I know what I am risking—my life.'

'Thank you, Ari.' Deor felt extremely humbled and grateful that Ari was willing to take up arms on her behalf, to risk her life for her, and for Sam and Sage.

'It is my duty, not just because of what happened on Nebra, but as a human being now, here. To let anything else happen would be a failure by me as a human.'

'Thank you …' Deor said again.

'Deor,' Ari said, 'there is one other thing, though.'

'Yes?'

'My attendant, Missy. Five years ago, I chose her. My father said I could choose an attendant when I was thirteen, and I felt a connection with Missy from the moment I met her, after she had been procured and brought here. I know now why I felt that connection, Deor. Missy also has the two-moons birthmark.'

CHAPTER 24

Ari was in a rush; she had to move fast. 'Missy!' she yelled when she located her in the villa. Then she checked herself and looked around. She couldn't risk others hearing. Missy was putting clothes away in Ari's bedroom. The light still streamed in from outside, but the shadows it cast were getting longer.

'What is it, Ari?' Missy asked nervously, pausing with the clothes.

'No time to explain! Just come with me!'

Ari led Missy out of their villa carefully so as not to arouse suspicion. Thankfully, Veronica was nowhere to be seen. She quickly led Missy back towards the amphitheatre. Fuscus would be back sometime soon. She had to bring Missy to see Deor before he came back and became suspicious.

'That birthmark on your foot,' Ari said as they hurried along. 'I've never really asked you about it. But I have the same birthmark. Until today, I've never known why. I just assumed it was coincidence, some sort of relatively minor birth defect.'

'You have it too?' Missy asked. 'Where?'

Ari pulled down the waistband of her skirt and lifted her

light shirt up slightly to show Missy her birthmark on her hip.

Missy's eyes widened. 'What does it mean, though?'

'Do you ever have dreams?' Ari said. 'Not normal ones, but ones that seem very real, more like a memory? And do you have them repeatedly?'

Missy looked perplexed, but nodded in reply. 'I have a couple of them, actually. One of them I don't like at all. I die in it.'

'Where are you in that dream? Here in Titus? Or somewhere else?'

'No.' Missy appeared uncomfortable at the memory of the dream. 'It's somewhere else, somewhere I don't know. And I'm there, but I'm not me. I'm someone else.'

'Fire and destruction?'

Missy stopped, eyes wide with shock. 'How do you know this?'

'Later,' Ari said and beckoned Missy into the amphitheatre and down to the cells. They rounded a corner and suddenly stood in front of Deor's cell. Missy and Deor locked eyes. Neither spoke. They just looked at one another in shock. Missy's face turned as pale as a summer cloud.

'Arunet ...' Deor eventually said. 'Is that you?'

'Deor?'

Deor reached for Missy through the bars, tears in her eyes. They embraced through the bars, the bond of childhood broken by a five-year gap, but unbroken in their hearts.

'You're alive!' Deor cried. 'I'm so happy you're alive!'

'What are you doing here?' Missy asked. 'Why are you in prison?'

'They took Sage. On the Day of Procurement. Sam and I are here to rescue her.'

'Looks to me like you're the one who needs the rescuing!'

Missy chuckled a little through her tears.

Ari smiled at the appearance of the cheekiness in Missy. She usually kept it in check, apart from the rare occasions when she let her guard down.

'She sure is,' Ari said. 'And I don't want to cut short your reunion, but we have very little time to discuss things. Fuscus is going to return soon, so we can't stay. Me bringing Missy here to visit an Alcyonan prisoner will be viewed with great suspicion. Missy, can you show Deor your birthmark?'

Missy removed her shoe and showed Deor her two-moons birthmark.

'I never knew...' Deor said. 'Did you not notice mine, when we were kids?'

'I did,' Missy replied, 'but I never brought it up. I was kind of ashamed of having a birthmark, so I hid it from view, and I didn't mention yours. Mostly yours was hidden under your clothing anyway.'

'Yes, it was, mostly,' Deor said, 'for the same reason.'

'In my dream,' Ari said, 'I gave you the brand on your foot, Missy. But I can't remember what your name was.'

'Her name was Phela,' Deor said.

'Yes ...' Missy nodded thoughtfully. 'I know that name ... Phela. I think you're right. But why are we all having the same dream?'

'Because it really happened,' Deor said. 'In our last life. We were all there together, the three of us and four others, on another planet called Nebra. We all died there, and we all branded one another with the two moons so we wouldn't forget. So we would remember and see each another again in this life, while attempting to rebuild Nebran society here on Earth.'

'Nebra ... yes ...' Missy nodded thoughtfully.

Ari knew what she was experiencing, because she'd experienced it herself not one hour ago. Memories of Nebra were unlocking in her mind. In the time it had taken her to get from the amphitheatre to home and back again, other memories had opened up in Ari's mind. Memories of her family and her life on Nebra.

'And, Missy,' Ari said, drawing her back to the present, 'this is why we have to get Deor out. And Sam. And Sage. We have to get them all out of here, and get the three of them back to Alcyone.'

'Back to Alcyone?' Missy asked.

Ari nodded. 'Yes. And, Missy, this is the most important thing. You need to think carefully about this: I need to know if you want to go with them, to go back to Alcyone.'

'You want to know if I want to help break Deor, Sam and Sage out of these cells and flee Titus, back to Alcyone?'

'Yes.'

'We'll be killed!' Fear flooded Missy's voice. 'Especially us from Alcyone! They'll torture us first, then kill us!'

'If Deor and Sam stay in these cells, they will die,' Ari said, trying to remain calm. It was vital that Missy understood the gravity of the situation. 'They are going to be forced to fight to the death on night two of the games. And if they don't fight, they'll both be killed.'

'Oh no …' Missy's eyes widened in horror as the enormity of Deor's situation sank in.

'So I need to know, Missy, are you in? Will you help me break Deor and her brother and sister out of here and outside the city walls? With me with them, we can get them through the west gate, and we should be able to get them across the border. It'll be a day's hike.'

'And what from there?' Missy asked. 'Do you mean I

would have my freedom? What if your father finds out?'

'He will find out,' Ari said, 'but hopefully not before we're long gone from Titus. We'll cut across country to avoid towns. I used to explore that countryside as a girl; I know some ways. My father doesn't know this, but I've been to the Alcyone border before, several times. I used to ride there in the morning and return in the evening.'

Missy's jaw dropped. 'You did what?'

'There's a lot of things my father doesn't know about me …' Ari had explored those borders many times, always feeling a pull there, though she never knew why.

'Including that you were Nebran in your last life,' Deor said.

Ari nodded. 'Including that, and we're not letting him find out about it … So, Missy, are you coming with us?'

'Am I coming with you … Ari … are you planning on leaving Merope as well? Will you go with Deor into Alcyone?'

'Yes, that's what I want to do,' Ari said. 'If Deor will have me. I can't live in Titus any longer.'

'Then I'm going with you,' Missy said. 'After all, I am your attendant.'

'No, Missy'—Ari had thought about this also—'you are not my attendant. Not anymore. In fact, I will no longer use your servant name, Missy. Your name is Arunet. I never knew that. We never should have taken you from Alcyone. All of this has to end. All of it.'

'When will we do this, then?' Deor asked.

'The morning after tomorrow,' Ari replied. 'Day one of Merope Week and the games. The day of the summer solstice, so the day will be longest. There'll be a service at dawn in the new forum dedicated to the temple of Pleid at the western wall. So people will be out early. That will help us to blend in. We'll need to leave early, before dawn. I need some time to plan this properly. Arunet, let's get home quickly, before anyone realises that you're gone.'

Arunet again hugged Deor through the bars of the cell, and Ari did the same.

'Thank you, Ari,' Deor said.

'Don't thank me yet. You can thank me when we're safely over the border.' As she said this, Ari instinctively turned to her left. Something was there in the shadows. She sensed something. Ari strained to look, but she couldn't see anyone. 'Who is there?' she called out and hurried up to the end of the corridor, but there was no one there. She looked around the corner and saw shadows moving at the end of the corridor, but again, nobody was there.

'What is it?' Arunet asked.

'I don't know. I thought I saw someone; I'm not sure. Maybe it was nothing.'

CHAPTER 25

The night was at its darkest, but Sage lay awake in her cell. The bed was hard, more a bench than a bed, so sleep was sporadic and restless anyway. The girls in the other cells were quiet, and so was the corridor. The guard had been quiet for a good while. Probably asleep now. The other three girls in her cell were also asleep, though Anthea, the girl from the Mid North, never slept much and never deeply. Even when she was asleep, Anthea tossed restlessly, turning and muttering. Her words were always distressed, even when they made no sense. There was no peace in Anthea. What had her life been like back home?

Sage waited a little longer, but no sound came from outside, so she quietly rose from her small bed. Noiselessly, she took the key from her pocket and opened the lock. She opened the door fractionally, slipped out into the corridor, and shut it again. The corridor was empty in both directions. At one end was the guardroom, its door closed.

Her heart beat hard in her chest, but Sage tiptoed down the corridor away from the guardroom, staying close to the cells on her side of the corridor. If the guard woke and came out, the shadows would hide her—hopefully. In the cells she passed, the girls all slept. She only dared glance into their cells as she crept by. Let sleeping Alcyonans lie.

The dirt floor kept her footfalls fairly silent, though her feet would be dirty when she returned. But she hadn't washed since being taken from Alcyone, so that didn't matter. Everything was dirt down in these cells, from the floor to their feet and hands and a covering of it on their clothes. She rounded a corner into a new corridor of cells, making a mental note of which way she'd gone. She sneaked down this new corridor, looking inside each cell briefly to see who was there. A rumour had spread from cell to cell about two prisoners from Alcyone. In this corridor, no luck; all were occupied by girls who had been procured. Sage turned right again into a new corridor, again mentally noting her path. She crept along it, and in the third cell down saw a man lying on his bed. Her heart leapt in her chest. Joy and sadness fought for attention inside her, as even in the dim light, she could make out his face.

'Sam!' she whispered. 'Sam, wake up!'

Sam, only half asleep, sat up in his bed. 'Sage?' he whispered, sounding confused and excited. 'Am I dreaming? Is that you?'

Sage produced the key from her pocket and tried it in the lock. Perhaps one key controlled all locks; perhaps there were different keys for different sections. No way of knowing except to try.

'What are you doing here?' Sam whispered, coming to the cell door.

Sage turned the key in the lock. It opened! She thrust the door open and hugged her brother tight.

'What are YOU doing here?' Sage whispered back.

'Rescuing you!' Sam said, trying not to laugh at the

absurdity of his comment.

'Well,' Sage whispered, 'I'm the one with the key. It looks like I'm here to rescue you! Is Deor here too?'

Sam nodded. 'Yes, they caught us both. We were making our way here to save you, and Dolus betrayed us to the patrollers.'

'Oh no … Where's Deor?'

'I don't know. All I know is that when they put me in here, they took her further down this corridor.'

'Well, come on, then'—Sage led her brother into the corridor—'let's go and find her!'

Noiselessly, they crept down the corridor past more procured girls. One of them sat up and looked at Sage in shock, but she didn't speak. In the last cell of the block lay a sleeping woman.

'Deor!' Sage whispered. 'Deor, wake up!'

Deor sat up in bed. A look of shock and surprise flooded her face, immediately replaced by happiness. 'Sage!' she whispered back. 'How are you here? Sam! Sam, what's going on?'

'We're breaking out, that's what's going on!' Sage tried the key in the door, and again it opened the lock. She led Sam into Deor's cell, and all three rushed to hug one another. Nobody spoke as they held one another for what seemed like minutes. Deor had tears on her face, but Sage did not. They had a breakout to accomplish.

'No time for crying, big sister!' Sage said. 'We need to work out how to get out of here! I'm here to rescue you both!'

Deor laughed a little louder than she intended to. 'We do,' she said, 'but we can't just leave now; we'll be caught for certain in the daylight. We have to have a plan, and I have some good news.'

'Can't we just escape now?' Sage asked.

'No, we can't. This way is better, Sage,' Deor said. 'Trust me. I can't explain it all now, but just be ready tomorrow night when it's getting towards dawn. I have an ally who will help us escape. An hour or two before dawn. But Sage, how did you get a key?'

'I stole it from the guard.' She grinned, knowing Deor would be proud of that.

Deor laughed. 'Of course you did! You're incredible, Sage! But we can't leave right now; it won't work. We stay in our cells tonight and stay out of trouble. And Sage, I'm going to need that key.'

The three siblings headed back out into the corridor. Sage led them around to Sam's cell. 'Look at us!' she whispered. 'We're reverse escapees! Whoever heard of people trying to break *into* a jail cell?!'

Sam snuck into his cell, and Sage locked the door behind him as quietly as she could. She whispered goodbye to him, then led Deor back around to her corridor. They tiptoed past the cells of sleeping girls, but when they reached the cell next to Sage's, a girl sat up in bed and spotted them.

The girl stood. 'You're out of your cell … You're escaping … Please, take me with you!'

Sage shushed her. She was being far too loud. Others were stirring in their beds.

'Take me with you!' the girl called out, louder this time.

'Be quiet!' Deor hissed at her. 'We are not escaping!'

They needed to be quiet or the guard would wake, but others woke and joined in the call.

'Take me with you!' said one from the cell opposite.

'Let me out! I want to go home!' said another.

Within moments, a dozen or more girls were pleading for rescue, making a racket. Sage looked at Deor. Her sister was glancing from cell to cell with a panicked expression. They couldn't quiet them all down at once, but Sage had an idea. Moving quickly, she opened her cell door and let herself back in. Anthea sat up in bed, watching, and the other two girls were waking. Sage quickly locked the door behind her and turned to Deor.

'Deor!' she whispered. 'Catch!' Sage tossed the key to Deor, who caught it as she turned. 'Go!'

A yell came from the guardroom. The guard, woken by the cacophony, flung open his door.

Deor mouthed the word 'Goodbye' … and promptly vanished.

A collective gasp of shock came from the girls in the cells nearby.

The patroller stormed down the corridor. 'What is all this racket?' he demanded. 'Who is responsible for this?'

One of the girls in the cell opposite pointed across at Sage. 'That girl was out of her cell!' she yelled.

The little cow …

The patroller turned to Sage. 'Were you out of your cell, little maggot?' he said.

'She was!' the girl across the corridor called out. 'And there was another woman with her, and that woman disappeared! She vanished!'

The patroller turned away from Sage to the girl across the corridor. 'What the hell are you talking about?'

'She vanished into thin air!'

Other girls called out in agreement, supporting her.

'She vanished!' yelled one.

'She was right there!'

'What do you mean, she vanished into thin air?' the patroller yelled, turning from cell to cell in confusion.

'She did!' yelled another.

'I think she was a ghost!' cried another girl.

The patroller spun from person to person, trying to make sense of what they were saying. Eventually, a thought occurred to him. He came to Sage's cell and tried the lock. It was locked. He turned to face the rest of the cells. 'How did she get out of her cell if the door is locked?' he yelled.

'She had a key!' one yelled.

'She threw it to the ghost!' yelled another.

Other girls tried to answer, but he yelled them down. 'Silence!' he roared. The girls fell silent. 'I don't know what game you're playing at, but it stops now! The next girl who makes a sound gets the rod!' He took his baton from his belt and held it up threateningly. No one dared speak. Sage watched as the girls across the corridor began slinking back to their beds.

'And you, mountain rat,' the guard said, turning to Sage, 'I've got my eye on you.' He turned and walked back down the corridor towards the guardroom.

Sage let out a breath at last as the guard got further away. That was close. She looked to where Deor had been. A faint trace of footprints appeared in the dirt, heading back towards her cell.

CHAPTER 26

The morning before the opening of the games dawned bright and clear in Titus. Ari welcomed this. She enjoyed the sunshine greatly, and as she walked down the strata alongside her villa, a smile spread across her face. She'd been down to the western gate of the city before dawn to see what happened. The gate opened, as it was supposed to, right at dawn, with just one guard responsible for it. That was great. She could definitely talk her way past him tomorrow morning. Beyond that gate, the road led west, and off it, trails led through the fields and woods she knew well. The escape was coming together.

Ari breathed in the morning air. Titus was beautiful, especially in summer. She would miss it, because if she did escape to Alcyone, she could never return. She headed south, past a long pavilion that was the previous emperor Bathus' forum. Bathus was her grandfather. He'd died before she was born, leaving the title of emperor to her father, Barritus, upon his death. For thirty years, Barritus had been emperor of Merope, and every year Titus had grown bigger, especially since the invasion of Alcyone and the plundering of their resources. Lately, there'd even been talk of expansion into other parts of the world. The expansion of Titus had always made her proud. They were the height of civilisation on this planet; she knew that. But was the means of attaining that civilisation something to be proud of?

Ahead of Ari stood another temple dedicated to their god, Pleid. His face was engraved on the portico at the front, and on the top of its arched dome, towering over twelve large granite columns, a statue of Pleid loomed over the city. In the morning light, he cast a long shadow from east to west.

Beyond the temple lay a long pool of water, which people sat by to rest or toss a coin in, hoping for Pleid to grant them a wish. Along its sides were carved depictions of battle, predominately images of the conquering of Alcyone. Her father was depicted in several of the reliefs, always in military uniform, always at the head of the battle. At the far side of the pool, on the southern wall, was a depiction of Titavius in his great battle in the south, in which he claimed all the now-Meropan lands. He was also depicted at the head of the battle, slaying many foul-looking, dark-shaded people. Ari knew little about this battle. At school they were taught that Titavius and his army slayed a rank and vile people who lived in the south, ridding the land forever of their stain. Titavius was an unquestioned hero of Meropan society. She had never questioned that story. Now, though … Just who were those people?

At the end of the pool, Ari turned eastward, and the amphitheatre loomed in front of her. She stopped in her tracks, her attention drawn not by the amphitheatre but by the familiar face standing in front of her, awaiting her arrival.

'Hello, Ari,' Dolus said casually, smiling.

His blonde hair was longer than when she'd last seen him,

and he was more tanned—though he was always tanned, growing up as he had on the east coast of Merope. A flutter of nerves and fear flashed through Ari's body. What did he know? He'd captured Deor and Sam, so was he here to make sure they were executed? She couldn't let on about anything she knew.

'Hello, Dolus,' she said as casually as she could manage. 'What brings you to Titus?'

'Well, the games, of course,' he said, as they walked on towards the amphitheatre. 'That's where you're headed now, I presume? My spies tell me you are the main man now when it comes to the games.'

'The main woman,' she said. 'My father put me in charge to ensure it all goes off smoothly.'

'And will it, Ari? Will it all go off smoothly?' Dolus looked at her with a strange, questioning expression. What did he know?

Ari measured her response carefully. 'So long as Fuscus does exactly as he's asked, then yes, I think it will.'

'Glad to hear it.' Dolus took his stare away from Ari and looked ahead to the amphitheatre again. 'How are my two spies coming along, then? Deor and Sam. I assume you've met them?'

'Coming along? Fine. They're in the cells. They'll remain there until night two of the games.'

'Have you spoken with them, Ari?' Dolus asked, putting his hand on her forearm and stopping them both from walking.

'Yes, of course, though I can't get much out of them. They won't trust a Meropan, you must know that. Though they trusted you. How did you manage to get them to trust you, Dolus?'

'Trust me?' Dolus said, surprised. 'Why do you think they

trusted me? I merely tracked them and brought them in.'

'That's not how I've heard it told,' Ari said. 'I'm told you came to Remit with them, as a group, then handed them over to the patrollers there. Is that not what happened?'

Dolus smiled at her with a curious expression. What was he thinking?

'That's more or less true,' he said, holding her gaze and his smile.

'Okay, then, so how did you get them to trust you?'

'I'd been tracking them for some days.' Dolus kept his eyes steadfastly on hers. 'On the Western Road, I eventually approached them. I posed as a merchant from the east coast heading to Remit to buy things my family needed. They bought it, and no doubt saw it as an opportunity to find out some things about Remit. They asked most about Titus, though, especially the procured girls. What they're taken for, where they're taken to, all those sorts of things. I fed them all kinds of erroneous information, which they ate up. That's how I gained their trust.'

Ari studied Dolus closely, but he was too difficult to read. Was this story true or not? He almost certainly knew more than he let on.

'Now it's my turn for a question, though,' Dolus said. 'Ari, you never were very good at lying. I know you've spoken more to the prisoners than you let on. I know you will have noticed the birthmark on Deor's shoulder, and of course I know that you have the same one on your hip.' Dolus touched her hip where her birthmark was.

Instinctively, she pulled away.

Dolus chuckled. 'There's no need to answer that. I can see from your reaction that you now know what that birthmark means. You didn't before, but you do now. Deor told you about it, didn't she?'

Fear gripped Ari. She didn't respond. Her plans were crumbling before her. If Dolus knew about this, then it would be easy for him to go to Vespus. Perhaps he already had? She looked around to see if there were any patrollers coming, but she couldn't see any.

'She told you a fantastic story about being reborn from a place called Nebra, didn't she, Ari?' Dolus held Ari's gaze and still smiled his inscrutable smile. 'You and she and five others, all there on that final day, all dying together on Nebra. You fought a war with Remus. And now you're all here to rebuild Nebran society, in Alcyone. And Remusans are here in Merope to rebuild Remus. Alcyone is the hated enemy of Merope, just as Nebra was the hated enemy of Remus. She told you all of this, right, Ari?' Dolus came closer to Ari's face as he spoke.

Sweat beaded on Ari's brow. If Vespus found out that Ari knew she was reborn from Nebra, he would have her disappear, with or without Barritus' permission. There was no doubt about that.

'It's a hell of a story, Ari,' Dolus continued, his face within centimetres of hers. 'With a very dangerous message, don't you think? Very dangerous. Daughter of the emperor, actually a Nebran reborn in Merope? Who is it more dangerous for, Ari? You? Or the empire? It's clearly dangerous for you. Imagine if Vespus knew. But it's dangerous for the empire too—their own emperor with a Nebran as a daughter … And an Alcyone-sympathising Nebran at that …' Dolus stared into Ari's eyes, his smile gone.

Panic rose within her, but she couldn't let Dolus see that. There was no point in lying, though. Dolus knew all about the Nebran and Remusan past. 'Yes,' she said eventually, 'Deor did tell me all of that.'

'And what are you going to do, now that you have that information?' Dolus asked.

'Nothing. The games go ahead as planned.'

Dolus laughed. 'As I said, Ari, you never were very good at lying.'

'Well, I'm an honest person,' she said, annoyed. 'I find it difficult to lie, while others find it very easy, don't they, Dolus …'

'I know you have something planned,' he continued, ignoring her barbed comment. 'I know you're going to try to rescue them. Set them free. Send them back to Alcyone. It's the right thing to do as a human being, right?'

'Oh no …' It all fell into place. 'You were there … yesterday. You heard us … at the end of the corridor …'

'That's right.' He nodded. 'I heard it all. You're breaking them out, tomorrow morning before dawn, and fleeing the city by the western gate.'

'Dolus, please,' Ari begged. 'You have to forget what you heard. If you care about me at all, you have to let this go. They'll be killed, both of them.'

'Let it go?' Dolus looked shocked. 'Leave you be? To try to break the prisoners out and let them go free, back to Alcyone? That's what you want me to do?'

'Please, Dolus. You must. You have to let me do this! It's wrong for them to be put to death. I have to stop it.'

'Ari, I have no intention of letting you go,' Dolus said, his face even closer to hers now, 'because I will be helping you.'

Ari froze, trying to process what he'd just said. 'You … you what?' was all she could find to say.

'To help them escape, Ari. I will be helping you. You're going to need some assistance if they're going to get back home to the Mid Territory. And you're going to need someone like me who knows his way around Alcyone, secret ways, ways we can avoid the patrollers once we cross the border.'

'You will help us? Why? And how do you know your way around Alcyone? Secret ways? What secret ways?'

'There're ways the patrollers don't know about, Ari. My people in the Coastal Territory have come up with some pretty interesting ways of going places undetected.'

'You're … you're not from Merope? You're from Alcyone?'

'Let's just say, Ari,' Dolus said, smiling again and looking off to the west, 'there's a lot you don't know about me.'

☾☾☾

Later that morning, Ari still puzzled over the events that transpired with Dolus. She'd been excited and relieved. With his help, they had a greater chance of escaping Titus alive. On reflection, though, she now wondered if she could trust him. After all, he was an agent in the Merope Guard, a trained spy. How could she trust anything he said? He may just be infiltrating their group in order to expose them, winning further favour with the likes of Vespus and her father. If he wanted to do that, though, why wouldn't he just reveal their plan to them? Why go to the trouble of infiltrating their group? She didn't know the answers, but she would have to be on her guard, because she couldn't fully trust Dolus.

For now, though, she had to stick to the script. She was here to organise the games. Fuscus had arrived with the riders, and she'd organised each of them to have one practice race each. The first two were readying their horses in the arena, so Ari headed there. Fuscus stood in the centre of the arena with two officials manning their platforms on each side. Finally, Fuscus was getting some things done—though the games'

279

success was a lot less important to Ari now than it had been just one day earlier.

'Riders!' Fuscus yelled as Ari joined him in the centre of the arena. 'Mount your horses! You represent the glory of Merope; ride like the riders of old who conquered our enemies! Ride for the glory of Merope!'

Fuscus fired a gun into the air, and the race was on. Each rider urged their horse on as the officials watched and counted the laps. After five laps, it was clear that one of the riders was trying to cheat. He wasn't staying close to the arena's outside fence, gradually shortening the distance he needed to run by coming further into the centre of the arena. Fuscus fired his gun in the air, signalling for the race to stop. The riders came to a halt, and Fuscus strode over to the rider in question.

'Rider!' he demanded, his belly wobbling as his small feet shuffled through the sand of the arena. 'Why do you try to cheat by running off your line?'

'I could not help it!' the rider said. 'My horse veers in when he runs! He naturally runs in that way and so runs away from the fence!'

'Do you think the glory of Merope is best represented by people cheating at races, rider?' Fuscus asked.

'No, sir!' the rider replied.

'Then keep your horse on the correct path, or you'll find yourself in the first and final events of tomorrow evening! No one will disgrace Merope by cheating! Back to your positions!'

The riders restarted their race, and this time the offending rider was able to keep his horse on its path. Ari congratulated Fuscus on his successful training, and he seemed pleased at that. She didn't care about him, though; her mind was occupied elsewhere.

The morning proceeded as planned, with all riders

practicing their race, but Ari was distracted the entire time. She spent the afternoon with Fuscus going over plans for the final days of the games, though it was an exercise in futility for her. All she could think of was whether or not they would succeed in their mission. Come the final day of the games and the possible boat battle that Ari and Fuscus discussed, she was certain she'd either be in Alcyone or dead. There was no in-between for her.

CHAPTER 27

Deor lay awake in her bed, though it was the middle of the night. Sleep was not going to come. She'd briefly seen Ari the previous evening, well after everyone had gone home from the games practice. Deor had given her Sage's key, and they had confirmed their plan: Ari and Arunet would meet them well before dawn, giving them enough time to get out of the cells, sneak away to the west gate of the city and leave. There were many potential problems, though. The guards, for one thing; patrollers spotting them on the streets for another. Let alone if they came across Barritus or Vespus on the morning of the ceremony. Timing was key; they could not be delayed. If they left the cells too early, they would have to wait in the dark of the city, which was suspicious and likely to attract attention. Waiting until daylight wasn't an option either—much too risky. Ari would arrive before dawn, but they couldn't bear a delay.

So Deor lay and waited. The sounds of other prisoners sleeping came through the bars. At least her brother wasn't far away—that was comforting. He would no doubt be lying awake as well. And Sage was here, and safe.

The night drew out painfully slowly, like a bad dream from which you can't wake. Every movement outside had Deor convinced it was Vespus or Barritus come to tell her that the plan was discovered. Ari had told Deor about Dolus returning and offering to help, and she didn't believe his intentions to be genuine. So with every footstep she heard or voice in the corridor, her heart skipped a beat as she waited for Merope to mete out her final punishment.

(((

'Deor!' Ari whispered. 'Wake up!'

Deor jolted awake. She must have dozed off. Quickly, she rose and saw Arieitis and Arunet on the outside of the cell. Relief flooded her. They made it. However, standing next to them was Dolus. Anger instinctively rose in her for what he did in Remit, but she had to push it down.

'Hello, Deor,' he whispered. 'Don't worry, I'm here to help.'

'You betrayed us …' she whispered back as Ari noiselessly opened the cell.

'There was a lot I couldn't tell you,' he said quietly. 'But you can trust me; I am not lying to you. I never did. I am not Dolus the Deceiver; I am Dolus the Double-Agent.'

Deor looked questioningly at him, but let the conversation go. For now. She had to; they couldn't risk being discovered.

'I have something for you.' Dolus handed Deor her Alphym spears. He'd kept them all. He also had Sam's equipment. 'Perhaps that will help you trust me …'

The quartet made their way around to Sam's cell. He was awake, and they quietly let him out. Deor and Sam embraced briefly, while Dolus mouthed the words, 'I'm sorry, I'll explain

…' to him. Sam looked at him with narrowed eyes.

They crept quietly through the corridors of the amphitheatre, following Deor to Sage's cell. Outside, the night was still black, but the dawn was coming. As they turned into Sage's corridor, Deor froze. A patroller stood outside Sage's cell, and the door was wide open. She hurried them back around the corner to safety.

'What do we do?' Sam whispered.

'We have to keep going,' Deor said. 'We can't stop now. I have an idea. I'll hide, using my veil; and Dolus, you pretend to be transporting Sam as a prisoner, okay? Ari, you're overseeing them, with Arunet assisting. Then we improvise when we get to the cell.'

Dolus nodded. 'I can tell the patroller that we have to collect Sage as well.'

'Okay,' Deor said. 'Let's do it; come on.'

Deor felt in her pocket and found her jakelope baton. She ran her finger along it and felt the smallest breath of gossamer as the veil silently covered her. The look on Ari's face told Deor all she needed to know—she had vanished. Dolus and Sam assumed the positions of prisoner and guard, and they walked towards Sage's cell. The patroller watched them as they came but didn't say anything. When they got to the cell, Deor saw why.

'Oh no …' she whispered to herself.

Inside the cell, Sage sat on a small bed with Vespus seated next to her, stroking Sage's hair. She looked terrified. The other three girls cowered on the other side of the cell.

'Hello, rats,' Vespus said, glancing at them. 'I've been getting acquainted with your sister, Sage. What a pretty little thing she is. I've been telling her about all the things I'm going to get her to do when she's a servant in my household. They won't all be pleasant, I can assure you. In fact, none of them will be.'

Sam lunged forward, trying to get into the cell, but the patroller stopped him.

'You didn't think you would get away with this,' Vespus said, 'did you? What was the plan again, Agent Dolus? What did you tell me they were planning to do? Sneak out before dawn, avoiding detection somehow, and leave through the western gate?'

Vespus laughed an evil, malicious laugh. It contained no joy, as he himself contained no joy. The pleasure Vespus sought—and gained—in life was gained through the suffering of others, not through their achievements or their happiness. To see another suffer brought Vespus joy, but to make another suffer brought him the greatest joy of all. To be the architect of their despair filled the void within himself that he thought of as his being. And now, it brought him great joy to be able to thwart Deor and Sam's plans.

'Yes, that's right,' Dolus said, walking into the cell and over to Vespus. 'That was their plan.'

From within the safety of her veil, Deor looked with anger at Dolus. He could not be trusted ever. Silently and slowly, she took one of the Alphym spears from her pack.

'But I didn't tell you about this part of the plan ...' Dolus produced a knife from under his shirt, lunged forward, and with speed and power, plunged it into Vespus' heart. The old man gasped in pain as Dolus twisted the blade. 'The part where I lure you to your death, you evil old man ...' Dolus said, looking into Vespus' eyes.

Sensing the moment, Deor moved quickly as Vespus fell to his knees. She grabbed the patroller's gun from his hands, and as he looked in surprise at his empty hands, she tripped him with the spear and slung him to the ground. Sam responded by getting on top of him and wrestling the patroller to hold him down. Sam took the patroller's baton from his belt and raised it over his head. 'I'm sorry about this!' Sam said as he struck the patroller hard, knocking him unconscious.

Deor chuckled at his politeness, then nimbly rubbed her jakelope baton again and reappeared.

Sam took shackles from the patroller, quickly shackled his feet together, then his hands behind his back.

In the cell, Dolus stood over Vespus. Finally, he removed his knife, and the old man fell to the ground, dead. Dolus cleaned his knife on the senator's robes. 'Now do you trust me?' he asked, turning to Deor.

'Quickly, we have to go!' Ari said.

Deor rushed into the cell and hugged her sister. She couldn't linger, though. The incident had cost them precious time. 'We're getting out of here,' she said to the other three girls. 'We're going back to Alcyone. If you want to come with us, follow us now!'

Anthea rose, came to Deor and looked at her with trepidation.

'Hello,' Deor said softly. 'Would you like to come with us? What's your name?'

Anthea didn't respond.

'She doesn't talk much,' Sage said, 'until she gets to know you. She's my friend. Her name is Anthea.'

'Hello, Anthea,' Deor said. 'That's a beautiful name. My name is Deor. Come, we'll get you home.' Deor turned to the remaining two girls, who still cowered in the corner. 'Do you want to come too?' she asked.

The girls looked fearfully at Deor and shook their heads.

Deor bowed her head slightly. The situation would be very

overwhelming for them, and they'd just watched a man being killed. It was understandable that they were fearful of leaving.

'We have to go, before it gets light,' Ari urged.

Reluctantly leaving the other two girls in the cell, Deor followed Ari out of the cell and down the corridor towards the front entrance. It was still dark outside. They peered cautiously into the street. In the east, the pre-dawn glow appeared on the horizon. The sun wasn't far away.

They made their way out the front entrance, but a voice yelled from behind them. 'Stop! Stop where you are!'

Deor spun around. One of the guards had emerged from a different corridor, and he ran towards them. 'We have to hurry!' Deor said urgently.

'Follow me!' Ari said.

She and Dolus led the way, running towards the western side of the city. Deor held Sage's hand to keep her close, and Anthea held Sage's. They ran on together with Sam, following Ari, Arunet and Dolus.

'It's beginning to get light!' Deor called out.

People were emerging from homes. Many people. The guard behind them was slow, but when Deor glanced back, he was motioning to two patrollers who'd appeared to see what the commotion was about. They took up the chase immediately.

'Head for the forum!' Ari called out. 'Go to the dawn service! We have to blend into the crowd!'

They arrived at the edge of the forum. At the western end, Deor saw an enormous statue of Pleid facing east. In front of it was the newly built temple, and behind it, the city wall. Many people were already in the forum, including Barritus, who stood at a lectern, apparently ready to make a speech for the service.

'Stop them!' yelled the patrollers behind them.

Suddenly, Deor had an idea. 'Follow me, quick!' She changed direction and headed through the crowd and around the southern side of the forum, opposite where Barritus stood. He hadn't seen the commotion yet. A large bearded man and a woman sat behind him, Ari's brother and sister. The sun crept up in the east, and Barritus prepared to begin his speech.

Deor hurried them through the crowd to a platform that stood on the opposite side of the forum from the emperor. She climbed it and stood at the top.

Barritus looked up and saw her. Their eyes locked for a tense second as the emperor realised that she'd broken out. Deor stared back at him defiantly across the forum. Barritus held her gaze; then his eyes moved to her right, where he saw his daughter. 'Ari …' Confusion and anger claimed his expression.

Moving swiftly, Deor pulled the large Alphym spear from her pack and loaded her Minerva gem into the cavity. The sun continued to rise, and its rays shone straight onto the statue of Pleid at the western end of the forum, bathing it in the glow of the dawn on the summer solstice.

'We are not tools of Merope!' Deor cried, her voice cutting through the dawn silence and echoing through the forum. It bounced off the stone city wall and reverberated through the columns. The last of the sun emerged from underneath the horizon and lit Pleid in glorious sunlight. 'And Alcyone will take back her freedom!'

She threw the spear at the statue of Pleid. It cut through the air at great speed, not slowing or dropping from its path. Imbued with the magic of the Alphym and Deor's Minerva gem, it struck his face with intense power, and a great explosion rocked the forum. The colossal statue shattered, and the wall behind it blasted open, leaving a great hole in the city's western wall. The temple was in ruins. Smoke and dust rolled in a blanket across the forum. People coughed and held their ears from the noise, confusion gripping them all.

'Run!' Deor yelled.

Sam grabbed Sage, and Dolus grabbed Anthea, as Deor, Ari and Arunet led the way through the confusion and dust towards the rubble that had been that section of the city wall. Deor glanced back. The patrollers clambered through the crowd behind them. Shots rang out from their guns, causing people to scream and attempt to flee the forum, which slowed the patrollers' advance. Barritus pushed his way through the crowd towards them, a gun drawn and a murderous look on his face.

Deor had the lead on them all, though, and she, Ari and Arunet got to the rubble of the wall first. She saw her spear lying on the ground. It had shattered in the explosion, but she recovered her Minerva gem. They climbed over the rubble and out into the field beyond the wall. Sam and Dolus followed with Sage and Anthea running beside them.

'The Western Road!' Ari yelled. 'It's the fastest way away from the city!'

They sprinted across the grass towards the road, which headed away from the western gate, but the gate opened and patrollers poured through it. Barritus had joined the patrollers behind them, and they fired shots, narrowly missing. The patrollers flooding out of the western gate ran towards them, catching Deor and her team in the crossfire between the groups. They changed direction and ran across the open land, but they were still under fire from both groups of patrollers.

Deor tossed the gun she'd taken from the patroller to Dolus, then pulled a spear from her pack and threw it at the closest patroller. Sam had his bow and arrow out and pelted them with arrows, while Dolus returned fire with the gun.

'Get behind me and get down!' Arieitis called out to Sage, and Arunet did the same with Anthea. They all ducked down.

The return fire stopped the patrollers' advance, but it wouldn't hold for long. Bullets still cut the air, and the crew were lucky to remain unhit, though Deor noticed blood oozing from Dolus' left shoulder.

The patrollers on the road advanced again. Deor threw an Alphym spear at the man leading their charge. He narrowly avoided it, but it thundered into the shoulder of the patroller behind him, bringing him to the ground. Sam fired several arrows, taking two of them to the ground, but a bullet crashed into his right shoulder, causing him to drop his bow.

'I'm out of spears!' Deor yelled. 'We have to move!' She turned to run, but a bullet skimmed her leg, making her stumble. The group retreated as best they could, trying to get away from the advancing patrollers, one group led by Barritus.

Suddenly, his voice boomed through the gunfight. 'Ceasefire!' he yelled. 'Cease your fire!' The patrollers stopped advancing and stopped firing, waiting for their emperor's instruction. An eerie peace hung in the air after the deafening sound of gunshots moments earlier.

'Alcyonans!' Barritus continued, his voice the only sound in the early morning countryside. 'Surrender now, and your lives will be spared! You have with you someone dear to me, my daughter Arieitis. Return her and surrender, and I will spare all your lives!'

Deor and her companions stopped. She looked around at them. Sam's shoulder was leaking blood, as was her leg. Dolus was limping—he must have taken a hit to the leg, as well as the one to his shoulder. Arieitis and Arunet were unharmed and had ensured the same for Sage and Anthea.

'What can we do?' Sam asked, pain clear in his voice.

Deor turned to Arieitis, who again hunched on the ground with Sage. 'Ari?' she asked. 'What do you want to do?'

Ari paused for several seconds, thinking about her response. No other sounds could be heard. In the distance, Barritus waited with his troop of patrollers, as did the group that had been advancing from the road. The sun continued to rise, and the day grew warm. The hum of insects on this Meropan summer day momentarily took centre stage.

'I can't go back,' Ari eventually said. 'I can't go back there, and if you go back there, they'll kill you. My father will not honour his promise. You will all end up in the games.'

'Are you sure?' Deor asked, seeing the fear on Ari's face.

'Yes, Deor. I am sure. I have always been sure. This is not where I belong; this is not where I'm from. I want to go.'

Deor nodded her agreement. She'd only known Arieitis a short while in this life, but she felt the deeper bond that stretched back through time to Nebra for the two of them, and she had no doubt Ari felt it too. She'd felt linked to her from the first time she saw her.

'Alcyonans!' Barritus thundered from behind them. 'Do not court war with Merope! It is a war you will not survive!'

Sam took Deor's arm. 'Dee, what are we going to do? We need a plan, and we need it fast!'

No sooner were the words out of Sam's mouth, when suddenly they heard the thundering sound of horses rushing up on them from around the northern side of the city. Deor turned towards the sound. Seven Alphym riders arrived alongside them with lightning speed—Rohanë, Aafjë and Claude with four others.

'Quickly!' Rohanë called out. 'On a horse each!'

'What are you doing here?' Deor asked as she scrambled

onto the back of Rohanë's horse.

'We're here to help!' Rohanë said. 'Remember, not all Alphym think we shouldn't involve ourselves in the affairs of humans …' As he spoke, he opened his shirt a little, revealing a birthmark on his chest—the two moons of Nebra. 'Come! We must go!'

'Open fire!' Barritus yelled from behind them, and the patrollers fired immediately.

Dolus again joined Aafjë, and Sam joined Claude on his horse. The other Alphym helped Ari, Arunet, Sage and Anthea up on their horses.

Deor heard someone cry out. She turned towards the sound. Blood poured from Ari's back where she'd been shot as she settled onto her horse. One patroller had come closer than the others and now stood up from behind a bush, about to fire again. Deor screamed, rage enveloping her, but without a spear she could do nothing. Dolus, however, on the horse next to Ari, raised his gun and shot him. The patroller fell backwards, dead.

Ari's rider quickly shifted her so she sat in front of him, and he held her to stop her falling from the horse. She was alive, but blood soaked her back already.

'Go!' Rohanë cried, and the horses sped into action, flying over the firm ground of Merope.

More patrollers, these ones on horseback, appeared along the Western Road and galloped towards them. Bullets came at them from both sides again, but the patrollers could not account for the speed of the Alphym horses. They missed, and Deor and her companions were quickly out of range. The patrollers on horses attempted to chase them, firing on them as they did, but within moments they were too far away, as the Alphym horses sped away from them over the green grass of Merope.

'Across the plains!' Rohanë called out. 'Make for the valley at the north of the mountains!'

The seven riders urged their horses on further, putting many kilometres between themselves and Titus in a short time. Deor turned to look at Ari as they rode. Blood was all over her clothes now, and her rider still held her close before him, but Deor couldn't make out Ari's face to see if she was conscious or not.

'She needs help!' Deor said to Rohanë.

He nodded, and after riding for a little longer, Rohanë signalled for them all to stop. They were clear of the danger for now. They dismounted, and Ari's rider helped her down.

Deor raced over to where she sat on the ground, her eyes closed. Claude was already tending to her wound. He'd poured some Alphym water on it to inspect it, but he looked worried.

'Ari, can you hear me?' Deor asked.

Ari's eyes opened at her voice. 'Deor ... I can't feel my legs ...'

Deor choked back tears. She turned to Claude. 'Can you help her?'

'The bullet is deep inside,' he said. 'It went through her spine and is in her organs. Plus, she's already lost so much blood. I will try; I will do my best.'

Aafjë brought a medical kit over to Claude, and they worked together on the wound, trying to close it over to prevent blood loss. They bandaged her, which stopped the immediate bleeding, poured more Alphym water over her back, and whispered some words into her wound.

'Deor,' Ari said, 'how far are we? From the border ... I want to see Alcyone again. I want to set foot in it ...'

'With the speed of our horses, we can be at the border in

an hour,' Rohanë said. 'The valley at the foot of the Asman Range lies dead ahead. We can cross there.'

Dolus nodded. 'I know people in the Northern, good people, largely free of patroller interference. They can help us. They can help Ari.'

'Then there's no time to lose,' Rohanë said. 'Claude, Aafjë, have you finished what you can do for her for now?' The two Alphym nodded a despondent agreement. There was nothing more they could do. 'Then let's ride, quickly!'

The riders remounted and set off for the border, due west. Rohanë led the way with Deor at his back, and Ari's rider followed alongside. The horses glided across the grassy plains of northern Merope, quickly putting many kilometres behind them. To their south, in the distance, Deor spotted some small towns along the Western Road, but the riders stayed well clear of them.

The plains turned to hills, then flattened out again. The riders skirted around the north of a small forest. In the distance, Deor caught a glimpse of the sea. She could see settlements dotted along the coast, near the sea, but they quickly vanished behind her.

Deor didn't speak, but she watched Ari the whole time, noticing her fading in and out of consciousness. Her rider held her flawlessly, easily balancing both himself and her on his elegant horse, but with every minute that passed, Deor's spirits fell. The colour was draining away from Ari's face little by little, making her stunning, golden-brown hair look even more beautiful against her paling complexion.

The grass became greener as they approached the fertile soil of the Northern Territory of Alcyone. Eventually, the group came to the top of a long rise, and below them lay a valley. They had reached the northern end of the Asman

Range. To their south, in the distance, Deor could see the final two mountains in that range, between which lay the border of the two nations. Deor thought back to the map, all the way back in the room at the Great Hall. The line of that border extended through here, through the valley below her and up to the ocean in the north. They sat on their horses and looked down into the valley, into Alcyone.

'Ari!' Deor said, sliding off her horse. 'Ari, look! We're at the border. Alcyone lies below!'

With difficulty, Ari opened her eyes. She turned her head away from Titus and towards Alcyone. Realising where she was, a smile broke out on her face. 'The Northern Territory,' she said softly. 'This is my favourite place …'

'There's no patrollers here,' Dolus said, 'because there's no road. This part of the Northern isn't much watched. The valley is clear.'

They remounted and rode carefully down into the valley and down into Alcyonan territory at the bottom.

'We're home,' Deor said, relief washing through her. 'We made it out.'

'Ahead, there's a lake.' Dolus pointed. 'There, surrounded by pine trees. On the far side of that lake is a small town. Let's head for the lake, get some water and shade, and give the horses a break for a while. Then we can get things we need in the town.'

'The horses will ride all day when they're needed,' Rohanë said, but then he turned to look at Ari. 'But I imagine the humans may benefit from some rest.'

Happy to be back on Alcyonan soil, Deor and the group made their way to the lake. Deor stopped and caught her breath as she saw it. The lake was filled with glittering clear water and was surrounded on all sides by towering pines, except for here on the eastern side, where a clearing and a small smooth-sanded beach sat at the edge of the lake. Water lapped gently onto the beach.

Arunet helped Ari off her horse. She was still conscious, but barely. Deor helped her carry Ari to the nearby pine trees, and they sat together in the shade. Deor and Arunet supported Arieitis so she could sit up.

'How are you feeling, Ari?' Deor asked.

'I don't know. I can't seem to keep my eyes open. Where are we?' She turned to see the lake that stretched out in front of them. 'It's beautiful.'

'We're in Alcyone now,' Deor said. 'In the Northern Territory. This is where all the farmers live.'

'They make the best tea …' Ari said, smiling.

Tears ran down Arunet's cheeks, and Deor tried without success to choke her own emotions down.

'Yes, they do …' Arunet said, kissing Ari's forehead.

Ari smiled as her friend embraced her.

'Thank you, Deor,' Ari said, turning to her. 'For bringing me here. I am home now.'

Deor couldn't hold back her emotions any longer. Tears streamed down her face as she leaned in, holding Ari and kissing her forehead as well. She and Arunet sat together cradling Ari between them, three friends who had perished together on Nebra, now reunited here on Earth. They held her in silence as Ari exhaled a long breath, her head nodding onto her chest, and quietly passed away.

CHAPTER 28

'Here lies Arieitis, of Nebra, Merope and Alcyone, loved by all.'

Sam and Dolus had procured a headstone from the town on the lake as well as some medical supplies to treat the wounded, while the others prepared a grave for Ari. They buried her on the edge of the pine forest surrounding the lake, in Alcyonan land. The Alphym added some spells to protect the stone and bring flowers to the grave.

'Every summer solstice,' Aafjë said, casting the spells, 'on the anniversary of her death, flowers will bloom on her grave, and remain there until the winter solstice, six months later.'

The afternoon shadows had grown long; they had to move on. They didn't know if Barritus would send patrollers into Alcyone to look for them, but they didn't want to take the chance.

'Can you get us to the Gap of the Sea?' Dolus asked.

'We can,' Rohanë replied, 'but then we must bid you farewell.'

'Thank you,' Dolus said. 'From there, we'll be okay. We have people there who can take us further.'

Deor said her last goodbye to Arieitis, where she lay now at rest, and the group rode away from the lake, the horses again making light work of the journey. Just before sunset they arrived at the small town that overlooked the Gap of the Sea, a place where the northern coastline cut in, forming a perfectly circular cove surrounded by steep cliffs on all sides.

Deor felt weary, not just physically but emotionally. The loss of Ari bore heavily on her soul. Arunet was also suffering. She'd lost so much in her life, and now she'd lost the one person in Merope who was her friend.

'We ride back to the south tonight,' Rohanë said as the remaining six members of the group gathered their things. 'We cannot go further and risk being seen by too many people. Our existence still needs to be kept a secret for now. Though after today I suspect that may become more difficult. I hope you can make your way back to your home from here without any further trouble.'

Dolus nodded. 'I have contacts from my home in this town. They'll help us.'

Deor embraced Rohanë as they said their goodbyes. 'Thank you,' she said, 'for coming to help us. Though I now know why, Xander.'

Rohanë smiled. 'Xander, that is correct. But Rohanë now, of the Alphym. I am still Nebran somewhere inside, though.'

'And thank you to all of you for everything you've done for us,' Deor continued. 'We are humbled that your people would put yourselves at risk for us.'

'You have friends in the Alphym,' Claude said, 'but remember the words of our king and queen: we do not encourage war.'

'Neither do we,' Deor said, 'but it may be that war is the inevitable path down which we are headed.'

'War can always be avoided,' Rohanë said, 'and perhaps, Deor, this is where your path can diverge from Lore of Nebra.'

The horses and riders set off back the way they'd come and were soon out of sight, their graceful equine forms disappearing into the early evening like a whisper disappears on a breeze.

They stood at the edge of the town, perched high on the clifftop. Below them was a circular beach of sand, and the water of the cove glittered silvery blue in the early evening light. Only the mouth of the cove along the ragged coastline broke the perfect circle, and it looked like the ends of two arms wrapping around the whole cove.

'What forces transpired to create such a beautiful thing?' Sam asked aloud, though more to himself.

'The eternal tide,' Deor said, 'breaking through the barrier of the coastline cliffs, then endlessly returning, reborn anew each day, washing in to work away at the shore.'

'We don't need Pleid to create beauty in this world for us; nature has already taken care of it,' Sam said.

The group admired the view for a little longer before heading into the town. Dolus seemed to know it quite well and led them to a small house near its border. He went inside, while Deor and the others waited in the street. They hadn't seen any patrollers in this part of Alcyone as yet. Why were the people here left alone so much more than back at home?

After a few minutes, Dolus came out with an older man, likely in his late forties, Deor guessed, but it was hard to tell, because a lifetime of being in the sun and on the water had tanned and weathered his skin. His blond hair matched Dolus', just a little greyer and thinner. There was no mistaking it; this was Dolus' father.

'Everyone,' Dolus said, 'meet my father, Damos. He is, as

always, both pleased and annoyed to see me. I promise, Father, I did not mean to be away so long this time.'

'Every time,' Damos said as they made their introductions, 'he says he'll be a week, just a week … and every time I worry more and more once that week passes by.'

'Come,' Dolus said after the introductions, 'we leave tonight. My father will sail us around the coast under the cover of night, all the way to the Mid Territory. We'll be there by morning.'

Deor was stunned. 'You would do that for us? Through the night?'

'Yes, Deor,' Damos said. 'We in the Coastal Territory are sailors and fishermen and women, we prefer to use the ocean to travel when we can, especially now with the presence of patrollers in every territory. We sail from the Coastal to the Northern and back, regularly. That is one way we avoid the patrollers.'

'We've made a deal with some of the people here in the North,' Dolus said as they made their way down towards the water, 'for the benefit of both of us. We sail here when we need to, and they sail to us when they need to. The patrollers won't let us cross territories by land, so we do it by sea when they can't see us. Under the cover of night.'

'Is that how you got to the Mid Territory?' Sam asked. 'When you first came with Leon, weeks ago?'

'No, we made the mistake of walking,' Dolus said. 'We had no way of knowing where we could dock in the Mid. And that's why we were seen. We'll be sailing more and more, though. Our Meropan resistance needs connected territories, which is exactly what Barritus and Vespus have been denying us. They've been keeping us as separated entities, so no unified resistance can form. This deal between the Coastal and the

Northern is the beginning of that unification. Next is the Mid; then we have to work out what to do about the Mid North …'

'Anthea will organise the Mid North, won't you, Anthea?' Sage asked, taking her friend's arm. Anthea blushed in reply.

'Come,' Damos said in the same tone his son had used moments before, 'this is my boat. We can board now. You'll find cabins below that you can rest in. They're not much, but they're dry and watertight. We'll set off straight away; the winds are favourable.'

Deor climbed aboard the boat and took a seat towards the front. She was tired, sore, hungry and emotionally empty, but she didn't want to sleep. Damos and Dolus pushed off and set sail, expertly guiding the ship out through the mouth of the cove and onto the ocean. They turned westward, seeing the last rays of the sun as it set over the ocean ahead of them, and let the northeasterly breeze fill their sails. The boat surged through the darkening sea as the stars began to come out above. A clear night, good for sailing.

Sage wasn't in a sleeping mood either. She took a seat up front next to Deor, and Anthea sat at Sage's side, still silent. Deor looked at the coastline sliding by as the boat sliced through the water, leaving Titus further and further behind. After a while, the coast changed; the land and cliffs disappeared, and an enormous river mouth opened up.

'The Alcyone River,' Deor said, pointing it out for Sage and Anthea. 'Our river flows all the way from the Southern Mountain, at the very bottom of our land, through four of our five territories until it empties out into the sea here. It gives life to all the lands around it. Sam and I saw where it begins, high up in the Southern Mountain at an enormous waterfall.'

Sage smiled. 'I would love to see that … Is it beautiful?'

'Very beautiful.' Deor put an arm around her sister. 'It's

the most beautiful place I've ever seen, and it's the home of the Alphym people.'

Anthea tapped Deor on the shoulder.

Surprised, Deor turned to her.

'What is a river like?' Anthea asked.

Deor smiled and stroked Anthea's hair. 'Anthea,' she said warmly, 'I promise you will get to find out.'

DEDICATION & ACKNOWLEDGEMENTS

This story is dedicated to my children: Daisy, Sam, Eliza, Olivia and Rose. It was written for them and named for them. It is also dedicated to the memory of my mother, who always pushed me to explore my potential fully.

I want to especially mention the help of—and give a writing credit to—my daughter Eliza. In late 2024, I first mentioned the idea for this story to her, and awkwardly asked her if she thought it sounded too strange.

'Dad,' she replied, 'have you seen some of the things people write about these days? It's not too strange …'

She convinced me to write the story and helped with the creative process every step of the way. Her creative drive was instrumental in the creation of the characters, storyline, relationships, plots and subplots. The world of Alcyone and Merope doesn't exist without her input, her imagination, her creativity and her story sense. And, of course, her support throughout. Thank you, Eliza.

AUTHOR BIO

Hi, my name is Cameron O'Brien. Thanks for taking the time to look at my book. I have been interested in fantasy and sci-fi stories all my life, and always wanted to—one day—write my own books. Until recently, I did not feel as though I was ready.

Then, in 2023, something tragic happened, and I got thinking a lot about life, the universe and everything; and in that time a story idea came to me. The idea bounced around in my head for a while. At first, it was just Deor and her backstory, but it began to develop.

In late 2024 I began writing it, and about three months later a draft was complete: 88,000 words. I reworked things, got editorial help (thanks, Tahlia Newland!), reworked more things, and eventually—here we are. Deor, Sammu, Dolus, Sage and everyone else came to life.

Their story is now being told.

A Note from the Author

If you enjoyed *Two Moons: The Eternal Tide*, I would be immensely grateful if you could leave a review where you purchased it. Even just a few words will help others decide if it's the kind of book they'd like to try out.

Also, we are building up a Two Moons community. If you want to be involved, sign up at https://www.camobrien.com/join-the-community, and as a bonus I will send you a free short story set just after *The Eternal Tide*, exclusive only to members of the Two Moons community. Your information will never be shared, but you will be able to receive updates about when new stories in the Two Moons universe are coming out and other bonus material.

So come on and join the community!